D1035491

PRAISE FOR

On Fire Island

"I can't stop thinking about *On Fire Island*, Jane L. Rosen's dazzling story of enduring love, gut-wrenching loss, and unlikely friendships. I read it with an enormous smile on my face and tears in my eyes—it's as funny as it is poignant, nostalgic as it is sharp. A beautiful tribute to the summers of our past and to Fire Island. Unforgettable!"

—Carley Fortune, *New York Times* bestselling author of *Every Summer After*

"It's clear that Jane L. Rosen poured her heart into writing this novel. The result is a captivating story about love and loss that's as magical and memorable as Fire Island itself."

—John Searles, *New York Times* bestselling author of *Her Last Affair*

"With her trademark humor and eloquence, Jane L. Rosen transports us to a summer paradise. . . . Don't miss this one; it's perfect." —Annabel Monaghan, author of *Nora Goes Off Script*

PRAISE FOR

A Shoe Story

"A smart, sensitive, and incredibly satisfying romantic comedy."

—Elin Hilderbrand, #1 *New York Times* bestselling author of *28 Summers*

"Read *A Shoe Story* and fall in love . . . whether for the first time or all over again."

—Katie Couric

"*Beach Read* meets *The Notebook* in this utterly absorbing Greenwich Village tale of first loves and second chances."

—Jo Piazza, *New York Times* bestselling coauthor of *We Are Not Like Them*

Titles by Jane L. Rosen

ON FIRE ISLAND

A SHOE STORY

ELIZA STARTS A RUMOR

NINE WOMEN, ONE DRESS

On Fire Island

JANE L. ROSEN

BERKLEY
NEW YORK

BERKLEY
An imprint of Penguin Random House LLC
penguinrandomhouse.com

Library of Congress Cataloging-in-Publication Data

Names: Rosen, Jane L., author.
Title: On fire island / Jane L. Rosen.
Description: First edition. | New York: Berkley, 2023.
Identifiers: LCCN 2022041891 (print) | LCCN 2022041892 (ebook) |
ISBN 9780593546109 (trade paperback) | ISBN 9780593638071 (hardcover) |
ISBN 9780593546116 (ebook)
Subjects: LCGFT: Novels.
Classification: LCC PS3618.O83145 O5 2023 (print) |
LCC PS3618.O83145 (ebook) | DDC 813/.6—dc23/eng/20220912
LC record available at https://lccn.loc.gov/2022041891
LC ebook record available at https://lccn.loc.gov/2022041892

First Edition: May 2023

Printed in the United States of America
1st Printing

Book design by Kristin del Rosario
Interior art: Beach art © Depiano / Shutterstock.com

For everyone who's ever missed
the ferry by one minute.

Author's note: While Fire Island is an actual island made up of seventeen different communities, Bay Harbor, where this novel is mainly set, is a fictional representation of one such town. As is its neighbor, Oceanview.

On Fire Island

prologue

In ancient Hebrew, the word for *tomb* and the word for *womb* are one and the same. This is what the Rabbi (and bestselling author) I met at the Random House Christmas party pointed out to me when I told her I was dying.

"We are born twice," she assured me. "Once from the womb and once from the tomb."

It may have been wrong of me to bring up such a somber subject at such a festive occasion, but she was a rabbi at a Christmas party, and I was curious about her views on the afterlife. Besides, I was confident, after my recent diagnosis, that I would not be seeing her again. Though I was wrong about that. She visited me weekly in the months before my death and even officiated at my big send-off.

I am not one to believe anything that I cannot see with my own two eyes.

"Julia is a skeptic," my father would often say, a trait that was evident since I attended my first magic show—my sister's eyes were wide with awe, mine were narrow with doubt. But the

Rabbi, or possibly desperation, made me a believer. And I left this world, after just thirty-seven years in it, convinced I would be heading toward another.

Between the two worlds, it turned out, there was one last summer . . . on Fire Island.

Part One

What a lovely place this is; it's got water all around it.

—MARILYN MONROE,
when first visiting her acting coach, Lee Strasberg,
on Fire Island

one

Fire Island

No one is quite sure why the narrow, thirty-two-mile barrier beach off the coast of Long Island is called Fire Island, but there is much conjecture on the topic. Many believe the name is tied to its origins—a violent winter storm in 1690 that broke through the mainland of Long Island, creating four separate inlets. The Dutch word for *four* (*vier*) is pronounced somewhat like fire, so that mispronunciation may be responsible. I tend to prefer the version that states the name is derived from the fires that pirates set on its shores to lure unsuspecting ships onto the great sandbar before looting and pillaging everyone and everything on board. Although I am a pacifist, that version is considerably more interesting to me than a Dutch typo.

The backstory of the island's name, as intriguing as it is, is eclipsed by the astonishing history of its many waves of inhabitants. What began with Native Americans, pirates, and moonshiners eventually gave way to a rapid succession of authors, actors, communists, artists, and an entire enclave of LGBTQ+ vacationers.

As a lover of the written word, I am most taken with the list of authors who've roamed its shores. Legendary scribes, from

Truman Capote to Tennessee Williams, spent time on Fire Island, if not writing, I would imagine, at least thinking—which, as an editor, I know is half the battle. The poet Frank O'Hara was struck and killed by a dune buggy on its beaches in 1966, a notable distinction on a virtually car-free island. Mel Brooks and Carl Reiner are said to have drummed up the premise for their infamous comedy sketch, "The 2000 Year Old Man," as teenagers there in the 1940s. And a decade later, Arthur Miller played softball on the field right across from my house, while his wife, Marilyn Monroe, sat in the stands.

It was in that house across from the ball field, ten wonderful years ago, that the love of my life, author and sportswriter, Benjamin Morse, got down on one knee and presented me with an advance copy of his second novel, opened to the dedication. It read:

I love you, Julia. Marry me?

I said yes.

Ben and I had our first kiss on Fire Island the summer before he proposed, and we knew instantly that it was "our" place. It's a common phenomenon. People need to be romantics to fall in love with a narrow strip of land that could be washed away by one big wave, and where their only mode of transportation is a bicycle or their own two feet.

At first glance, Ben and I make an odd couple. We undeniably call to mind Beauty and the Beast: me, petite, with dark shiny hair and my button nose perpetually buried in a book, and him, with his clunky towering frame, unruly locks and moody, brooding demeanor. Though I always found him to be sexy—sexy like an unmade bed. Intellectually, on the other hand, we are completely in tune and have an uncanny ability to finish each other's sentences—not surprising since for most of our marriage I was also his editor.

The decision for us to collaborate wasn't so much a choice on either of our parts as a natural progression. It began with an author passing pages to their spouse—a common occurrence even when publishing is not the family business—and grew from there. A year into our marriage, when Ben's editor hinted at retirement, the writing was quite literally on the page. His publisher agreed to assign someone else to deal with the financial components of the job and I came on board to fill the rest of the role. I had been looking to make a move for a while, and it was very exciting for both of us. Plus, as far as my career went, Ben had always felt like the one who got away. Even with two of my authors on the bestseller list at the time and one a Booker Prize winner, adding Ben to my list felt like a crowning achievement.

When I first heard the name Ben Morse, I was technically a newbie. I say technically because while I had only been in publishing for a year and a half at the time, I had considered myself an editor of sorts since the ninth grade when Ellen Crown's mother (an editor at Alfred Knopf) spoke on career day. By the time she was halfway through with her presentation, I was all in, and my intention never swayed.

I immersed myself in the classics, writing tiny notes in the page margins and highlighting character traits, conflicts, and points-of-view. While the other girls were obsessing over *Titanic*'s Jack and Rose, I went to sleep dreaming of Cathy and Heathcliff or Elizabeth Bennet and Mr. Darcy. I got a greater high poring over my friends' English assignments than smoking a blunt with them in Sheep Meadow. And nothing thrilled me more than a prompt with a small word count. To me, editing felt like the best kind of puzzle.

My first real job, after graduating summa cum laude with a degree in English from Sarah Lawrence College, was at Sopher-Grace, a midsize publishing house run by a sexist tyrant. The narrow-minded managing editor, who inserted the fact that he was a Yale man into nearly every conversation, had a huge ego with little taste or talent to back it up. While others found him a charming throwback to a *Mad Men*–like, three-martini-lunch era of publishing, I found him pompous, misogynistic, and, in fact, not a very good editor—and he knew it. He also knew that firing me without cause would land him in hot water with HR, so he tried other tactics, like tasking me with reading a 120,000-word dramatic tome written by a sportswriter from the *Daily News*, which no one else wanted to tackle.

"Any plans this weekend?" he had asked on a Friday afternoon, as I failed to slip by his open office door unnoticed.

"Nothing much," I lied, not wanting to get personal and admit that I had a blind date courtesy of my nana Hannah, who had been pushing me to go out with her neighbor's grandson, the Doctor, for months.

"Now you do," he said, handing me a cumbersome box containing a double-sided copy of the aforementioned five-hundred-page sweeping saga spanning three generations of a poor Irish family.

I canceled my plans, dealt with Nana, who I was apparently "pushing to an early grave with my lack of interest in settling down," and barely slept the entire weekend, and not because I wanted to impress my jerk of a boss—I couldn't put the book down. I immediately fell in love with its protagonist and developed an instant fascination with its author.

My nana was incorrect in her analysis; I had an interest in settling down. It was just that all my crushes of late had been on fictional characters who instilled unrealistic expectations when it came to my real love life. I went to sleep that weekend dreaming of my nineteenth-century Irish lover and woke itching with an unyielding curiosity about the man who had created him.

I excitedly pitched *A Long Way to Tipperary* at the office that Monday, thrilled by both the prospect of editing it and that my boss's plan to discourage me had backfired. I detailed my vision and explained how perfectly I felt it fit on our list. I comped it to epic bestsellers like Ken Follett and Pat Conroy and came just short of promising him the next Hemingway. My boss agreed to get to it *tout de suite* (his words, not mine) and then strung me along, as if he were in the process of reading, for weeks. Until one day, when I learned from *Publishers Weekly* that Random House had acquired it in a preempt. Telling my boss, who still hadn't read it, "I told you so," was of no consolation. I was frustrated and heartbroken.

The book landed on the *New York Times* Best Sellers list within weeks of publication and I witnessed one person after another lugging around the hefty page-turner everywhere I went. The *New Yorker* did a piece on Benjamin Morse, dubbing him the city's new Renaissance man on account of his ability to craft both epic love stories and gripping sports pieces with equal pizzazz. In the interview, he unsurprisingly attributed his passion for sports to his dad and surprisingly attributed his intimate understanding of the romance read to his grandmother, who had lived with him growing up. He said that as her mind aged, he would let her recount entire tales to him from memory as if they were true stories. The anecdote made me think he was a nice guy.

The entire thing would still eat at me if it hadn't led to a promotion. Word of the debacle rose from watercooler gossip to the editor in chief, who called me into her office and said that the next time I discovered the next big thing, I should bring it directly to her. No more middleman. A few months later I did, and soon became one of the youngest women to be named editor at my publishing house. It took weeks to wipe the giant grin that exploded with pride and amazement from my face every time I caught my name on my new office door.

JULIA GOLD, EDITOR

Still curious about Benjamin Morse, I followed him on social media. His meager display of incongruent images of ball games and book PR gave me little insight as to who he was as a person. I even read some of his articles, trying my best to reconcile the guy to land the first post-scandal interview with Tiger Woods with the one who infused just the right amount of titillating lust and tender longing into the pages of his novel.

I yearned to meet him in person and tell him how much I loved his work. While my insides would sometimes twist and turn when meeting my favorite authors, I hadn't fangirled on a novelist this much since my childhood obsession with Judy Blume.

Then, on a cool spring night, while waiting for the aforementioned doctor, whose company I had been infrequently keeping and even less frequently enjoying, I finally had the chance when Benjamin Morse ponied up next to me at the bar at The Odeon. It wasn't lost on me that literary greats like Tom Wolfe and Jay McInerney were known to have patronized the downtown eatery and had possibly even warmed the same stool that Ben Morse was sitting on. I wondered if that weighed in his decision to choose this particular restaurant, and if so, whether it was out of phoniness or nostalgia. I hoped it was the latter.

He looked younger than I'd expected. His success and proclivity to use old-fashioned language in his writing often made me forget he was just five years older than I was. He ordered, without a menu.

"A New York strip, rare, with a side of fries and a Scotch and soda, please."

It was just what I imagined Ernest Hemingway would order. I drained my glass of merlot and garnered the nerve to speak to him.

"Sorry to bother you, but are you Benjamin Morse?" I asked, already knowing the answer. To be fair, he was taller than I imagined.

"Hey," he curtly answered with a dismissive grin.

"I'm Julia, Julia Gold," I said, which brought just a nod in return.

"I want you to know that you broke my heart," I added.

He looked annoyed, as if he had heard this same refrain a dozen times or possibly as if he were just full of himself and didn't want to chat at the bar of a busy NYC restaurant where chatting was not only tolerated but expected. I guessed he knew that Tom Wolfe and Jay McInerney frequented The Odeon, and he came here ironically. I felt the sinking feeling of disappointment burn in my belly.

"I'm sorry I killed off Patrick O'Reilly," he said, adding, "you know they aren't real people though, right?"

I could have left it at that, since clearly my fantasy of Benjamin Morse far outweighed the ornery real thing, but for some reason I didn't want him to think of me as just an ordinary fan.

"Not in that way," I explained. "I'm an editor at Sopher-Grace. I read you on submission."

"Well, you were the only house we didn't hear back from, so I guess you didn't like it."

"I loved it actually, ergo the broken heart."

"But you didn't throw your hat in the ring?"

Finally, he spoke like he wrote. This made me smile, even though I was pretty sure he would not measure up to my lofty expectations.

"My boss didn't back me up," I admitted.

"Maybe you need a new boss."

"I got one, thanks."

His steak arrived, and he navigated the perfect bite. I looked to the door for my date and adjusted myself as not to interrupt Ben's meal. Soon *he* reengaged.

"Did you ever read the final version?"

"I did."

"And?"

"And it was good."

"Just good?"

Truth was, I wouldn't have killed off Patrick O'Reilly either. I wouldn't have given him and Erin O'Malley a happily ever after, but I wouldn't have offed him, a detail that wasn't in the early draft I had read. I certainly would not tell him as much.

"What? Was it the ending?" he asked impatiently. "Most people love it, you know. Only a few readers have said otherwise."

I decided he must be one of those authors who combs through Goodreads and Amazon for negative reviews. My Hemingway comparison that had seemed so promising when he ordered a Scotch and soda came to a hard stop. I doubted Papa Ernest would give a crap that Suzy from Schenectady was disappointed in the ending of *A Farewell to Arms*.

"It's good, really. I mean, how many weeks have you clocked on the bestseller list now?"

In a case of perfect timing, my date, the Doctor, entered and caught my eye.

"My friend is here. Very nice to meet you!" I exaggerated.

I wished I hadn't had to.

That night I returned home to a new follower on Instagram and a private message that read,

Curious about how you would have ended it.

I had thought about this before but spent more time contemplating if I should answer than how I should answer. In the end I decided it was in no one's best interest to edit a book already in print. I went to sleep without responding.

In the morning I woke up to another message from him.

> **Sorry if I was rude at the bar last night. I'm obviously insecure about the ending.**

It's hard to know if neurotic people become authors or if becoming an author makes people neurotic, but either way the result is the same. As familiar with this particular human condition as I was, I responded with real insight and praise, stroking his ego and soothing his self-doubt as I had found myself doing often with many an author facing criticism. Soon a back-and-forth between us developed. What began as typical publishing industry therapy morphed into shoptalk, followed by chitchat and eventually flirtatious banter. Somewhere in between it all the real Ben Morse, with his boyish charm and his powerful observations, grew on me, and eventually the reality of him excited me more than the fantasy. Tired of obsessively checking my Instagram messages, I gave him my cell—and each of us later admitted to texting and deleting multiple iterations of the question "*Should we meet in person?*"

That summer, I took a share in a house on Fire Island with my old roommate from Sarah Lawrence, Sarah Lawrence. (Yes, her name and the name of the school were one and the same, and yes, it had made her an instant campus celebrity—which she thrived on.) I'd never been to Fire Island, but Sarah Lawrence had been a part of a group house there every summer since graduation. The vibe of the house, which had been founded on beer pong, cold pizza, and shots of Jäegermeister, had matured with its residents, now more interested in charades, clambakes, and chardonnay. It was finally approaching my speed, so when a spot opened, I grabbed the chance to perk up my social life a bit. I spent too much time reading and way too much time texting with Ben Morse. He was no better, by the way. Writing epic love stories on trains, on planes, and in hotel rooms while covering games and tournaments and even the Olympics seemed to render his personal life nonexistent.

Sarah Lawrence was pacing back and forth across our itsy-bitsy room in her teeny-weeny bikini, the smell of her, courtesy of her sacred tube of Bain de Soleil Orange Gelée, penetrating my nose every time she trudged by. She was obviously eager to get to the beach, though too passive-aggressive to say it with actual words.

I looked up from my current entertaining exchange with Ben and blurted, "Go to the beach, Sarah. I'll meet you there."

"Is it that author again? Will you ask him out already?"

"I will, soon."

"Bullshit!" she called, as she grabbed my cell and took off with it to the bathroom.

Five minutes later she returned, announcing, "Benjamin Morse will be on the noon ferry."

I probably changed six times before picking up Ben at the dock that day, which was quite a feat, since I'd packed only three outfits. I'd never experienced anything close to what I was feeling when his ferry appeared in the distance. My heart froze in my chest, and by the time the boat came close enough for me to read her name—ironically enough, the *I'M HERE*—I thought I might pass out from nerves. As it turned out, I wasn't the only nervous one. Ben had also tuned in to the discrepancy in our sizes and our uncanny resemblance to Beauty and the Beast. He'd convinced himself that the chemistry we had clearly established through the written word would never fly in person.

And so it was, on that hot summer day, many, many months after I had first read his manuscript and fallen in love, Benjamin Morse exited the ferry with a shy, blushing smile and a handful of wild clary—the same flowers that Patrick O'Reilly had given Erin O'Malley after they first made love in the fields of Tipperary. How he found a bouquet of wild clary before making the afternoon ferry was beyond comprehension. I ran to him.

When I reflect on that weekend, I always seem to see it through a hazy lens, offering only a fuzzy recollection of first touches, first smiles, and first inhaling of the scent of him, a woodsy mixture of the salty bay and a summer campfire. When his lumbering arms enveloped me in our inaugural hug it filled me with a feeling I had never experienced before. I belonged in his arms. I badly wanted to stay in them forever.

It was his maiden visit to Fire Island and, while I was a newbie myself, I was sufficiently familiar with the simple lay of the land—a grid-like arrangement of beach-themed streets traversing the narrow strip from the bay to the ocean—to find my way around. The bay side boasted a small town dense with bars, restaurants, boutiques, and three separate ice cream shops, each with a perpetual line leading to its door. The ocean side contained a vast and beautiful beach dotted from one end of the thirty-two-mile island all the way to the other with colorful towels, colorful people, and an abundance of gratitude.

We spent most of the day by the ocean in the company of my housemates, playing Kadima, riding the waves, reading, and basking in the sun. We took part in the group barbecue dinner and stayed for a few rounds of charades. I picked *A Tale of Two Cities*—which Ben quickly guessed from my miming a tail. For his turn he quite hysterically got stuck with *The Vagina Monologues.* If I hadn't been into him before, watching him attempt to act out the word *vagina*, without one, made me fall even harder.

He suggested a walk and an ice cream cone before the last ferry, and we ended up sitting on the swings at the playground on the Great South Bay, each with a scoop of Moose Tracks to distract us from the narrative running through both of our heads—*Where is this going?*

"I have to make the boat," he said, slowing down his swing and jumping off. He grabbed the chains of mine to slow it down too. The moon was full, and its light caught his shy smile.

"Can I kiss you goodbye?" he asked softly.

"You can kiss me hello," I responded breathlessly.

His mouth was sweet and cold, and we kissed on that swing for what felt like hours. He never made the last ferry boat.

Back at the house, I crawled into the barely twin bed next to a sleeping Sarah Lawrence and gave him mine. His legs hung off the end, and I marveled, again, at the difference in our sizes. A sliver of light from the full moon outside illuminated our faces enough to stare into each other's eyes (and souls) until our lids became too heavy and we both drifted off.

The next day, we rode the Long Island Rail Road back to the city together, holding hands the entire way. And we didn't let go until this past Tuesday night at Sloan Kettering hospital, when I quietly left the earthly world for good.

two

My Funeral

Even though we knew the end was coming, Ben and I did not discuss the funeral or what I wanted. Knowing my control-freak mother as I did, expressing my wishes seemed as pointless as when I asked for a small bat mitzvah and ended up making my grand entrance into the ballroom of The Pierre Hotel on the back of a camel. I took it as a lesson, and when it was time to marry, Ben and I eloped. It was a transgression that my father understood and my mother never forgave. I was certain that my funeral would be seen from the same vantage point, my mother's, with little consideration for what my barely half-Jewish, fully heartbroken husband would need. It was wrong of me not to tackle the subject with my family in advance. I just didn't have it in me, even though I had nightmares that my mother would open up my coffin, yell "Is that what you're wearing?" and apply her signature Dior red lipstick that she'd been unsuccessfully pushing on me since the tenth grade.

In the Jewish religion, the preference is for a burial to take place within twenty-four hours of death. So it was the very next day that Ben stood at my graveside funeral. I was shocked that he won the debate between an intimate graveside service versus a multilevel extravaganza at Riverside Memorial Chapel, but apparently, even my indomitable mother was not on her A game after losing her firstborn child. It was the only argument she had lost in years, although, in her characteristic fashion, losing may have been her plan all along.

The trade-off for the smaller funeral was Ben's promise to commit to seven full days of shiva—the Jewish time of spiritual and emotional healing. On hearing the deal he made, well, let's just say, if guilt existed in the afterlife, I'd have been riddled with it for not making my wishes clear in advance. It was a bad trade, and poor Ben had no idea what he was in for. My new Rabbi friend, who was thankfully present for the conversation, tried to warn him. She said, "When someone dies in the prime of their life, there are many, many people who want to pay their respects. It's going to be hard to manage at the cemetery, and you are going to be flooded with visitors at your home." Ben thought he knew better and stood his ground. I guess you rarely know better than a rabbi.

The funeral service was brief. My Rabbi friend spoke beautifully about my life cut short. She acknowledged my inner light and my dry wit that she had gotten to know over the past six months, my success as an editor and my love for books; Modena chocolate; Fire Island; our rescue dog, Sally (named for the book, *Sally Goes to the Beach*); and, of course, my husband of nearly ten years, the now five-time bestselling author, Benjamin Morse. No one stood up and recounted funny stories because, first, that is not something that's really done at a graveside service, and second, a funeral for a thirty-seven-year-old is not likely to have you laughing at remember-whens. I think you need to be at least seventy before the guests leave feeling as though they had attended a roast at the Friars Club.

Ben scanned the sweltering scene with his hollowed eyes, determining that he had done no one any favors, himself included, by getting his way on the service. He steadied himself and took a deep breath in as the Rabbi read the beautiful poem "We Remember Them," by Sylvan Kamens and Rabbi Jack Riemer responsively with the crowd:

At the rising sun and at its going down; We
remember them.

It was brutally hot, even for late June (not for me, by the way—a very nice perk of my new condition). My mother began to rock back and forth and back and forth, the ridiculously high heels she had worn for the occasion digging deeper and deeper into the ground. Someone noticed and placed a folding chair beneath her, and even though it wasn't a good look for her—sitting while everyone else was standing—she acquiesced. It reminded me of a camp visiting day in Maine when the temperature reached a record-breaking 105 degrees. My mom, who never went anywhere without perfectly coiffed hair and a face full of makeup, rose from her lawn chair and walked directly into the lake, right in her Lilly Pulitzer.

At the blowing of the wind and in the chill of
winter; We remember them.

My sister, Nora, traditionally a mama's girl, took my usual spot, wrapped in our father's arms. I hoped she would help to fill the void of my passing by becoming closer to our dad. She was crying, but as I watched her then, all I thought of was our hysterical fits of laughter in the dark when we were young and shared a bedroom.

At the opening of the buds and in the rebirth of
spring; We remember them.

My high school friends stood in a row, holding on to each other for dear life, old grudges between them instantly dismissed. A montage of memories played out in front of me, from sneaking drinks at bat mitzvahs in bandage-style dresses to throwing our shared fake IDs out the bathroom window of Webster Hall for the next group to enter with.

At the blueness of the skies and in the warmth of
summer; We remember them.

There were many people there from Random House and the publishing world in general: publicists and editors, authors and friends. Ben's agent, the indomitable Elizabeth Barnes, was visibly rattled, which surprised me as I had never even seen her blink. I was happy for Ben that there was such a nice turnout, though he didn't seem to notice.

At the rustling of the leaves and in the beauty of
autumn; We remember them.

Out of all the groups in attendance it was our Fire Island friends who felt nearest to my heart. The lot of them huddled close to one another for collective strength. All except for my nearest and dearest, our neighbor, Renee. She had stepped to the side and was clearly having a hard time keeping her composure. Losing her marriage and her best friend in one year had cracked her exceedingly strong resolve. Her ex-husband, Tuck, walked over to her and put his hand on her shoulder for comfort. She swatted him away—no dismissing grudges there. I homed in on the newest addition to the group, baby Oliver, who was just six weeks old. His moms, Pam and Andie, were a part of our inner circle at the beach.

As long as we live, they too will live, for they are
now a part of us as; We remember them.

Before long the sun-beaten crowd loaded themselves back into their cars, where the procession to return to the city spanned two exits on the parkway. Ben could tell, upon leaving, that most people hadn't had the chance to express their condolences, and it panicked him. It takes a lot to keep a Jew from paying a shiva call, and not having had a face-to-face exchange with the bereaved was top of the list (maybe second to top—word had gotten out that lunch was being catered by Zabar's). He knew that many would feel the need to tell him in person how sorry they were for his loss—a mouthful of condolence followed by a bagel with whitefish salad, and they would leave satisfied that they had fulfilled their commitment. That notion, along with the conversation on the way back to Manhattan, pushed him over the edge.

It was odd to see Ben sitting in the limo alongside my sister, my parents, and my maternal grandmother, without the link that was me. He really didn't fit in without me beside him. I could tell it was hard for him to stomach the sight of my grandmother, alive and kicking at ninety, while I was gone so young. She began questioning everything about the upcoming shiva, from the kashruth of the food to the *female* Rabbi. Ben was clearly longing for a do-over.

More and more often lately, nonorthodox Jews, like us, seem to sit shiva for less than the traditional week. Ben's family was not religious at all, and when his father died a few years ago, they sat shiva for three days and thought it was the most pious thing they'd ever done. His mom was not Jewish, and he was never bar mitzvahed.

When he met my family for the first time, Nana Hannah, my father's mother, came right out and asked him, "Are you Jewish?"

I squirmed while he answered truthfully.

"My father is Jewish and my mom is Protestant, but we were raised Jewish—culturally, at least."

I thought she would give her standard answer, "You are what your mother is," but she didn't. She asked him a question that no one had ever asked him before.

"Who do you believe in, God or Jesus Christ?"

He didn't have an answer, so she plowed on.

"I assume that you and my granddaughter have had sex?"

The whole family, who were now glued to this inquisition, jumped in to stop her.

"I have a point," she insisted, raising her hand in the air like a traffic cop.

"When you are at your most fulfilled moment in sex, do you scream out Oh God or Jesus Christ?"

"Oh God," he replied sheepishly.

"Okay, how about when you're flying on an airplane and there is horrible turbulence? When the plane lands safely, what do you say to yourself?"

"Thank God," he responded.

"One more. You're a sportswriter, right?"

"I was. I recently took leave to concentrate on writing novels and to spend more time with Jules." He looked over at me lovingly, and I wasn't sure if he was for real or trying to score points with Nana Hannah. He hoped his affection and accomplishments would distract her. It didn't. She continued her inquisition.

"What football team do you root for—Jets or Giants?"

"Whoever is playing against the Pats."

Nana laughed. "Nice. Mets or Yankees?"

"Yankees."

Nana Hannah shook her head and laughed some more. "Mets or Yankees he's sure of!" She continued, "You're home on the couch watching the Yankees. Bottom of the ninth, tie score, two outs, bases loaded, and the phone rings. You get up to grab it and catch your pinky toe on the corner of the cocktail table. What say you?"

"Jesus Christ!" he proclaimed, laughing along with everyone else.

Nana Hannah stood up and kissed Ben on top of his head, officially proclaiming him to be Jewish enough. Ben had adored her since that moment and was very sad when we lost her a few years later. I knew it was out of some sort of respect for her and her sweet proclamation that day that he had agreed to be a part of the elaborate mourning rituals—because he had assured her that he was Jewish enough.

Ben stared out the window for most of the ride to the city, clutching the unlit candle whose flame, he was told, would burn for seven days, guiding a part of my spirit on its journey toward the afterlife.

The Rabbi had taught me that everything has a soul and that every soul has five dimensions. One of those dimensions, the

Ruach, translates to the words *spirit* and *wind*. I clung to this often in my last weeks on earth. It comforted me.

I am the wind, I thought, in the moment.

Back at the hospital, I only realized I had passed when I could no longer feel Ben's hand cupping my cheek. At first I attributed it to the morphine, but it soon became obvious that I would never feel his touch again. As I realized it, I saw Nana Hannah, clear as day, coaxing me to come join her.

From what I could tell so far, you are given two choices when you die: go right ahead to see the people who have passed before you, or stay with your person until you are ready to go. I missed Nana Hannah something awful, and it was hard not to run to her, but after everything I'd been through I yearned for one last summer, with Ben, on Fire Island. It was obvious that he needed that too. As Nana Hannah faded from sight I wondered if I would spend eternity in limbo.

three

The Shiva Fugitive

The skyline rose in front of us as we crossed the bridge. Ben hadn't grown up in the city as I had, but about forty-five miles away in Jersey. His delightful, childlike reaction to the sight of the Manhattan skyline, even after years of seeing it rise into view, always delighted me in return. Today he was devoid of expression.

The shiva would take place at our apartment, another detail that I found worrisome. Ben had wanted to be at home for the week, as opposed to being held hostage at my parents' palatial pad, but when the Rabbi announced our address at the funeral, I could see the shiver of fear it sent down his spine. It wasn't an overreaction: all of those people strolling about our new two-bedroom, peeking into the room we had once been decorating for our baby, empty except for an orphaned treadmill and errant splotches of nursery paint colors, as if my dying wasn't pity-inducing enough.

The limo stopped at the corner of Columbus and Seventy-Second. Everyone but Ben piled out. My sister had been sobbing uncontrollably since we'd crossed the bridge, and Ben never even turned toward her. Normally, he cared for my sister very much, but I doubt he'd even heard her crying.

My father slid back into the car and put his arm on Ben's shoulder in encouragement. I questioned where my dad was getting the strength. His composed-mourner act was a little suspect and left me wondering if he had uncharacteristically helped himself to a taste of my mother's Valium.

"Cousin Shirley has everything set up. Nothing for you to worry about. C'mon, son," my father said, coaxing Ben out of the car.

I had never heard him call Ben "son" before. I'd never heard him call anyone "son" before.

Ben gave in and dutifully followed, more zombie than man.

When the elevator opened on our floor, my formidable cousin Shirley blocked them in the hallway like a linebacker. She was carrying a traditional tin wash cup and bowl that, along with her accent, resembled an artifact from a Polish shtetl. Ben tried to avoid her, but even he didn't have a chance.

"You must not enter the house until you have washed your hands," she insisted. "You cannot bring death into the house!"

He made two fists, pulled them to his chest, and pushed past her. He wanted to keep my death with him. I worried he may never wash again. The others consoled Shirley and apologized for Ben's behavior. They all washed their hands. Twice.

Ben entered the apartment and grimaced at the covered mirrors and traditional low mourners' chairs. My great-uncle Morris saw Ben's bothered reaction and approached him.

"Benjamin, if there is anything I am sure of in this world or the next, it is that Jewish practices of mourning are invaluable. If you follow them, they will help you get through this."

Morris mistook Ben's blank stare for interest and launched into a lengthy explanation of each detail. I knew better. When he finished, Ben asked the question that had clearly been plaguing him since he walked through the door.

"Where's my dog?"

Uncle Morris smiled. "In your bedroom." He placed a loving hand on Ben's shoulder. "I'm sure Sally will say all the right things."

As Ben shut our bedroom door behind him, Sally, our sixty-pound bordoodle, jumped him and cried as if she knew what had happened. Ben locked the door and lay on the bed. Sally snuggled next to him, her head in his lap. I've never been so thankful for rescuing that dog as I was on that day. I immediately pardoned her for the Manolo Blahnik incident in exchange for Ben not having to be alone.

He reached over for my pillow and placed it over his face. At first I worried he was trying to off himself, but as he took long deep breaths through his nose, I realized it was infinitely sadder. He was inhaling my scent. He sat up abruptly, his eyes fresh with panic as he pulled off the pillowcase and folded it up as compactly as possible. Sally followed him to the surprisingly empty kitchen, where he walked over to the cabinet that housed the ziplock bags. He removed a large one and squeezed in the pillowcase, sealing it to protect my smell from fading. The ziplocks sat next to the poop bags, prompting Sally to wag her tail in anticipation of a walk. Ben smiled at her, a real smile that seemed to come with a cartoonlike light bulb overhead. He grabbed the Fire Island Ferries schedule taped to the fridge and shoved it and the pillowcase in his pockets. He clipped on Sally's leash and took a deep, cleansing breath for strength. In the kitchen doorway his gaze went from the front door to my family to the yet-to-be-lit yahrzeit candle on the entranceway credenza. The Rabbi's words, "This candle will light the way for Julia's soul," ran through his mind. He suddenly wondered if the things the Rabbi had been filling my head with for months were more than mere words to ease my fears. He wondered if I was with him.

I wished so much that he believed. I'd explained to him many times over the past few months that death was not the end, that my soul would not perish with me but live on eternally. I even asked him to join me and the Rabbi on occasion to hear her expertise on the Kabbalah, the afterlife, and death itself, firsthand. It made me much less fearful of dying, and I knew it could make him less fearful of losing me. After a while, I stopped talking about it. He wasn't a believer, and I needed to be all in. I was determined that, when the time came, I would not go kicking and screaming but in fact go gently into that good night. This is not to say I didn't try to live; God knows I tried to live. But when there was no possibility of doing so, I wanted to leave in peace.

Ben now found himself praying that it was all true. He decided he couldn't risk taking off without the yet-to-be-lit candle, if so, possibly leaving me behind. He waited for a heated discussion among my family members to distract them, which took all of two minutes, slipped the candle under his suit jacket, and left, mumbling "Walking the dog," to anyone who may have been listening. As he exited through the revolving door of the lobby downstairs, he anticipated being weighed down by the afternoon heat, but he felt immediately lighter. He hurried to the corner, turned, and headed for our parking garage, where he officially became . . .

The Shiva Fugitive.

four

The Pretty Way

Rush hour had already begun when Ben escaped the city. Between the gridlock and having to pull over on account of not being able to see through his tears, there was no way that the Shiva Fugitive was catching the four o'clock ferry. As he usually did when he realized we weren't making the boat, Ben took an alternate route out east, the "pretty way," as we had taken to calling it.

The pretty way, a two-lane highway called the Robert Moses Causeway, is a bucolic slip of mid–Long Island road flanked by the Atlantic Ocean on one side and the Great South Bay on the other. If you were dropped there from above, you would probably guess you were somewhere on the coast of California or the Florida Keys. Long Island often gets a bad rap—people think of strip malls and endless traffic, but parts of it are breathtaking. Driving this length of road offers the opposite aesthetic to sitting in traffic on the Long Island Expressway, plus it had the added benefit of not passing the cemetery again. I pictured him seeing the exit and pitching a tent next to my freshly dug grave.

An archipelago of tiny islands appeared on the bay side dotted with quaint cottages where residents travel to and fro on motorboats. On the ocean side, the Atlantic peeked out between breaks in the beachgrass-covered dunes. Each glimpse of the sea took your breath away, again and again and yet again.

In normal times, we would open all the windows, allowing the week's tension to be washed away by the cross breezes of the ocean and the bay, but these were not normal times. I wished Ben would at least crack his window, but he seemed dead set on not breaking the seal of grief.

With hours until the next ferry, and an overwhelming desire not to interact with other humans, Ben pulled the car off the road and onto the dunes, where he sat and watched the waves lapping the shore. Like the sea air, the ebb and flow and ebb and flow of the ocean usually took away his stresses, but short of a tsunami, there was no wave big enough to accomplish that today.

I watched Ben and Sally and the waves for a bit, and found myself wishing that things had been different between us. While I was grateful that we had spent so much time together—especially considering the hard stop that my death brought to the relationship, I sometimes wished that I hadn't been Ben's editor. While it had been a beautiful and very successful partnership, Ben would now lose his wife and his editor in one fell swoop. Either on its own would have been hard enough for him to bear; together, he was completely lost. He was supposed to turn in a new book proposal in the fall, the third in a three-book deal. Looking at him now, that seemed like an impossibility.

I thought about how different we might have been if Ben hadn't given up his reporting job to become a full-time novelist. If he had been following a busy schedule of sporting events, prioritizing "the game" over birthdays, anniversaries, and even Thanksgiving, we would have been an entirely different type of pair. I had always looked at those "we have separate lives" couples with curiosity—the ones you find at cocktail parties standing at opposite ends of the room, deep into tales of their individuality. Ben and I stood so close to each other at cocktail parties that we may as well have been one person. In the spirit of the original celebrity super couples like Brangelina and Tomkat our host would often introduce us as Benlia, and we would all laugh about it. It wasn't funny now. It had been years since either of us had spent a night apart. Even when I was in the hospital, he never left my side. I was frightened for him.

Ben let out a guttural sigh. Sally whimpered in response, and I decided I needed a break. I bailed and headed to the 4:00 p.m. ferry without them. It was selfish on my part, but hey, you only die once.

five

The Usual Suspects

People sometimes asked me why we put down roots on a barrier island where the threat of "one big wave" always loomed large, and I usually just smiled and shrugged, not wanting to reveal the secret. It's not the beauty of knowing that the ocean is just mere steps away from wherever you are, or the benefit of living sans cars and therefore without traffic and pollution. It's not the sound of the noon siren that reminds you to head to the market to pick up lunch, or the charm of the familiar scene when you get there. It's not the fountain of youth effect that being surrounded by water seems to imbue, or how the minute you set foot on the ferry the weight of the world wafts away in the summer wind. And it's not the sunsets over the bay, or the anglers lined up in the morning surf, or the fawns that dutifully follow their mamas across the ball field. The secret, the real secret of what makes this narrow barrier island so special, is the people.

Fire Island is a haven for warm souls and mismatched pairs, for neighbors, lovers, and kooks, and kook-loving neighbors. It's a community of people who spend the winter dreaming of their return. If you were lucky enough to have been born to it, odds are you would find its sand between your toes for the rest of your days. And if you came upon it through your own volition, as I did, your odds could be similar. It was a magical place, and if you believed in it, if you felt the magic, you could become a lifer as well.

I really never thought I would see it all again, and as I arrived at the ferry terminal—nothing more than a parking lot, a ticket booth, and snack counter—I nearly kissed the ground.

There was a small crowd waiting for the boat, many of whom looked as if they had come straight from my funeral. An interesting selection of the usual suspects. I scanned the group and homed in on Pam and Andie and baby Oliver. I had yet to get a good look at him. I peeked into his carriage but could barely see him bundled up under a hat and blanket. Even though they had him dressed for winter in June, I knew they would both be great moms. They had so much love to share.

Pam and Andie had known each other forever, literally forever, but only became a couple about six years back. Their coming-out trajectories were very dissimilar. Andie could barely remember a time that she didn't know she liked girls, changing her name from Andrea to Andie sometime in the fifth grade, while Pam got with every guy she could straight through college. She joked that she was a bit of a slut, but in the end she was just trying to feel something, anything, which she didn't until the first time Andie kissed her.

"Oh," she had said out loud in the elevator of the Brighton Beach apartment building where both of their grandmothers lived.

Andie and Pam had known each other since they were kids, and the last time she had done something scandalous in the elevator with Andie, they had gotten chased by the building's super for pressing all the buttons. At ten, she thought it quite thrilling. Their kiss topped it.

Andie took a step back.

"Oh, what?"

"Oh my God," she clarified.

They both laughed. The Q train could not make it to the city fast enough after that. They spent the rest of the weekend in bed.

When Pam relayed their meet-cute story to me, she riffed on the famous Billy Crystal quote at the end of *When Harry Met Sally*: "When you realize you want to spend the rest of your life with women, you want the rest of your life to start as soon as possible."

Pam's grandmother—Bubbe Bertie, as she liked to call her—recognized something in Pam that she had yet to let herself discover. When I spent time with her bubbe, the few times I had, I figured that looking at her granddaughter may have been a bit like looking in the mirror. My guess was that Bubbe Bertie would have lived a very different life if she were born a few decades later and that she wanted more for her granddaughter. In the spirit of another eighties rom-com, *Crossing Delancey*, Bertie fancied herself a Jewish matchmaker and invited her neighbor and her neighbor's granddaughter (Andie) for Shabbat dinner one night, when Pam was coming from the city, hoping the two women would reconnect.

When hearing of the surprise guest Pam said, "Bubbe. This is awkward. I haven't seen her in years."

"I think you will have a lot in common," Bertie insisted.

There was no use in arguing. There was never much use in arguing with Bubbe Bertie.

As kids, Pam and Andie were thick as thieves. Both girls grew up in the suburbs, Pam in Jersey, Andie on Long Island, and both were shipped to their grandmothers' apartment building in Brighton Beach on school vacations, while their parents worked. What may sound like torture held some of their greatest childhood memories.

For two kids from the suburbs, an apartment building in Brooklyn may as well have been Disney World. They played sidewalk games with the neighborhood kids, like hopscotch, jump rope, and handball, while the bubbes sat on lawn chairs, relishing the faint sea breeze coming off the ocean just a block away. They rode their scooters up and down the boardwalk, and when the weather was bad they scooted in circles around the lobby. When they were old enough to cross the street, the bubbes gave them a couple of bucks to walk over to Mrs. Stahl's Knishes, a tiny shop tucked under the elevated train on Brighton Beach Avenue. Pam still dreamed of the crispy cushions of mashed potatoes and onions. Andie would always get the smelly kasha flavor instead of potato—even though the neighborhood kids would turn their noses up at her "old lady" choice. She didn't care. She had always danced to the beat of her own drum. It was one of the things Pam admired most in her. Pam, on the other hand, had always been a conformist.

As they tell it, on one particularly hot spring day when they were around sixteen, Andie smuggled a bottle of Boone's Farm wine in her overnight bag and the two of them snuck out in the middle of the night and headed for the beach to escape the heat of their grandmothers' stifling apartments. They took off their shoes under the boardwalk, dug their feet deep into the sand until they reached the cold layer, and passed the bottle of cheap sweet wine back and forth till they felt light and tipsy. They lay back on the sand. The wind had picked up a bit, and Andie turned on her side and looked into Pam's eyes with a serious expression. She reached out and tucked a few errant hairs behind Pam's ear. Pam felt a stirring in her groin that she had never felt before, and it frightened her. She jumped to her feet to counter it.

"Let's go," she'd insisted, already on her way back to the building. Sixteen-year-old Andie followed, feeling as if she had crossed a line but still too young and inexperienced to put it into words.

After that, other than quick hellos in passing during Jewish holidays, they didn't see each other for years. Until that kiss in the elevator, when everything changed.

"You hungry?" Andie asked Pam now, at the ferry dock.

"Not really," Pam replied.

"White or red chowder?" Andie inquired.

"White."

We all laughed.

Hungry or not, the first ferry ride of the season was not complete without a cup of clam chowder from the snack-bar window. Nothing compares to that first spoonful after months of longing for it—thick with chunks of potato, bits of bacon, and dollops of nostalgia. I would have been envious but, lo and behold, I seemed to have lost that emotion as well. C'est la vie, c'est la mort.

We stepped in line at the snack counter behind Matthew Tucker, the sixteen-year-old son of my across-the-street neighbor Renee—the one who shuddered at her ex-husband's touch at the funeral. I looked around for Renee but didn't see her or her ex, Tuck, anywhere. I was surprised Matty was on his own, though he wasn't completely—his cat, Houdini, was strapped to his back in one of those pet carrier backpacks. It was usually Renee's job to bring Houdini out at the beginning of the season. I looked around for her again, then imagined her trying to keep her distance from Tuck at the shiva at our apartment in the city. I was sure she was questioning what she was doing there since Ben was nowhere to be found. I was sure that many people were wondering the same thing right about now—especially our friends and work colleagues. For Ben's sake, I hoped the widower card was on par with the cancer card—I hadn't done anything that I didn't want to since my diagnosis.

The kid behind the counter looked at Matty familiarly.

"Extra crackers, right?" he asked.

"Yeah, thanks," Matty responded, adding the obligatory, "how was your winter?"

"Awesome, man. You?"

Matty knew there was little worse than asking the standard question "How was your winter?" and receiving the shit truth in return.

I hoped no one would ask Ben the "How was your winter?" question. I assumed that my death was common knowledge by now, while Matty's problems, I thought, were more on the q.t. Not for me, by the way: his mom had fully shared every hideous detail of their divorce as it transpired.

"Yeah, pretty awesome too," Matty lied.

Matty's winter had sucked. I could search for a more sophisticated word but *sucked* sums it up too perfectly to bother. Back in September, Matty's straight-as-they-come father "Tuck" Tucker broke his mother Renee's heart by running off with his twenty-seven-year-old assistant, Lola. You may think that sounds apropos for a guy nicknamed Tuck Tucker, but his moniker wasn't a cool pet name lovingly given to him by his college frat bros or his best friend since kindergarten. He literally asked people to call him Tuck and corrected them when they called him by his given name, Arthur, until they finally gave up and gave in.

Tuck is a forensic accountant and Renee is a divorce attorney; pitting the two of them against each other registered a solid 8.9 on the divorce Richter scale. It was truly a cataclysmic event. They nearly killed each other during the proceedings, and both parents blurred all boundaries and shared terrible things about the other with poor Matty. In the end, neither party could bear to give up the one material thing that the other cherished the most. And so, they put the house on Fire Island into a trust for their only child. Obviously, the house still belonged to all of them. Matty was just a kid, and his parents paid for its upkeep and could come and go as they pleased, but legally it was considered his. Tuck and Renee were supposed to rotate their time there—switching up every two weeks. But Tuck still wanted to be with Lola, and Lola wanted no part of Fire Island. Lola, who aspired to an influencer lifestyle, fancied herself a Hamptons girl.

Apparently whatever Lola wants, Lola gets. Tuck rented them a "cottage" in Sagaponack. It was doubtful he would be on Fire Island all summer, and I doubted Matty would leave to visit him in the Hamptons.

"All aboard, Bay Harbor!" the ferry captain beckoned as everybody fell into line. I was excited to get on the boat—excited to be on the water once again.

six

The Four O'Clock Ferry

Pam and Andie pushed their baby and a ton of baby gear aboard the four o'clock boat. The twinkle of anticipation for Oliver's inaugural ride, not to mention the warm chowder, helped erase the lingering sadness in their eyes from the day's event. I was glad they had skipped the shiva and headed straight out to the beach. I would have done the same if I were them.

The ferry boats have interior seating below and open-air seating up top. In keeping with their nor'easter dress code for little Oliver, Pam and Andie remained down below. Ben and I only ever sat down below during an actual nor'easter.

I followed Matty, who tossed his bag onto the piles of provisions and climbed the stairs to sit up top with Houdini. Within minutes, an older man, Joel Mandel, slipped into the powder-blue metal bench behind him, his cronies watching intently from afar. They had all been at the funeral, along with Joel—their suits and sports jackets were a far cry from their usual T-shirts and gym shorts or sweats. Joel greeted Matty with a hard tap on the shoulder.

"Matty, Matty, how are you, my young friend?"

"All good, Joel. You?"

"Just came from your neighbor Julia Morse's funeral, so—what can I say? Not so good."

"Must have been aw-awful," Matty stammered.

"It was awful," Joel continued. "We all went."

It was bizarre to hear a review of my funeral in person, but oddly satisfying to know that my death affected people. Selfish as that sounds, it would feel horrific to spend thirty-seven years in a place and not be missed when you leave. Before I was diagnosed, when death was just a punch line, I remember Ben contemplating the topic. He joked while surveying the crowd at one of his book launches, "These people will probably be at my funeral, but they'll only cry if I'm in the middle of writing a trilogy. When *you* die, there won't be a dry eye." I doubted the first part of his statement was true, but the second was now fact.

Joel motioned to the men sitting a few rows back. They all shot a quick wave to Matty. He shot one back.

"We didn't go back to Ben's apartment afterward. None of us could bear anymore."

"I couldn't bear choosing who to stand with, my mother or my father, so I skipped the whole thing," Matty admitted.

"I'm sure Ben will understand."

I knew he would. Ben wasn't one to judge. Joel squirmed in his seat and looked back at his friends. They were all watching the conversation with great interest, and it was easy to figure out what was going on.

In our small town, the men, especially, can mostly be divided into three groups—ballplayers, tennis players, and beach bums (surfers and volleyball players included). It doesn't matter what age you are, what religion or sexual proclivity you subscribe to—these are the basic categories. The men here, along with Ben and Matty, (though both could surf and hit a tennis ball well enough) were in the ballplayers' group. And Matty, with his powerful stick and cannon arm, was a star. A star they had all helped to create and all took pride in. His father, on the other hand, was a horrible softball player—a fact that had never stopped him from insisting on a spot on the roster for the big Labor Day Homeowners' Game against the neighboring town. It was this fact—and the intensity of that game—that had Joel Mandel and his cronies all up in Matty's face.

"So, talking about your parents," Joel asked nervously, "is it true?"

"That my parents divorced this winter?"

"No, Matty, please, that's none of my business."

Matty waited a beat to let Joel squirm. I was obviously completely correct in my analysis, and now Matty seemed to have figured it out as well. He put Joel out of his misery.

"That I got the house in the divorce and will officially be able to play in the Homeowners' Game instead of my father?"

Joel tried to hold in a smile, but it was useless. A huge grin broke through. He looked back at his teammates and shot them two thumbs up. The men, all three in their fifties or sixties, high-fived each other like teenagers. Matty turned to look at them, and they quickly stifled their reactions.

"Sorry, Matty. It's been years since we won the big game and, well, your father's a nice guy and all, but the Strikeout King did plenty of damage."

"My father's a prick."

"Yeah, well, sorry about that too, kid. See you on the field this weekend?"

Matty nodded, and Joel stood and patted him on the shoulder again, this time more in empathy than salutation. Matty drowned his sorrows in his soup until the shore appeared in the near distance. He squinted, looking for his best friend, Dylan.

Every year, Matty rose from his seat as the ferry reached the harbor and waved his arms back and forth over his head like a madman, or a mad boy, really. And every year, his best friend, Dylan, would return the favor from the shore, jumping up and down like a puppy spotting its owner. Today was no different. Add in the catastrophic shifts since summer last, the predictable sight of Dylan greeting him from the dock filled Matty with a palpable sense of relief—and me with love. When I was lucky enough to witness these two in action, they had always tugged on my maternal heartstrings.

Dylan's father, Jake Finley, was the ferry captain. He looked out at Dylan from his vantage point, towering over Matty, and shook his head. I had no doubt he was considering what kind of trouble these two would get themselves into this summer. The list of past infractions was long. Especially for a strict single parent like Jake.

Matty took in Jake's barreling legs. They were the size of tree trunks, especially compared to his own father's, which were more like twigs.

"Hello, Matthew," Jake said, barely acknowledging Matty's response as he walked away.

Things had definitely changed between Jake and Matty in recent years. Not that he was ever warm and fuzzy, but when they were young, Jake would let Matty and Dylan ride the ferry back and forth for fun and would even allow them to sit in the captain's chair and steer a bit. And on his rare days off, he'd take them out fishing on the Boston Whaler he kept docked at the market. Those youthful days of innocence were long gone. Matty was definitely cautious around Jake now that the two kids' summer antics had elevated to fooling around. I knew from Renee that Jake was mostly misunderstood. Yes, he was as big as a lumberjack and strong as a longshoreman, but his heart was a lot softer than he let on. There was no doubt he was feeling the weight of his baby girl leaving the nest.

Yes, Matty's best friend, Dylan, who could skim a rock on the bay and make it skip seven times if it skipped once, was a girl. At least she was until a couple of summers back when, to everyone's great shock, a woman with breasts, a bikini, and a belly button ring showed up at the ferry dock.

Breasts aside, Dylan and Matty had been best buds since I arrived on the island. But, since postpubescent teenagers can rarely put breasts aside, it recently began to escalate into something different. The two spent many hours last summer kissing and groping on chilly August nights. Ben and I embarrassingly witnessed them making out on the bleachers or at the beach on more than one occasion during Sally's nighttime walk or when returning home from dinner in town. I knew they rarely saw each other over the winter, and Matty's parents seemed clueless about the change in their relationship status. The two kids usually picked up right where they left off, and I hoped, for Matty's sake, this summer would be the same. He'd certainly weathered enough change lately.

Matty tossed the cardboard soup container in the trash and bounded down the stairs of the ferry to be the first one ashore to meet Dylan. Seeing her was the only thing he had looked forward to in a long while. Dylan was extraordinary—like lightning in a bottle.

Part Two

Summer is, after all, the season of escape:
the landscape in which to contemplate, alone,
our failures and our possibilities; the safety valve,
the frontier that none of us wants—or can afford—
to see closed.

—JOAN DIDION,
"American Summer," *Vogue*, May 1963

seven

Dylan Finley

Most year-round residents experienced a mix of happiness and dread as the summer people arrived on the island, but for Dylan Finley it was pure happiness. The main source of that happiness was the chance to spend time with her best friend, Matty.

Dylan navigated the crowd, setting herself up in a prime spot to greet him, as she had been doing for years. She used to make her dad phone her up at the first sight of Matty and his parents on the mainland, but Jake hadn't acquiesced to that in ages. Now she just waited for Matty to text her. Aside from the standard check-ins for Christmas and whatnot, the two barely kept in touch over the winters. When scrolling back, his text that morning of "Meet me at the 4 o'clock ferry?" had been the first he'd sent her in months. Although he did call a few times this winter to vent about his parents' sudden divorce.

Dylan took in the crowd. It was the typical bedlam.

For starters, let me explain that everyone basically knows each other here. So, the happy people getting off the boat have only seconds to call out "Hello" and "Goodbye" and "Why are you leaving on such a glorious day?" to the not-so-happy people waiting on the dock for their ride back across the bay. When the boisterous exchange of passengers is complete, the new arrivals fan out onto the sidewalk, most dragging their bags over to the adjacent wagon park. There are usually a spattering of guests being picked up by their hosts, whose big welcoming smiles usually mask their true feelings: *Why did I invite them, and when are they going to leave?*

I recognized the three Fauser sisters waiting with empty wagons, hoping to make a few bucks carting people's belongings to their houses. I saw Bonnie Zucker with a beaming smile on her face, searching the throngs for her children and grandchildren. A deckhand tossed a prescription from the pharmacy on the mainland down to Ruth, the zinc-faced doctor's wife, and another passed a large box of fresh mozzarella from the Italian grocer in Bay Shore to one of the kids who work at the town's beloved market.

Everything seemed to be as it always was, though of course it very much was not.

Dylan controlled herself from charging the boat when she saw Matty debark, mostly because she was aware of her father's watchful eye, I'm sure. Matty must have been aware as well; when he reached her they hugged cautiously. Dylan grabbed his duffel and threw it in the basket of her bike, while Matty gave her a once-over, landing on the bikini top peeking out from under her denim shirt.

I wondered if she just threw on the outfit without a second thought to meet her BFF or contemplated every aspect of her appearance in the mirror to meet her BF. My gut said it was a combination. She caught him looking, and he blushed.

"Nice pegs," he teased, motioning to the fresh additions of two metal tubes sticking out from either side of her back wheel. He swung his leg over her rear tire and stepped on them for a lift home. Dylan scanned the crowd for Matty's mom or dad before shoving off.

"You're alone?"

"Except for Houdini." He turned his back so that Dylan could say hello.

"My mom's coming later tonight, she let me come out alone—you know—it's part of the broken-home dispensation package," Matty joked.

Dylan joked back, "That and the not-so-broken home."

Matty had obviously caught on that he was in the "I'm sorry that we failed you" post-divorce window, where it was possible to get away with nearly anything. Dylan hadn't been in that window for years.

Jake yelled out to her through the fence, "In the house by seventeen hundred hours, Dylan."

"Yes, sir!" she called back, making a sarcastic salute.

"My grandma is coming for dinner," she explained to Matty.

"That's OK. I'm kind of excited to be alone in my house for a little."

I was sure each of his parents had been hovering over him for months. Either out of worry, or out of making their case. Poor kid.

As Matty and Dylan rode the sandy sidewalks in silence for the five-minute trip from the dock to his house, you could almost feel their bond reignite. They arrived at the ball field on our corner, where Matty's eyes nearly popped out of his head. He jumped from the bike before it fully stopped.

"What the hell is that?"

Dylan disembarked and leaned her bike against the backstop fence to join him—gaping in awe at the forty-five-foot net that had been erected between the field and the tennis courts over the winter. She had watched it go up (there's not much to do in the off-season), but it still amazed her. I thought it was pretty unbelievable as well.

"You didn't hear about the twenty-five-thousand-dollar net?"

I had, but it was obvious that Matty had not. Ben and his friends had been placing odds all winter over who would be the first to hit one over it. They were considering starting a pool.

"Wow, no, I didn't. I guess it will stop the balls from flying over the fence."

"That's the hope—though I always kind of loved it when they did."

We stood, myself included, and reflected on the monster shots of seasons past: the smack of the ball hitting the bat at that sweet spot, followed by loud cries from the players on the field of "Heads up!" and even louder curses from the pissed-off tennis players ducking for cover as an errant softball descended from above. We were all a wee bit disappointed that the show would now be over.

Matty took the sentimental moment to reach down, touch Dylan's face, and kiss her briefly on the lips. She took an odd step back in response. It obviously hurt his feelings, which embarrassed him. He blushed.

"What's up, Dyl?"

"Nothing—I just have to get something off my chest."

His face instantly filled with worry, as if he were kicking himself for thinking that she was still in the same place she had been when he left. It had been a long year, and she very well could have a boyfriend. I hoped an unwelcome surprise wasn't coming his way—he'd had more than enough unwelcome surprises of late.

Dylan attended high school off-island, so there were endless prospects in the boyfriend department, aside from the possibility of someone local. Matty worked a summer job as a delivery boy at the market with another kid—Corey—who was a year-rounder like Dylan. I hoped it wasn't him. I didn't care for him at all—he never bothered shutting the screen door behind him or thanking me for a tip. I knew Matty didn't like him either. Poor Matty.

Dylan was really taking her time answering, staring at her feet and kicking the dirt around home plate. Embarrassment, about what I didn't know, landed firmly on her cheeks. Matty noticed too.

"Dylan, don't worry about it. I thought we would start where we left off, but if you're not into it, that's cool."

Dylan laughed, and her complexion went from crimson to scarlet. I was beginning to feel for her more than Matty—the pull of the sisterhood and all.

"No, no. That's not it. I want—I mean—you know how I'm going to college in September?" she managed.

Dylan was a year older than Matty and two years ahead of him in school. She had skipped a grade on account of being really smart and also because the Fire Island elementary school had so few students that they combined grades when she was young. By the time she went to Bay Shore Middle School she was way ahead of the other kids. She was headed to UC San Diego in September to study marine biology, and while she presented now as insecure and green she was anything but. She was the epitome of competence and confidence. Dylan Finley never met a race she didn't win.

Matty had had enough of this uncomfortable exchange.

"It's cool, Dylan, I get it."

"You don't get it. Between growing up here without my mom, and only being seventeen when I start school—I feel like everyone is going to be so much more experienced than me."

"Please, Dylan, I'm sure those California kids have nothing on you—in class or in the ocean."

"That's not the experience I'm talking about."

She was obviously upset, he was obviously confused, but like the good egg he was, he gave her a comforting hug. Dylan relished it for a bit and then broke away, blurting out her big admission in one breath.

"I don't want to go away to college a virgin!"

I laughed, surprised by her proclamation, but Matty was speechless. Now they both looked down, shifting their weight from one foot to the other on the dry sandy clay, little clouds of dust wafting through the silence. It was likely the first time there had been any awkwardness between them. And the longer Matty was silent, the more foolish Dylan felt.

I don't know what Dylan expected, but I knew this reaction wasn't it. It was as if, as ridiculous as it may seem coming from the mind of a sixteen-year-old, having sex with Dylan had obviously not occurred to him. I guess it was because they weren't actually boyfriend and girlfriend. From what Ben and I had witnessed the summer before, it always seemed very aboveboard, if you get my drift. Like they had covered every inch of territory on the island apart from each other's bodies, which just stood as another one of their many adventures. Actual sex was a huge leap from there. Though I got what Dylan was feeling. Like I said before, Dylan Finley never met a race she didn't win—until now, I guess. I was sad she was thinking of her virginity that way, but not all that surprised.

I wanted to shove Matty or yell at him to snap out of it, but Dylan stepped in and did both.

She pushed her hands into his chest and shouted, "Matt! If you don't want to do it with me, just say so."

He recovered, but not well. "No, no. It's fine."

Dylan became angrier. "Fine? Don't do me any favors."

"No, I mean, not fine. Of course I'll do it."

He touched her cheek again, and it brought a small smile to her face.

"I would love to do it with you, Dylan."

Dylan's smile widened, and she kissed him gently on the lips. The whole interaction felt a bit forced on both sides, very perfunctory. Maybe it was just nerves.

"Do you want to come in?" he asked, in a very half-assed way. He had a lot to wrap his head around. To his obvious relief, she tapped on her watchless wrist.

"Seventeen hundred hours, remember?"

He smiled at her and said, "OK. See you tomorrow, Dyl Pickle," in homage to their usual nightly exchange.

"Not if I see you first, Hazmat," she responded, as she had a zillion times before.

As she rode off, I took a good look at the four corners where I had lived. While the ball field looked visibly different on the outside, the three houses that surrounded it were forever changed on the inside. I wondered how the summer would play out and how much of it I would see.

eight

The Eight O'Clock Ferry

When the eight o'clock boat came and went without Ben on it, I imagined his eyelids becoming heavy and his fighting to stay awake, parked on the beach exactly where I had left him. I could picture his inner turmoil—feeling the exhaustion wash over him but knowing that setting an alarm in order to make the ferry would mean turning on his phone and being on the hook for the dozens of missed calls and texts that would surely be waiting for him. His absence in the city would be worrisome to say the least, especially to his own mother, whose heart ached for him and his loss as if it were her own. I hoped he would wake up in time to make the last boat of the night, aptly named the "dead boat," whose only purpose was to wait at the dock on the other side in advance of the morning departure. Once on board the passenger-less vessel, it would be easy for him to sit downstairs, unnoticed by the captain and the one crew member above—his shiva-fugitive status would remain intact.

Luckily my trip to the ferry wasn't a total loss, as Renee stepped off the boat and, just as quickly, out of her heels. She was still wearing her funeral outfit. I was surprised she hadn't gone home first to change, but when you want to be at the beach right away, there is little that can stop you. As far as I knew it was the first time she'd been back since the divorce. My last memory of her and Tuck together was us all lying on the beach one late afternoon. Renee resting her head on Tuck's potbelly, Tuck twirling her hair in his fingers, both so seemingly content in the life they had built together.

She began walking toward her house, but after half a block turned around and headed to town. My guess was she was hungry and knew nothing much would be waiting for her at home. Besides, it had definitely been the kind of day that required a good strong drink or two if she were to have any chance of falling asleep later. She stopped in to the first restaurant in town, Matthew's, and sat down at one of the small tables that flanked the bar.

"A bowl of clam chowder, extra crackers, please."

Like mother, like son.

"Anything to drink?" the server asked.

"Tequila and club soda. With a lime. Actually hold the soda and make it a double."

The drink arrived first, and when the chowder came she requested another. It was a lot for her, she didn't usually drink hard liquor. She looked around. It had been a while since she had been there. Matthew's was the place to be when she was younger, especially on Thursday nights for Margarita Madness. She had hostessed there the summer before her dad sold the house, and whenever she looked back on that time an uncontainable smile sprouted across her face. Tuck didn't particularly care for Matthew's, so she hadn't been back in years. Nothing had changed, from the old-salt decor to the thickness of the chowder. She was thankful for that.

A group of twentysomethings were playing darts in the corner.

One of them caught her staring and smiled. She felt his eyes still on her as she finished her soup. It wasn't odd, in my opinion at least. Even in the full throes of grief, her hair down and messy, her eyeliner smudged, Renee was still gorgeous. A few minutes later, the guy approached, darts in hand.

"Want to play winners?" he asked.

"Are you winners?"

"I am."

He was adorable. Scruffy with a shy smile. His Levi's looked older than he did, and he wasn't wearing any shoes. Renee had painfully slipped her shoes back on when she entered the restaurant, and she was literally dressed for a funeral. The tequila had just begun to soothe the ache in her heart, a little, and for some reason that she didn't quite understand she kicked off her shoes again and agreed to play. She was good at darts. Darts was a big thing in most of the bars on the island, so she'd had her share of practice during her younger years. Plus, I doubted she was in any rush to go home to the street where her best friend and her husband no longer lived.

She won the first game, which prompted her new friend, Gabe, a drummer from Brooklyn who had an upcoming gig on the island and planned on staying the week, to insist on a rematch. Three games later the place emptied out and it was clearly time to head home, though Renee still didn't want to.

"What now?" she asked Gabe, madly out of character.

"A slice to soak up the tequila?"

They waited on line at the pizza place with more young people. She was too buzzed to be embarrassed in front of the few she recognized.

"That kid used to babysit for my son," she told Gabe.

"How old is your son?" he inquired.

"Sixteen. How old are you?" She laughed.

"Almost thirty."

He was still at the age where you made yourself older instead of younger. After thirty I started doing the opposite.

"I was almost thirty ten years ago," she responded—peeling off a couple of years as she did.

"Was it a good ten years?" he asked.

If he had asked her that question a year ago, she would have said it was a great ten years. She'd had a happy marriage, a loving husband, a beautiful boy who had grown into a fine young man, and a killer career doing just what she'd always wanted to do—helping women exit unhealthy relationships intact, both emotionally and financially. Her success had helped her to slay her childhood demons and assure that she would never need a man, or anyone else, to support her—financially at least.

But now she answered with "That's a loaded question."

"Want to eat on the beach, check out the starry night?"

Another loaded question.

"OK, sure," she said, clearly wondering if the words she heard coming out of her mouth were her own. I was questioning them too from the never-paint-outside-the-lines Renee I knew and loved. I couldn't wait to see where this was all going.

They only ate a few bites on the beach before the pizza ended up in the sand, a casualty of his lips brushing against hers. It took her by surprise but was totally welcome and followed by a more passionate kiss and then a frenzy of wet and warm tongues and teeth connecting and teasing, and fingers, his, playing in her hair. I could almost see the thought *What am I doing?* run through her head, before running out just as quickly. As far as I knew, it was the first man, other than Tuck, that she had been with since she was in her twenties. Thanks to the combination of tequila and emotional numbness, she let herself go in a very atypical way. I was happy she had the chance to escape from her mind, to feel something besides sadness and regret.

"Was it a good ten years?"

If she was thinking of any of it, it all disappeared as the drummer's hand reached under her skirt.

I left and headed to the dead boat in hopes of finding Ben.

nine

The Dead Boat

The midnight ferry appeared with Ben aboard under a dark sky. Despite the way the drummer had sold the starry night to Renee, there was only a sliver of a moon and a few stars to light it up. Ben was thankfully still gripping the candle but worried that he hadn't yet lit it. I was in the dark on this as well. Was my soul looking for that particular flame to light my way to heaven? I wanted to at least stay the weekend.

More tears came for Ben, as he stared blankly out the ferry window. Sally did her best to keep up the pace, licking each away as it escaped his eyes. Thank goodness he had our dog. Her presence infused a small thread of warmth in his hollowed heart, assuring it wouldn't implode from sheer emptiness.

It was very dark out, but Ben knew every inch of the way from the dock to our house by memory. His gait was unusually heavy. Each step looked as if he were about to fall off the horizon. The darkness was a reminder of the unlit candle, and I could see a fresh layer of panic come over him. He pulled the ziplocked pillowcase out of his pocket, opened up a little corner, and stuck his nose in, inhaling my scent before quickly resealing it. He'd once said that burying his nose in my neck and inhaling deeply transported him to childhood visits to his grandma's house in the country, the ethereal essence of the morning grass after a rain—he'd said I smelled like watermelon air. It was that kind of description that surprised me, both in his writing and in real life. He was a true enigma, my husband, with his clenched jaw and brooding eyes in contrast to his tender heart.

He was careful not to turn the outside light on when he reached the house. Even though it was after midnight and everyone was asleep, he still worried about drawing attention to himself. He was certain that, for him, it was best to grieve alone. He lifted the mat up for the key, but it wasn't there. Attention be damned, I could see he was close to screaming at the top of his lungs. He jiggled the door handle, and the door popped open. It wasn't surprising, really. Everyone from the plumber to our neighbors knew where we kept the spare key. It was a testament to the simplicity of owning a house on a car-free island where the action peaks at drunken fisticuffs and stolen bicycles. Though I heard people talking at the funeral about someone breaking in to houses in the middle of the night just to have a snack and take a load off. The *Fire Island News* dubbed the unknown person "the Goldilocks Interloper."

Once inside, Ben set the candle down on top of the fireplace mantel and struck a long match to light it, wondering if there was a prayer for the occasion. He made one up, a mishmash of things he had heard over the years in synagogues and churches, hoping that doing his best would count for something, and followed it with a tearful and heartfelt amen. His efforts touched me, though they came with uneventful results. Nothing seemed to change for either of us.

Ben must have been hungry. He hadn't eaten since the morning, and even then he didn't do more than pick at whatever was put in front of him. We hadn't been to the beach in months, so there wasn't a morsel of food on the horizon until the market opened in the morning. I prayed he would sleep until then. He kicked off his shoes and stripped to his T-shirt and boxers, without even bothering to turn on the light. He slipped into our bed, which he expected to be cold but was oddly warm.

Even after the big nap in the car, Ben's eyes looked heavy with the possibility of more sleep, a state far preferable to him now than being awake. He closed his eyes and tossed and turned before feeling a large lump move in the bed next to him—a lump that was most definitely not Sally.

Who's been sleeping in my bed? I thought as images of the aforementioned Goldilocks interloper rushed to mind.

Ben screamed and jumped a good five feet in the air, flicking on the light switch as he descended. The lump screamed back.

"What the hell, Ben!" Our eighty-year-old neighbor, Shep Silver, cried out as if Ben were the intruder. Sally ran in to investigate—too little, too late.

"Jesus, Shep, you scared the crap out of me!" Ben exclaimed.

"You scared the crap out of me!" Shep hollered, placing two fingers on his racing pulse, possibly concerned, but just as possibly to be dramatic.

"What are you doing here?" Ben asked, betting on the latter.

"What am *I* doing here?" Shep sat up and pushed himself back to the headboard and continued, "You nearly gave me a heart attack! This is *my* house."

Ben looked like he might explode, literally explode. My first thought was that the old man, whom we had bought the house from ten years earlier, had finally lost his marbles. His behavior had always been odd, but this was beyond. His wife of fifty years,

Caroline, had passed away over the winter too, and if Ben was feeling this adrift after ten years of marriage, I figured Shep must be fully out to sea.

Ben took a few deep breaths and tried to set things straight, explaining in a kinder tone, "It's not your house anymore, Shep. I bought it from you over ten summers ago. You know that. You gotta stop calling it your house."

Houses rarely changed hands on the island, and when they did, they were usually inherited or sold to a longtime renter with the inside scoop. A house hadn't sold to a stranger on our block in years; Ben and I were the first newcomers in a long, long while. The fact was that once you arrived on the island and planted yourself there for a few summers, it became a part of your DNA, your third arm, your fourth child, your favorite uncle. Nobody seemed to leave unless they died—and even that I'm not so sure of anymore.

Shep put on his glasses and began his protest, confident in his evidence.

"Benjamin, when you get a delivery from the market, what does it say on the box?"

Poor Ben barely answered, "'Old Silver House.'"

"Correct. And when you run out of gas for the barbecue and order a new tank, where do you tell them to bring it?"

"The Morse house," Ben answered with misguided confidence.

"OK. And they say?"

Ben grimaced. "'Where's that?'"

"And you say?"

"The old Silver house."

Shep stood and puffed out his chest like a rooster before

pounding it with his fists. "Old Silver, old Silver house! When I'm dead and you're dead and the next guy who owns this house gets a delivery, it will probably say the old Morse house. You'll have your day, Ben. You hungry?"

Ben shook his head in disbelief and answered, "I am, but there's nothing to eat. I haven't been here in months."

"There's plenty," Shep answered as Ben threw on a pair of sweatpants and grudgingly followed him to his own kitchen.

I've always had a soft spot for the curmudgeonly old man across the street and his beautiful wife, Caroline, with her silver hair and British accent. I was hopeful, before she unexpectedly passed away over the winter, that she would be the one to keep an eye on Ben for me. I never imagined this scenario. I knew I should feel bad for Ben, who went to such noble efforts to be alone, but I was happy that he wasn't.

"I didn't expect you back yet. I've been sleeping here for a couple of weeks, figured I would head back home when my girls visit in August—they both promised to. I've always liked this house better than that debacle across the street," Shep admitted. "You know it was Caroline who wanted to build that big house—room for all the kids and the grandkids, she said—meanwhile they come out for one week, if even, and I'm alone in that big house while all of my memories are over here in this one."

And there we had it, a hearty spoonful of Shep Silver's somewhat warped, somewhat logical reasoning. It also didn't help that, aside from hanging a hand-painted LOVE SHACK sign on the front gate, Ben and I had barely changed the place since we bought it. Houses on Fire Island traditionally come with the entire contents included, and Caroline had beautiful taste. An Eames chair, a mid-century-style sectional, an antique farmer's table, there was no reason to replace any of it. Plus the house had good bones: a simple ranch built by an artist in the fifties, it had high ceilings, big windows to let the light in, and walls paneled in rare pecky cypress wood. Point being—it looked very much as it had when Shep had raised his family there.

And then there were the memories he spoke of, the ones from before the decades-old rift between Shep's two daughters began. That rift prevented the Silver sisters from even sitting beside each other at their mother's funeral, let alone concurrently filling Shep's house across the street with his children and grandchildren.

I like to think we had helped fill the void for Caroline and Shep over the years, at least a little—sitting with them at the beach, enjoying cocktails or having them over for barbecues and vice versa. Typical generational divides are blurred in Fire Island, more than any other place I've been. Who's to say your favorite people need to be your own age? I think it's the way it should be.

"You'll see soon enough, Benjamin. Your memories are all you have," Shep warned.

Ben winced at the words he knew to be true. He sat on a stool at the kitchen island as Shep opened the fridge. It was full. Shep noticed Ben's surprised expression and filled him in.

"No widower goes hungry in this town, I imagine. Every day the ladies bring over more and more food—I've named them the Brisket Brigade." He lay the choices out on the counter.

"Mindy Shapiro's casserole surprise. You remember her husband, Jerry? He escaped a few years back."

"Didn't he die?"

"Sometimes it's just a means to an end." Shep grinned.

I swear I saw a faint smile cross Ben's lips as Shep continued announcing the buffet.

"Dotty Brown's fried chicken, Millie Holtz's corn salad—I could swear they all want to get in my pants. At least the ones who brought the covered dishes."

Ben looked at him skeptically as he explained, nodding with conviction, "They get a second shot at me when they come back to pick up their casseroles."

Shep piled an assortment of food on a plate and put it in the microwave as he continued, "It's Caroline's fault, you know. She was always telling everyone how good I was in bed."

I was grateful I'd never been on the receiving end of that conversation but pondered who would have their sights set on Ben now that I was gone. There was a fair number of divorced and single women in our town and the next who I could picture vying for his attention (or inattention as the case may be). Another thing I should have brought up in the last few months: don't rush, but don't wait too long. Not that we ever had that kind of conversation. Whenever I tried to discuss life without me, he shut me down.

"We won't go hungry this summer, I imagine, either of us," Shep pointed out as they waited for the microwave to ding.

When it did, Shep put the plate, with a little of everything, in front of Ben, along with a fork and a napkin. He held up a beer. Ben declined.

"Just water, please."

Shep inspected Ben while he ate. It was obvious how hard it was for him to swallow even a bite—nausea and despair pushing back against the hunger. Watching Shep watch my husband, I had to admit that Ben appeared to have aged ten years in one. It was hard to look at him. I noticed at the funeral that most people couldn't hold his abandoned gaze for long. It was like staring into the sun: you could only do it for a minute before you had to turn away. But not Shep. Shep wasn't intimidated by Ben's grief. As with everything he did, he took it straight on.

"You really look awful, Benjamin. You should try to get some sleep."

"I actually slept today, in the car after the funeral, for the first time in weeks."

"I'm sorry I wasn't at the funeral." Shep's strong facade cracked, along with his voice. "With Caroline gone . . . there's only so much—"

Ben interrupted him, aiming to curtail his misery. "Don't worry. I understand. You must really miss her."

"Hell, I missed that woman when she left a room."

Ben pushed his barely eaten plate away. Shep scraped what was left of it into the garbage.

"You'll eat tomorrow—we can even have a catch if you want," he offered sweetly.

Ben's eyes widened at the thought of it.

Shep encouraged, "Let's get some sleep."

I wondered if Shep would head home now that Ben had arrived, but he didn't seem to be going anywhere.

Ben looked toward our second bedroom, but he needed to sleep in the bedroom that we'd shared. He studied Shep's tired face and asked, "Have you been sleeping OK, Shep?"

"I fall asleep OK, here in this house, but it's the waking up that gets me."

Ben looked confused. Shep noticed and responded sadly.

"Life can be pretty subtle, Benjamin, but not death. Death really packs a punch."

And with those last words of wisdom, the two of them turned in—together. I imagined Shep pulling up memories of Caroline in their first little cottage by the sea, and Ben thanking me profusely for my insistence on buying a king-size bed.

I wondered, now that he had been delivered safely home, albeit in the hands of an ornery octogenarian with questionable conduct, if it was my time to go. I stood by the candle and waited for my nana to appear again. There was no sign of her.

ten

The Bicycle Journey

After my diagnosis, I had shuddered at the thought of Ben sleeping alone in our gargantuan bed. We had endlessly debated the size when we bought it. Ben had fretted that we would never find ourselves tangled up together as we had in the queen-size—legs intertwined, a hand brushing against a breast or a thigh. Sometimes those errant touches would lead to us making love in the middle of the night—that soft and sensual type of lovemaking, not impaired by alcohol or the pressures of the day. And other times, it would have us peacefully wrapped in each other's arms till morning. I promised I would search him out in the king-size bed to initiate both scenarios, and he eventually agreed on the larger mattress.

"Room for little humans," the man at the mattress store had thrown in during our debate. We had both smiled nervously. As I swiped my Amex, I realized the salesperson was onto something. It was most definitely time to move on to the "little humans" stage of our lives. We had planned on having children but never got to the point of putting that plan into action. We were always too busy with work. I wonder now what life would have been like if we had taken the hint at the mattress store and tossed my birth control before its delivery.

Instead, I said, "Did you hear what the salesperson said?"

"Yeah—about the five hundred coils—very exciting!"

"Ha-ha, and no."

"Let's talk about it after our next deadline?"

I agreed. I didn't feel ready and was so happy with the way things were, but I think that was the day I first heard my biological clock ticking.

Now, as unexpected as it was seeing Ben asleep next to Shep (and Sally), I felt relief that he wasn't alone in the king-size bed. I watched as the rays of early-morning sun crackled through the giant bay window, stirring him awake. His hand immediately shot to his belly as death sucker punched him good morning. It was just as Shep had described. Sally awoke with a moan, and Ben patted her on the head knowingly.

"I feel you, girl, c'mon, I'll let you out."

She followed him dutifully, heading to her favorite spot between the garden and the deck to relieve herself. The screen door slammed behind them both, waking Shep. He too wrapped his hands around his belly as his own reality pummeled him in the gut. He called out the window to Ben.

"Bring back a couple of bagels and some herring—in cream sauce."

"I guess I'm going to the market," Ben reported to the dog, letting her back inside. He slipped on flip-flops with the T-shirt and sweats he had slept in. I would take odds he would wear the getup all day, maybe even sleep in it again tonight, yet alas, no one to bet against.

Ben walked to the shed to get his bike and was immediately confronted by the thing that had haunted me more than the cavernous bed. My bicycle.

The bicycle is often a vehicle of romance in a car-free town such as ours, but today it was anything but. The first sight of my barely ridden, bright yellow bike with the matching plastic ducky horn and baby seat attached was as brutal as I had imagined it would be. Ben pulled it out angrily and dragged it to the back of the house, a little plot of dirt reserved for junk and firewood. He tossed it like an old horse put out to pasture and returned to the shed with a tear-stained face to collect his own bike. I had dreaded this moment for months, and even considered calling one of the local contractors to remove it before he arrived. But I worried that might have upset him more. Now I wished I had.

Ben bought the yellow bike with the baby seat as a grand romantic gesture in the fall when we were closing up the house for winter after our first obstetrician appointment. He had been slow to get on the parenthood train, and when he rode up our street, all smiles, squeezing the ducky horn, I knew he was fully on board. I had looked at it in awe. We were finally having a baby.

Watching other moms transport their children on the back of their bikes on Fire Island was one of the first things I thought of when anyone mentioned the joys of parenting. It was the first thing that Pam and I were able to bond over—maternally, that is—in the two minutes that we were actually pregnant together. The thought of us riding up and down the streets of Bay Harbor with our babies in tow had us both on top of the world.

I remembered our first summer in the house, asking Renee why she still had a baby seat attached to her bike. At the time, Matty was nearly eight, and certainly not climbing on for a lift, though I had seen tired kids that old squeeze their little butts in for a late-night ride home.

"I can't bear the thought of taking it off," she'd explained, and went into great detail about the joys of singing young Matty to sleep on it over the years with a medley of moon songs: "Moon Shadow" to "Moon River" to "I See the Moon and the Moon Sees Me." Renee was not naturally nostalgic, but even she couldn't resist the purity of this fleeting act.

The bike was a great marker of the passage of time on Fire Island. In fact, one's entire journey there can be distinguished by the state of one's wheels.

The training-wheel years don't last long, as the wheels' removal is closely tied to the self-respect of both parent and child. The backbreaking (for the parent) and tear-inducing (for the child) ritual of learning to ride a two-wheeler has its rewards for all involved—freedom!

Freedom comes easily in a town with few cars and fewer strangers. By the time a kid is seven or eight, even the most paranoid parents allow their offspring to go it alone. They needn't even come home for lunch, because as long as they can spell their name, they can charge a sandwich at the market and eat it on the dock with their friends, feeling like they're at least twelve. By the time they actually turn twelve, it is on to a bigger model with pegs and giant baskets for summer gigs delivering pizza or transporting buckets of clams retrieved from the sandy bottom of the Great South Bay. That bike will eventually be passed down, stolen, or beaten up by the ocean air, and though that kid is really not a kid anymore, when they step on their next set of wheels and pedal the sidewalks of Fire Island, they still feel like one.

That sense of freedom lasts a very long time—often right

until the day they drag their wheels over to Steve at the hardware store and announce proudly that it is time to attach a baby seat to the back. A wonderful moment that, in our case, tragically backfired.

I watched Ben as he made his way to the market. He rode so slowly I wondered if he would fall over. I imagined he wasn't ready for the outpouring of love and sympathy he was about to receive. When he reached the widened expanse of sidewalk between the ferry dock and the wagon park, he froze. Thankfully, after a few minutes, Matty pulled up, nose to nose.

"Hey, Ben," he managed, not really knowing what to say.

Ben answered back with an indistinguishable sound, before looking down to hide the tears that had formed upon seeing him. Matty gripped Ben's shoulder in sympathy. The two had been playing ball together for years, with Matty starting as somewhat of a team mascot before surpassing most in skill. Like Ben's friendship with Shep, age was never much of a factor.

"Are you going to the market?" Matty asked.

Ben barely nodded.

"Want me to pick up what you need instead?"

The offer thawed him.

"Yeah, thank you. Some coffee, the *Fire Island News*, a couple of bagels, and something to put on them."

"Got it."

"Oh, and Shep wants some pickled herring. Not the kind in a jar, the kind from—"

"Behind the deli counter—got it."

"And charge it to my account. It's under Julia because there are those other Morses, on Bungalow."

"Do you want me to ask them to change it?"

"Why?"

Matty turned beet red, realizing he had said the wrong thing and no doubt picturing the wretched scenario for both Ben and the person checking him out with his dead wife's name all summer. Ben barely noticed and silently rode away.

I didn't follow him. I had no idea how long this afterlife visitation would last and there was no way I was missing one last trip to the Bay Harbor Market.

eleven

The Market

Born and raised on the Upper West Side of Manhattan, I've frequented my fair share of outstanding food markets. In fact, my childhood apartment on Central Park West was a five-minute walk to Zabar's, Citarella, and Fairway. If you are not familiar with these three Manhattan food Meccas, let's just say they are woven into the tapestry of the city as much as the Empire State Building or Carnegie Hall.

Every Sunday growing up, my dining room table overflowed with the usual cast of characters: my grandparents, my mom's great-aunt who lived below us, my father's widowed business partner, and babka from Zabar's, bagels from Fairway, and the most exquisite gefilte fish this side of the Hudson from Citarella. We would sit around for hours, noshing and kibitzing and passing around sections of the Sunday *Times*, owning our culture like the true Upper West Side Jews we were. Even with the Zabar's/Citarella/Fairway trifecta being such a big part of my childhood, my Fire Island provisioner was still my number one.

The Bay Harbor Market and Liquor Store, the only commercial

entities in our small town, were owned by a couple in their sixties, Les and Winnie Biggs. They were the third generation of the Biggs family to own the market. Les's great-grandfather had won it in a poker game back in the 1920s, when vaudeville actors and moonshine-makers filled the island.

Besides carrying everything one could need, it was arguably the best place to socialize other than the beach. A trip there, whether for a sandwich or a long list of groceries, always took twice as long as necessary on account of the chatting factor. The market itself was nothing much to look at: bright fluorescent lighting, a blue-and-cream-checkerboard floor, and narrow aisles flanked by white wooden shelves. But the Biggses' only son, Little Les, an unfortunate misnomer as he was anything but, made up for the weak aesthetics. He was beautiful. Tall with sparkling blue eyes, thick black hair, and square shoulders that aligned perfectly with his square jaw. And let's not even discuss how quickly he can open a produce bag!

From early on, it was obvious that Little Les was destined for great things. He was one of those boys and then men who walked with a purposeful stride—even before it became obvious where he was going.

From the first time he took his place behind the deli counter, the people lined up for him to make their sandwich. Before I tasted one, I was sure that the attraction, for the ladies at least, was in the handoff. The handoff always came with a slow, thoughtful, killer smile. Until I tasted one. It was a good sandwich.

The ability to craft the exact meat-to-cheese ratio, the right touch of salt and pepper, an ideal amount of shredded lettuce, avocado, tomato, and the expertly mixed and applied condiment was not his greatest skill. Baseball took that prize. Les was a great ballplayer. Not just Bay Harbor great, America great, and even Big Les gave in to letting his only son have a few hours off on weekend mornings to play in the town's game.

Little Les was a major league hitter with a gun of an arm who could whip a ball from third to first before the runner even hit his stride. He was so good, in fact, that to keep the teams fair he had to agree to bat lefty, and even then he stacked the odds.

By the time Les turned fifteen, he was dreaming of playing college ball and possibly beyond. And those dreams were soon achieved. He was recruited by the University of Virginia, and in his junior year there he left to play Double-A ball. A year later, he was playing Triple-A, and it was no surprise when he was called up by the Baltimore Orioles.

The Bay Harbor ballplayers chartered a bus and drove up for his first game. And even though he was only in for the last inning, and struck out, it was a dream come true for them all. He slowly made his way up the roster, and by his third year in the majors he was a starting player until one night when a drunk driver crossed a divider on the highway and sent his car tumbling down a ravine, ending his career and nearly his life.

He returned home to his spot behind the deli counter with a bum left leg and his twinkle extinguished. His stride was no longer purposeful, and he never played ball again, not even in Bay Harbor.

By the next summer, even the sandwiches suffered, and everyone was worried about Little Les. The town's greatest mavens got together over lime rickeys and canapés and decided that Little Les needed to replace his love for the game with another love. They each found a girl, a neighbor or cousin or cousin of a neighbor and invited them to the beach with an ulterior motive in mind. With every introduction, Little Les barely looked up over the counter until week six, when Sally Ingram introduced him to her niece from Westport, Connecticut, Darcy Miller.

"A pound of grilled artichokes and six sour pickles for now, please, plus two racks of ribs and a barbecued chicken for delivery later," Sally had ordered, adding, "Les, this is my niece Darcy, she went to Chapel Hill." She turned to Darcy. "Les played ball for UVA."

The two schools were legendary rivals. Les did a double take at the beautiful Tar Heel and joked, "I won't hold that against you."

Sally watched as his killer smile slowly expanded across his face. She had missed that smile.

Unlike the other women who'd been brought around to meet Les, Darcy, who was quite a catch herself, was not in on the scheme. She didn't bat her eyelashes and blush in front of the dreamy-looking former ballplayer in response to his killer smile and attempt at humor. This got Les's attention, and when their order of chicken and ribs came out of the oven at the end of the day, Les delivered it himself.

Les stayed for dinner, and possibly breakfast, I was told, and soon thereafter his turkey sandwiches tasted good again. Ben said the joy was back in them. I had noticed a big shipment from Hellmann's on the freight boat the day before, but I never mentioned it. He seemed so happy that he could taste the joy.

Now, I followed Matty in to the market, where he was greeted with open arms—well, not exactly. As usual, Big Les's hands were completely full.

"Hi, Les. How was your winter?" Matty asked, with genuine interest.

"Good, but too short."

Spoken like a man who worked sixteen-hour days all summer long.

Big Les got up every morning at 5:00 a.m. and crossed the Great South Bay to pick up fresh bagels and the morning papers. He was back in time to help unload the 7:00 a.m. freight boat. He never complained, but people on the receiving end of those early-morning papers and fresh bagels would adversely describe the winter as too long and the summer as too short. At least I always felt that way.

A handsome man with a weatherworn but welcoming smile, Big Les added, "The wife has your schedule," before getting back to business.

Winnie sat on her perch at the back of the store, answering the phones while searching for Matty's delivery schedule.

"Bay Harbor Market," she said into the receiver before quickly pulling the phone away from her mouth to plant a loving kiss on Matty's cheek.

Matty smiled hugely. I knew he was thankful that at least some things hadn't changed.

Matty grabbed a box of Lucky Charms and a quart of milk before heading to the most popular place to congregate in the store—the deli counter. There, Little Les was already crafting a sandwich. He wasn't the only one, by the way. There were always one or two other guys by his side. But a response of anyone but "Les" to the common question, "Who made my sandwich?" was usually met with a grunt of impending dissatisfaction.

Upon seeing Matty, Little Les wiped off his hands on his apron and came around the counter for a burly bro hug, exclaiming "Matty!" Followed by a rustling of his hair and a "Hey, you grew some!"

I'd noticed it too. There were a few years when the height difference between Matty and Dylan was like a textbook illustration for a puberty chart for boys versus girls. They once played Romeo and Juliet at the annual Bay Harbor Kids Shakespeare Festival. I'll never forget Matty on his toes for their fateful kiss. Now, at sixteen, he had finally surpassed her.

"How you holding up?" Little Les asked, clearly referencing Renee and Tuck's divorce.

"Good, good," Matty lied. "You?"

"Can't complain."

The main reason for his lack of complaint, Darcy and their adorable three-year-old son, the littlest Les, came by. She hugged Matty hello, leaving him to blush while discussing her plans with Little Les.

"Baby, I'm making the next boat. Do you need anything from the other side?"

Little Les gently touched her face and kissed her lips.

"I got all I need right here."

She leaned in—"I'll be back after lunch"—and out. "Bye, Matty. Sorry about all the crap with your parents."

Poor Matty. The off-season gossip trail ran deep.

As she left, Little Les headed back around the counter.

"What can I do you for?"

"Half a pound of herring with cream sauce, please."

"Pickled herring? Is your grandfather visiting?"

"No, it's for my neighbor . . . Shep."

Les Jr. pulled out the herring and scooped it into a container.

"Talking about your neighbors, you haven't seen Ben, have you? Half of his family has called here looking for him. It seems he skipped town after the funeral. He's not answering his cell, and his house phone is off the hook."

"What'd you tell them?"

"That I haven't seen him, which I haven't, but I'd like to know if he's here and if he's OK."

"He's here."

Les Jr. passed him the container of herring and spoke discreetly.

"Tell him I'll keep covering for him but that he may want to check in with his mom. She is pretty panicked."

"I'll hang up the phone when I get back. I got it."

"And I'm sorry too, about the crap with your dad this winter. I heard it from the girls at the register."

Matty looked over at the three girls, plus the longtime cashier Miss Sullivan, bagging and adding and weighing and gabbing, and physically shuddered. I guessed it was at the thought of them knowing it all. I got it. It was a ritual I used to love to listen to, as the register girls would collect the sauciest gossip of the year and spew it out in one long, tawdry diatribe. Not so funny now that my dear friend and her son were the principal attraction—and me, too, I guess. I'm sure my whole awful saga was hashed and rehashed behind that counter, though in a quieter tone.

"Catch you later, Les."

"Catch you later."

Outside, an old man pulled up on a brand-new tricycle looking even more curmudgeonly than I remembered him. I assumed it was because of the bike. The last phase of the bicycle journey, the one that sometimes comes with as much kicking and screaming as the first days without training wheels, is, ironically, nearly right back where you started. The tricycle. This time, an adult tricycle. A three-wheeler bought for you by your kids who worry that you are a bit "wobbly" on your two-wheeler, or, even more distressing, a used trike, given to you by the son or daughter of a guy who just yesterday you were playing tennis or poker with, who has now moved on to heaven, hell, or worse—a nursing home. It's your last bike, no matter how you spin it.

Matty greeted the old man by name, "Hey, Mr. Henry."

Mr. Henry grunted something inaudible in return and shuffled into the store.

twelve

The Mourning Paper

Matty dropped the paper on the kitchen counter with the bagels and put the herring in the fridge as if it were his own house. He had been at our place countless times and was obviously quite comfortable. I loved it. It wasn't uncommon to feel that familiar with the houses of Bay Harbor neighbors and friends. In truth, the beach town was just a more-monied generation away from a Catskills bungalow colony, with many of the same norms. I can't say for sure, but I don't think the same could be said of the other summer destinations of the Manhattan elite. I doubted the casual drop-in was a thing farther out east. In fact, I would guess the Hampton-goers had an entirely different definition of casual.

If challenged, I bet I could examine the contents of any random Manhattanite's suitcase and tell you just where she was headed. The largest, a piece of fine leather luggage or a Louis Vuitton duffel, filled with ERES bikinis, matching sarongs, Hermès Orans for day, Manolos for night—the Hamptons. A medium-size wheelie brimming with polo shirts and bright cardigans by KULE or J.McLaughlin, one-piece racers, tennis sneakers, and espadrilles—Connecticut. A large backpack or tote stuffed with three bikinis, a pair of cutoffs, jeans, a sweatshirt, Birkenstocks, and maybe a cotton button-down—but don't expect an iron—Fire Island.

Matty quietly hung up the kitchen phone. A bit of a mama's boy, he couldn't bear the thought of Ben's mom calling over and over again to a busy signal, in duress. Ben, meanwhile, grabbed the *Fire Island News* and turned to his favorite section—the police blotter. In between a missing cat and a noise complaint he found something worth reading out loud.

THE GOLDILOCKS INTERLOPER STRIKES AGAIN!

> Homeowners on Surfview Road summoned the police early Sunday morning to review evidence, including splattered pancake batter and eggshells, that the Goldilocks Interloper had visited their home overnight.

"Why do I have a feeling this is you?" Ben asked Shep.

"Nope, I only interlope here—and not really, even, because . . ."

"It's your house," Ben said, with what looked awfully close to a smile.

Shep flashed a boyish grin in return but was busy exploring our now ancient musical source—an iPod. The archaic device clearly amazed him.

"Shep—you have an iPod?" Matty asked, surprised that the old man was not still sitting in front of a Victrola, I assumed.

"It's Ben's. He has it all hooked up through his speakers." He said it as if Ben was some kind of tech genius to have wired it this way. "He has some Sinatra on here, and some Tony Bennett!"

Shep placed it in the dock and the song "Love Shack" by the B-52s, the inspiration for our house name, filled the room.

Ben looked up from the paper and joked wryly, "Though this seems fitting, no?"

Matty clearly found it funny, but only Shep laughed, and followed with, "Two jokes in one morning. Very good, Ben!"

Ben smirked at Shep, but Matty still appeared stricken. Shep hit him on the back with a little too much oomph.

"You can still laugh here, Matty. We're the same people we were before our hearts were wrenched from our chests."

"Sorry," Matty said. "Want me to show you how to make a playlist?"

"Don't mind if you do."

As Matty slowly explained the procedure, the phone rang.

"I think it's your mother," he proclaimed guiltily, avoiding eye contact with Ben.

"You're found. Get the phone," Shep advised.

Ben put down the paper, breathed deeply, and did what he was told.

We all sat glued to the one-sided conversation.

"Hi, Mom. . . . I'm sorry. . . . I texted you that I was OK. . . . Please don't come here. . . . I don't want to be distracted from my pain; I want to feel the pain. . . . I'm not alone, far from it. . . . No, it's the B-52s. . . . I actually think it is appropriate. . . . I am sitting shiva. I have the candle and . . ."

In a perfect display of good timing, the Tirschwells, our neighbors from down the street, came to the door. Ben waved them in with a genuine smile.

"People are coming to see me," he told his mother truthfully.

Annie Tirschwell placed a bakery box in his hands, quietly stating, "It's a babka."

Ben smiled at her while responding dryly to his mom.

"People with babka, so I have the candle and the people and a babka . . . I'm not making fun, Mom." He turned his back to the group and whispered into the phone, "This is the only place where I can breathe. Please, tell the others, I mean no disrespect. I won't survive if I'm not here. You should go back to Florida."

I wasn't surprised that once word got out that Ben was on the island a makeshift shiva would come to him. Sure, it wasn't formal like the one in the city, where countless relatives and friends were probably wandering around our apartment wondering where Ben was, as they piled pastrami and corned beef and coleslaw and the good mustard atop slices of rye and pumpernickel. Jewish deli meat aside, this less formal version was no doubt better for Ben, and not much different from normal times. People were always popping in and out of our house. Especially since it was so close to the ball field. I loved that part of Fire Island life—how things went from zero to sixty in an instant. I always had snacks and drinks and even party games ready for when the need arose.

The visitors came and went all day, and Ben waffled between passively engaging and actively ignoring them. The latter seemed to take more energy on his part. Renee came in looking almost buoyant, like a bottle that had been shut tight for forty-three years and had finally been opened. I studied her face and her eyes. Renee had most definitely had sex with the long-haired man-child the night before, and from the look of her, my guess was, good sex. This was a huge deal, as I'm pretty sure that she had never had good sex before. She had once told me that sex was "not that important to her"—which, if you ask me, is an indirect way of saying it wasn't very good.

I wondered if she came home and crossed off "one-night

stand" from the divorce bucket list I knew she had made to mark the end of her marriage.

"It's a thing," she had told me. "All of my clients make one."

Shep and Matty did their best to keep things light, even going as far as coordinating the music to match whomever walked through the door. Shep was a bad influence on Matty—not that the kid couldn't use a bit of bad influence. They played "Delta Dawn" when Ian Frenchman sauntered in. It was rumored that when his wife threw him out over the off-season, on account of his traveling too much, he moved into the Delta Sky Lounge at JFK. He ate, drank, and even showered there. When Dave Golden walked in with his much younger trophy wife, they played "Must Be the Money," and for Marty Kranz, a grown man who collected Cabbage Patch Dolls, "People Are Strange." It kept them both amused, but Ben barely noticed—until the proudly well-cushioned Smith sisters entered to the tune of "I like big butts, and I cannot lie." Even that got barely a rise out of him—though he was mature enough to tell them to cut it out.

In the end, I was the one responsible for Ben's only genuine laugh of the day, courtesy of the thrice-married widow Lisa Marlin-Cohen-Fitzpatrick. Don't worry, she only buried one husband. The other two marriages ended in divorce. Lisa Marlin-Cohen-Fitzpatrick was both a close and a low talker. It was a brutal combination since your need for auricular satisfaction pushed you to lean in and spatial intolerance pushed you to back up. Ben and I would bury our noses in our books at the first sight of her heading our way on the beach—our laughter making it difficult to get through the page. It was a wonder she got one man to marry her, let alone three.

One night, soon after my diagnosis and the discovery of Tuck's infidelity, Renee came over for dinner in the city. She was one of the few people who didn't treat me differently because of the *always whispered* cancer. Most people had no clue what to say around me. I would watch them struggle with regular conversation, dodging topics like vacations or babies, and steering clear of complaining about anything in their seemingly healthy lives. Renee acted normal, and I really appreciated it.

She partook in my selection of medical marijuana, pulled Ben's novel *One Day in Berlin* off the bookshelf, and read the steamy sex scene out loud in her most titillating voice.

It wasn't just to make me laugh; she was addressing my biggest concern: that Ben would be alone forever. She was convinced that the ladies would be lined up, hoping for reenactments of the way the book's protagonist, Hans, took the love interest, Ursula, in the luggage compartment on the Deutsche Bahn from Frankfurt to Munich. Ben used to jokingly reenact his love scenes with me as a funny way to initiate sex. It would make me laugh, at first, but by the time he got to the good parts I was no longer laughing.

"We must warn him to steer clear of Lisa Marlin-Cohen-Fitzpatrick," she said, no longer amused. That particular visit coincided with the widow Lisa Marlin-Cohen-Fitzpatrick's current divorce proceedings. Renee's colleague was her attorney and quite unprofessionally spilled the amusing details of her latest decoupling. The ins and outs of the first divorce had already run through the Fire Island rumor mill. Lisa had a record. She was a silverware klepto. Apparently, this is a real thing that costs restaurants thousands of dollars a year. Ordinary people who wouldn't dream of pilfering something from a retail store have no problem leaving a dining establishment with their utensils stowed in their pockets or purses. For some reason, which I found odd, considering the vast array of place settings she must have registered for and received over the years, Lisa Marlin-Cohen-Fitzpatrick made silverware stealing a sport. According to court papers, she had collected twelve place settings, over time, of a meticulous copy of Georg Jensen's cactus pattern circa 1931 that an exceptionally stylish restaurateur had commissioned for his bistro. It was the thing that put the final nail in the coffin of her second marriage. She and Seth Cohen were finishing up dinner with one of Seth's biggest clients when the maître d' escorted the police into the restaurant. They instructed Lisa—then, just Marlin-Cohen—to empty her purse.

"Call your lawyer," she begged her husband while being led out in cuffs.

He called a divorce lawyer instead.

Apparently that wasn't all there was to her fetishes. After we smoked a bit more, Renee let it spill that during divorce number two, she heard that Lisa had some rather unusual sexual preferences.

"That's all I'll say," Renee had proclaimed, blushing like a schoolgirl.

I was never much of a gossip, but for some reason the combo of my chemo brain and the anger I felt surrounding my current situation led me to enjoy this kind of catty conversation regarding someone else's self-inflicted misfortune. It obviously cheered me, and gave Renee a good excuse to break her colleagues' confidence.

"Come on," I begged, adding with a wink, "I'll take it to the grave!"

Renee couldn't resist making me laugh and spilled the whole X-rated tale involving baked goods, most specifically, banana cream pie. By the time Ben came home we were rolling around on the living room floor in hysterics, having decided that the widow Lisa Marlin-Cohen-Fitzpatrick would be the first to pounce on Ben after I passed—and how it was a shame that Ben didn't really care for pie. Ben found the conversation far from funny. In fact, he was furious, and retreated in a huff to our bedroom. His reaction, and the effects of the marijuana no doubt, made us laugh even harder.

I felt badly about it when I finally came to bed.

"I don't want you joking about this, Julia," he'd said. "It makes me feel you've given up."

I felt awful about it after that. Until now, that is, when the widow Lisa Marlin-Cohen-Fitzpatrick walked in at the tail end of the fake shiva carrying a banana cream pie. Ben stifled a laugh and excused himself with his usual alibi—walking Sally.

He whispered to Shep through a narrow grin, "Keep an eye on the silverware," before heading out.

thirteen

Keep Off the Dunes

That night, in search of Ben, who had taken Sally for a walk on the beach (a mere one hundred feet from the house, by the way), I passed two people making out on the dunes. I wavered between wanting to yell "Get off the dunes!" since disturbing these fragile hills is a near federal offense in our vulnerable beach town, and averting my eyes from the seemingly PG-13 exchange. In the end, I got caught up in the beauty of young love, remembering a time when Ben and I would roll around in the sand at night on the way back from this or that, too hot for each other to make it all the way home. But then I realized it was Matty and Dylan. It didn't completely surprise me, of course, after the conversation I'd witnessed. I was surprised though that they were in the dunes—especially Jake Finley's daughter.

Like Dylan, Jake Finley had grown up on the island and was known as the unofficial keeper of the piles of wind and water-driven sand that protected the natural barrier from the constant threat of nor'easters and hurricanes. He would even go as far as paying a few kids out of his own pocket over the winter to plant seagrass along our stretch of dune. Aside from Dylan, there was nothing Jake loved more than this island. Year-rounders, like him, felt especially protective of it.

There is an age-old hierarchy in Fire Island that I imagine is consistent from town to town. The year-round people, like Jake, resented the summer people, and the summer people resented the renters, and the renters resented the groupers, and the groupers resented the day-trippers. It is an island of rules, and outsiders did not always follow those rules—like keeping off the dunes, which was essential to the survival of the ecosystem. But year-rounders and summer people got annoyed by other things too, like littering or playing loud music. The people of Bay Harbor, especially, worshipped their peace; disturbing it was a near abomination. Yet nothing came close to disturbing the dunes.

I walked away from the scene of the crime and stumbled upon Ben and Sally sprawled out on the beach a few blocks east. Ben was lying on his back, staring at the starry sky. I tried not to think about the trail of sand they would bring into the house without me there to insist on a shakedown and lay beside them.

A few minutes in, Ben said, "Can you believe Shep is staying in the house—in our bed?"

It took me a bit to realize he was speaking to me, not Sally, who put her head on his chest as he continued.

"I know I can kick him out, but I feel badly for him, you know, sleeping in that big house all alone."

He, too, realized he was speaking to me completely, as if I were there, and laughed. "I think I'm losing it, Jules. Maybe it's good that someone is there with me, someone to talk to besides you—and Sally. Someone who will answer." He laughed again.

Sally had picked up her head at the sound of her name. She looked west and barreled over Ben's chest with vigor. Ben sat up to see what had caught her eye. In the distance, we could see Jake's dog, Charlie, charging down the beach—which most likely meant that Jake wasn't far behind. Though I was pretty sure there was nothing I could do, I raced back to where Dylan and Matty lay to try to warn them. I arrived to find them with less clothing on than before. Matty's shirt was tossed to the side, and Dylan's top nestled between blades of beach grass. Both were bare-breasted, with Dylan's bare breasts, of course, being the bigger issue. As I prayed things wouldn't advance, for a multitude of reasons, not least of which being that it felt wildly inappropriate to be standing over them, Dylan rolled off Matty and lay flat out on the sand, proclaiming, "Matty, wait."

He rolled on his side to face her.

"What's up?" he asked through chafed lips.

She turned to face him, her arms settled across her bare chest like Wonder Woman. Their faces were but an inch apart. They looked more like two little kids whispering secrets on a sleepover than consenting near-adults. Dylan continued very matter-of-factly, "I just want to say that I don't want to do it tonight. I mean, obviously, because we don't have a rubber—you don't, right?"

I was glad she was thinking of protection. From the surprised look on Matty's face, it was clear that he was not. He answered as if he was.

"No, I don't—but I'm sure I can get one."

"Not from any of our friends though, OK?"

"Do we have any friends?"

"Yeah, kind of. You know what I mean, I don't want any of the kids our age knowing my business, especially the city kids. Just promise."

"Cross my heart, hope to die."

Dylan laughed, and continued, "Stick a needle in my eye."

"My lips are sealed, my promise true!"

"I'll never break my word to you."

They did some funny hand-slapping, pinky-swearing ritual before falling back onto the sand laughing. They took a beat, staring up at the stars as they had on a zillion nights before.

"Hazmat?"

"Yes, Dyl."

"I only want to do it once."

Matty sat up.

"Once?" he asked, no longer playing it cool.

"Yes, once. I just want to know that it's over with."

"Over with? Jeez, Dyl—"

Dylan's black Lab interrupted the tedious discussion, charging the dune, knocking Matty on his back, and covering his face in kisses.

"Charlie, hey, boy."

Matty hadn't seen Charlie yet and was quite obviously thrilled by both his arrival and his timing. They laughed as I jumped up and down in the sand, trying to alert them to the obvious situation at hand, amazed that they hadn't yet put it together. Though, in all fairness, Charlie could have been on his own. He was one of those island dogs, unlike Sally, who knew the lay of the land as well as any human and would often wander around unattended. The locals all recognized him, but I can't count the times I saw visitors making chase to catch the "lost" dog. There was no catching Charlie unless he wanted to be caught.

Charlie playfully grabbed Dylan's bikini top in his mouth and took off with it toward Sally. Still naively amused, Matty and Dylan sat up just in time to see two bare legs the size of tree trunks, stepping toward them in weatherworn Timberlands.

"Oh my God, Matty." Dylan squeaked, "Pray for a rogue wave."

Matty closed his eyes and moved his lips in silent prayer as Jake called out, "Charlie!"

The trunks came closer as the sound of each step echoed off the sand—*kaboom, kaboom, kaboom, kaboom*. Dylan opened her eyes and looked at Matty, who was white as a ghost. Even though she knew she had more at stake than him, it was clear that he was equally scared. He tossed her his shirt and fell right back into his old role, in which she was in charge. She had always been in charge. He was just along for the glorious ride.

"What do we do? What do we do?" he whispered in a panic, as if he just realized that they were actually in the dunes.

Dylan threw on Matty's shirt, closed her eyes, tilted her head down and folded her body into as small a package as possible. She motioned for Matty to do the same.

"The invisibility cloak? I don't think that's gonna work this time, Dyl."

"Just try," she begged, falling back on their childhood response to trouble—of which they had their fair share. Matty gave in and copied her position exactly.

Jake bellowed, "Charlie!" as Ben made his way over from the other direction, calling out similarly to Sally.

They were both but twenty feet away from the impending catastrophe.

Fifteen feet.

Ten.

And then, Jake yelled: loud, strong, angry.

"HEY! GET OFF THE DUNES!" Followed by "Who's there? I see you!"

Neither Dylan nor Matty moved a muscle, their eyes still squeezed tight, their heads still buried.

Jake's towering stems stopped right in front of them, as he muttered, beaten and broken, "Dylan, is that you?"

Ben arrived, lucky for Matty, just as Charlie came flying back with Dylan's bikini top in his mouth. He dropped it at his master's feet like a proud dog back from the hunt and wagged his tail vigorously. He was infinitely alone in his joy.

fourteen

Does Sex Trump Lucky Charms?

As the morning sun peeked through our bedroom window, I watched Ben's new ritual, a wince of pain as his hands reached for his belly. Shep was making breakfast, but even the smell of bacon didn't draw Ben out. Sally, on the other hand, was duly inspired. She made a beeline to the kitchen and sat at Shep's feet in anticipation until a noise from the garden distracted her. It was Renee's cat, Houdini, who, per usual, took off at the sight of Sally.

Houdini was an inside cat who often escaped, ergo his name. I followed him home to Renee's, thinking I would finally solve the mystery of how he got out. I was quite disappointed to see that he just nudged open the screen door and walked in like anyone else. Inside, Matty was retrieving the Lucky Charms he'd bought at the market, looking no worse for wear from the night before. He was indeed lucky that Ben had been present to calm Jake down a bit and move things along. Poor Dylan must have had an awful time of it when they got home. She texted Matty saying Jake had not said a word to her yet, not one word.

Houdini jumped onto the counter and strode across, rubbing up against Matty's arm and purring.

"Hey, Houdini."

He grabbed two bowls, a spoon, and the milk and sat at the kitchen table. He poured the milk into the bowls, one for the feline and one for himself, and tapped on the table for Houdini to join him. He opened the box of Lucky Charms and chatted with the cat like the old friend he was.

"Houdini, I have a very important question for you."

I thought he was going to ask him where to get a condom; it wasn't gonna be easy in this one-horse town.

"Do you think sex will be better than Lucky Charms?" I was close, I thought, laughing. He was a funny kid, Matty, an old soul. It was hard to believe he was only sixteen, but only children often seem wise beyond their years, from spending so much time with adults, I imagine. Plus, city kids are usually advanced, just from being exposed to so much. I certainly was. He studied the back of the box while arranging an equal ratio of charms to cereal for the perfect first bite.

"Will I still find them magically delicious?" he asked Houdini, before shoving a spoonful into his mouth. He pulled out the inner bag, picked out extra marshmallow surprises, and tossed them into his bowl. A boy after my own heart.

"Trix are probably out of the question." He laughed through a mouthful of unicorns, blue moons, and red balloons. Houdini looked up at him, tiny beads of milk peppering his whiskers. Matty ran his hand across the cat's back while cracking himself up.

"Silly cat. Trix are for kids."

I understood his curiosity about adults eating kid cereal. Every time I strolled down the cereal aisle at the market, I mourned the Cap'n Crunch–loving days of my youth before arriving safely at the Kashi and muesli. And let's not even discuss Pop-Tarts—strawberry with white frosting dotted with sprinkles, cinnamon brown sugar, or chocolate—gooey and delicious from a two-minute stint in the toaster. What a waste of self-control that was.

By Matty's third spoonful of Lucky Charms, Renee entered the kitchen looking strangely flustered. She was acting jittery, even nervous—I'd never seen her present either of those emotions. Matty seemed to notice too. While it was odd, it was a vast improvement from the doomsday presentation she had been sporting since the divorce. To Renee, *divorce* was the worst word in the world.

Some people marry for love, some marry for money, but Renee married Tuck for sustainability. She simply never wanted to get divorced. She yearned for the sanctity of a traditional marriage, for having that one person standing beside her, or behind her, or in front of her—whatever the circumstance at the time called for. Her own childhood, paired with the hours upon billable hours of hearing other couples' war stories, made her all the more thankful when she finally stumbled on Tuck. Short, dull, reliable Tuck.

While I knew Ben was the one because he took my breath away, Renee's tell was the opposite—she breathed easier when Tuck was around. Short, dull, reliable Tuck, with the only girl in Scarsdale High history to win both most likely to succeed and prom queen on his arm. The first thing people said when they heard the news of his cheating was, "I'm surprised he had it in him." It was one of Renee's first thoughts as well.

Being keenly aware from her occupation of every sign of infidelity made it pretty simple for Renee to see when something was amiss in her own marriage. Plus, she had all the tools. When her antennae went up, she began tracking his phone and it didn't take long till she saw that he was a frequent flier at the Sherry-Netherland hotel. She waited outside until she saw him exit, with his assistant of all people. They kissed goodbye on the corner of Fifty-Ninth and Fifth. Renee was close enough to see his tongue sloppily jutting in and out of her mouth. She crossed the street to Central Park and threw up behind an oak tree.

She thought about asking the standard question you always hear in the movies—*Do you love her?*—but realized she didn't much care. It was the betrayal that fed her anguish. She packed up his things, left them in the hallway, and changed the locks. This isn't to say she wasn't upset; she was really quite devastated. She had lost control of her marriage, and control meant more to Renee than most anything else.

Though from the look she was currently flaunting, she might have let that go as well. She seemed loose. Renee was not loose. Her tendency to be tightly wound was the thing that had unraveled her marriage. At least that's what Tuck implied.

At my insistence, Ben had met Tuck for a drink one night after Renee had thrown him out. (It was before my diagnosis or I never would have pushed him.) Their personal connection was negligible, really. Ben only tolerated Tuck's company because of my friendship with Renee and his love for Matty. To Tuck, I imagined it was something more. Tuck was not a guy's guy and, to make matters worse, he wasn't particularly aware of his shortcomings. It was probably the reason he insisted on playing in the Homeowners' Game, even though he wasn't any good. Ben would say, "The great Tuck Tucker is a figment of his own imagination." Tuck had little self-awareness, though apparently a bit more when it came to his infidelity.

Ben didn't ask Tuck for an excuse when he met him for that

drink, but Tuck was quick to explain himself. He claimed that Renee had no interest in him sexually. That she lay there bored during sex, thinking about work. And it wasn't conjecture. On more than one occasion, just as they finished, he described how she rolled over and scribbled down notes on the pad on her nightstand. And they weren't about his performance. In contrast, Lola loved sex with Tuck—and it wasn't his imagination. It turned out that Lola was a screamer. Tuck made Lola scream. Tuck made *someone* scream was more the point. Ben didn't really have answers beyond that.

Renee was often transactional in her relationships and possessive with her time—doling it out like the aproned master portioned out gruel to the boys at the workhouse in *Oliver Twist*. I often teased her, calling her the queen of multitasking. I was sure that what Tuck had said was true, but there was no way I was breaking the girl code by admitting it.

"Did you ask why he didn't address these issues with Renee before looking elsewhere?" I inquired, speaking to the weak link in Tuck's excuse.

"No," Ben said, the way a husband does when trying to avoid saying the wrong thing. I wasn't letting him off that easily.

"I'm just saying, if he wasn't happy, he should have told her so. Don't you believe that?"

"Please don't do that thing that women do, where you question what we have because of other people's relationship failures."

"Please don't do that thing that men do, making ridiculous comments like 'that thing that women do.'"

He laughed. "You got me there, sorry. I didn't ask because I don't really care. Tuck is a giant dweeb, and I think Renee would be happier with someone else. Someone who makes her scream."

As if I had conjured him, the long-haired, shirtless someone-to-make-her-scream dashed down Renee's stairs—landing with a playful thud in her kitchen.

I guess she had to put one-night stand back on her bucket list. I was dying to know how the second night came about.

She looked painfully embarrassed and proceeded as if everything was as it should be.

"Good morning, Matty, how did you sleep?" she asked, while kissing him sweetly on top of his head.

"Fine," he replied, along with a quick glance at the kitchen clock. It read 9:00 a.m. He didn't return the question. He had no desire to know how she slept.

The man-child, who, as you can imagine, looked as different as humanly possible from Tuck, the wandering-eyed number-crunching bad lover, came in for an introduction.

"Hey, man, I'm Gabe."

Renee tried to get it together. "Yes, sorry. This is Gabe; Gabe, this is my son, Matty."

Gabe reached out for a fist bump, revealing a small yin-yang tattoo on his wrist that I hadn't previously noticed. Matty studied it while barely bumping back. The painful introduction continued.

"Gabe is a drummer," Renee relayed hopefully.

Relief inexplicably flooded Matty's face.

"A plumber!" Matty happily declared. "Are the toilets clogged again?"

Renee and Gabe laughed; Matty assumed with him, but it turned out to be at him. Renee spoke clearly and slowly.

"*Drum-mer.* Gabe is a drummer, not a plumber."

Matty mumbled, "Are we starting a band?" before drifting off into some sort of a drummer-just-screwed-my-mother coma. It was hard to watch, yet I couldn't turn away.

Renee continued, "Gabe has a show at Maguire's coming up, if you and Dylan want to come."

"Dylan is working nights this summer."

"Oh, well, maybe you'll come. It's alternative music."

She turned to Gabe in a consolatory fashion. "Matty loves that kind of music."

I was pretty sure Renee had no idea what alternative music was. She concentrated intently on an errant cuticle on her nail, studying it and biting at it instead of making eye contact with her son. I had never seen her like this.

The drummer finally spoke. "Come check it out, man, it'll be lit."

Matty focused on Gabe's bare feet. They had a faint line of dirt on their sides that almost seemed to be tattooed on, as if he had been barefoot for weeks, possibly years.

Thankfully for all, the familiar sound of a foul ball slamming into the house put an end to the torturous exchange. Renee jumped, Matty snapped to attention, and the drummer barely flinched. I guessed he was used to loud banging.

A familiar "Sorry!" drifted in from the direction of the ball field, alerting Matty that the first game of the season had begun. He excused himself with "Gotta go," grabbed his mitt, and headed for the door as the drummer picked up the box of Lucky Charms and shook it.

"When a man tires of Lucky Charms, he tires of life!" Gabe dramatically exclaimed.

Leaving Matty even more confused than he was before.

fifteen

Eight Men Out

Stepping onto the ball field on Fire Island is like stepping into an alternate universe where nothing else exists but that day's game—a seven-inning respite from reality. It comes in very handy when trying not to think about your wife's cancer, a lagging mortgage payment, a problem at work or, in Matty's case, his mother's sudden turn from lioness to cougar.

Matty stopped briefly at the pinnacle of the four corners where my house, his house, Shep's house, and the ball field converge. There was loud music coming from mine, an alarming—or at least odd—occurrence so early in the morning. He resisted checking it out and headed straight to the field, where a few of the guys were warming up. It was immediately clear that there weren't enough for a game. Matty really needed there to be a game.

The pitcher, a brass union attorney, hurled the ball across the plate, where it fumbled out of the catcher's mitt. The catcher, a famous voice-over actor (the red M&M and the Charmin Papa bear) ripped off his mask and threw it to the ground.

"It's so damn hard to align my bifocals with the catcher's

mask," he yelled in frustration, before retrieving the ball from the sidewalk.

They were both pushing sixty. Which is still considered one's prime on the Bay Harbor Ball Field. At another time, Matty would have appreciated the humor in the curmudgeonly catcher's complaint, but he had barely heard a word since the scrappy drummer appeared in his kitchen. The vacant look in his eyes refocused as he surveyed the situation.

I slid into the top row of bleachers, where I usually sat, as Pam strolled up, baby in tow. She looked up at me, and tears filled her eyes. For a second I thought that she saw me; it would be just like Pam to be sensitive to paranormal activity. The catcher noticed her tears and put his arm on her shoulder.

"You OK, Pam?"

"Just exhausted," she admitted.

"It will get better real soon," the curmudgeonly catcher promised, in an uplifting tone.

I really love these people.

"Where is everybody? I thought we'd have enough for a game," Matty hollered, clearly not feeling as sentimental as I did at the moment.

"Well, we would if the guys would come back from Ben's," the catcher whined as the pitcher explained.

"Eddie and Rico went to get Ben and Shep around twenty minutes ago."

"Want me to go check?"

"Joel just went to check."

A guy in the outfield yelled in, "That was ten minutes ago!"

Matty picked up a bat, leaning against the backstop.

"Pitch me a couple, and then I'll go."

He hit three balls over the right field fence, put down his stick, and headed for our house.

"Wow, someone's been hitting the cages!" the catcher remarked.

I imagined it was his father's face he pictured on that ball as he smacked it, though it could have been the drummer's.

We stood in the doorway of my house and surveyed the sorry scene in front of us. There was a lot to take in. The song "Everybody Hurts" by R.E.M. played in the background as six grown men sat around the living room in a disjointed circle on either side of Shep and Ben. It looked like one of those group-therapy sessions that the doctors at Sloan were constantly pushing me to join—ones with names like Stupid Cancer and Share. I always refused. Sitting in a circle wallowing in one another's misery didn't seem like a fun way to spend my ever-dwindling afternoons. From the look of this group, I was right.

I worried Matty would join the sob fest. He certainly had the material, but he kept his eye on the prize. He pulled open the shade on the living room window. Sunlight filled the room, and the men squinted, adjusting their red-rimmed eyes.

"What's going on in here?" Matty asked.

Most greeted him with blank stares, but one of them spoke over the depressing music. Tears pouring down his face. "My dog died."

"Mugsy? He's tied up on the fence at the field, where you should be."

"Not Mugsy. Mr. Chillypeppers. My mother said I was too young to hold the leash, but I wouldn't listen."

They all looked wrecked, ironically except for Ben and Shep. Ben was clearly suppressing amusement while Shep, in his typical fashion of not giving a crap about appearances, was actually laughing.

The next song came on, Johnny Cash singing "Hurt." I recognized the first few chords of the guitar even before he crooned the first line—

"I hurt myself today to see if I still feel."

I couldn't believe my ears. Matty walked over to the iPod and inspected it.

"And what's with the depressing music?"

Shep answered proudly, "I made a playlist!"

Right after SUMMER CHILL and JULIA'S DANCE MIX, it read HAH.

"'Hah'? It doesn't sound very funny," Matty observed.

"It's an abbreviation," Eddie explained while Joel, as always, tried to lighten the mood.

"Ever think about how the word *abbreviation* is so long?"

"It's not an abbreviation," Shep corrected him. "It's an acronym. You kids love those acronyms."

Matty asked Shep with his last thread of patience, "What does it stand for?"

"IDK, my BFF Matt."

Ben put us out of our misery, explaining "Hopeless and Heartbroken" as Shep smiled proudly.

"You said I should make a playlist. What'd you expect? Show tunes?"

"You know, it's beautiful out," Matty announced, ignoring Shep.

"So go back out," the guy crying about his childhood dog chimed in, still teary-eyed.

"Jesus Christ, I can't deal with this today." Matty turned around and left without another word.

I couldn't blame him. It was madness.

Outside, the same guys were still running batting practice with the addition of a few more. Les Jr. passed by in a golf cart and stopped to say hello as Matty reached the corner.

"Hey, Matty."

"Hey, Les."

The last time Matty saw Les anywhere near the field was during his last year in the majors, when he surprised everyone at the Homeowners' Game. The other team joked it would only be fair if he batted blindfolded, and so he did. They tied a bandanna around his eyes, spun him around a few times pin-the-tail-on-the-donkey-style, and he still batted it out of the park. It was hysterical, and if Les's career had not ended as it did, the story would have been shouted from the Bay Harbor rooftops for years to come. Now it was only occasionally whispered.

"Looks pretty quiet out here. Don't have enough for a game?" Les asked.

"Half the guys are in Ben's house crying."

"It *is* crazy. Both Julia and Caroline in such a short time."

"I know, but they should come out. They're making them feel worse."

"Want me to try?"

"Couldn't hurt—I guess."

We went back in with Little Les. The guys were now looking intently at Rico, a longtime Fire Islander and professional trumpet player.

"So 'drop dead' was the very last thing you said to him?"

"I'm afraid so."

Rico looked down to avoid eye contact. The others commiserated as Les attempted to bust up the party.

"What's going on in here, guys?"

The room responded with general grunts, "Hey, Little Les" and other assorted nonanswers.

"Just a little morning mourning," Shep volunteered with a smirk.

"I heard you're trading sob stories. Want to hear mine?"

To that came a resounding "No." They all knew it, and to this group, Les's baseball trajectory was beyond tragic.

"Come on out to the ball field. You can even pitch a few to me . . . blindfolded."

This perked them all up.

"Shep, come watch," Matty added.

The men looked to Shep for direction as he was widely considered the unofficial Commissioner of the Ball Field—it was even rumored that in the old days he took it upon himself to mow the lawn every week. He stood and everyone followed. I knew these guys were a bunch of nuts, really, but this morning's histrionics were next level. And though Ben and Shep had no intention of playing yet, with Ben still figuratively sitting shiva and Shep fully in his court, they made it out to the field to watch. I sat right between them. Shep whispered to Ben.

"I saw Little Les tossing a ball to his son a few times this spring. But I never thought I'd see this again."

Me neither, I said, slapping the old man on the back to zero reaction. I guessed that having a kid who wanted to play catch put a wrench in Les's plan to never pick up a ball again.

Eddie pulled his bandanna off his head and tied it around Les's eyes. He took the plate, and the show began.

"Careful not to hit me, Roger—no more extra avocado in your sandwiches if you do," Les warned as the catcher set him up perfectly.

Roger stood at the plate in his pre-pitch stance, pulled his arm back, and yelled "Pitch!" as he released the ball.

The ball glided over the plate, and the crowd shouted, "Swing!" but Les didn't connect.

They tried again. "Pitch!" "Swing!" Miss. And again. "Pitch!" "Swing!" Miss, before Les announced, "Just a couple more, guys—I have to get back to the store."

Les connected with the next pitch but hit a foul into the brush in front of Matty's house. The men still fell into "kid-table syndrome" when it came to Matty—they expected him to fetch foul balls and probably would until they took some other "fatherless" youngun with potential under their wings. He didn't fight it. Knowing him, he probably found comfort in his role—especially now that there was little tradition he could rely on.

As Matty gingerly climbed through the brush, Renee, clad in a bikini and colorful pareu, exited the house looking pretty fabulous. The drummer stood by her side in nothing but a red Speedo. I was immediately curious about the suit. Was it Tuck's? I doubted it. Tuck was a swim-trunk type and, aside from being a lousy softball player, he wasn't much of a swimmer. The only times I even saw him in the ocean were on green-flag days, where it looked more lake than sea. And even then, his trepidation upon entering was palpable. The other choice was that the drummer wore a Speedo under his jeans so as to always be prepared for a dip. It wasn't a bad plan when shacking up on a thirty-two-mile sandbar. The notion made me like him even more. Yes, I already liked him, and yes, it was completely shallow of me. The guy was hot and just what my friend Renee needed.

Shep homed in on the red Speedo too and questioned Matty on his return.

"Who's the suit?" he joked, looking at Joel and Eddie for a reaction. They both obliged until Matty's sullen face doused their amusement.

"A one-night stand, I guess."

We all took a closer look. Gabe, the drummer, was holding two beach chairs.

"Looks like he's going for a second night," Joel observed as the pitcher called out, "Matty! We're not getting any younger here!"

That was for sure.

Matty tossed Roger the ball and took a seat on the bleachers.

"I knew my mother would date eventually . . . but I figured someone who looked like my father or one of his friends . . . not Peter Frampton."

I loved the old-time Peter Frampton reference—the kid always knew his audience. I said it out loud, but of course no one heard me. I didn't care. It was better than that awkward IRL feeling when you realize no one is listening so you fade out your voice to save face. Apparently, there's no room for shame in the afterlife. Though I would like to share my thoughts with someone. I wondered where Caroline was. Why was I the only dead person here?

Shep patted Matty on the back. "Sorry, kid, where'd she find him?"

"I don't know—in town, I guess. He's a drummer—he's playing at Maguires next weekend."

Well, at least there's an end date.

Joel couldn't resist an opinion. "Sure is a one-eighty from your accountant father."

Matty looked like he was about to cry, and I felt for him, really I did, but I was still happy for Renee. No matter how successful, intelligent, and beautiful she was, she had to know that her new title, "Poor Renee," was the first thing that came to mind when people saw her as of late. Like Tuck's infidelity was somehow her fault.

As if to prove my point, one of them tastelessly chimed in, "Just like that, from dumped to humped in one night!"

Everyone but Matty laughed.

They were all team Renee, not team Tuck. But above all, they were team Matty.

Shep really felt for the kid.

"You could bunk with us, Matt. I mean, no room in our bed, but we've got the extra bedroom."

Joel looked at him dubiously.

"What?" Shep defended himself. "It was my house first."

The pitcher called out, "Pitch!" shifting their attention back to the field.

They all stood and watched the ball ascend toward the plate.

"Swing!" they yelled, with bated breath.

And then, *PING*—the best sound in the world reverberated through the air as Les's bat perfectly connected with the ball, propelling it over the forty-five-foot net and onto the tennis courts.

The tennis people yelled in protest while our guys erupted in cheer. Les whipped off the bandanna; his signature smile crossed his face as he took the bases in stride, bum leg and all.

The men chanted in unabashed delight, "Little Les! Little Les! Little Les!"

I watched the scene unfold with joy, which increased tenfold when my awestruck gaze reached my husband. I expected more of the same melancholy from him, but there he was smiling like the rest, totally feeling the ovation. Even he couldn't resist the collective thrill of watching a man who thought his glory days were behind him hit a home run over a forty-five-foot net, blindfolded.

I knew Ben's venture into joyfulness was just a dalliance. His shoulders, which were now on par with his ears, would soon slump back down under the weight of his grief. But, for a moment, I could see the future. I could see a place where it would be OK to leave him behind.

sixteen

Digging It / Not Digging It

The sounds of Chance the Rapper and Kendrick Lamar riffed through Renee's living room where Norah Jones and Alabama Shakes had once reigned supreme. It made me laugh to hear Renee rapping about hacky sacks and Rascal Flatts, but she seemed to take to it. Under other circumstances, Matty may have enjoyed the switch, but he decidedly embraced anger instead. Though not enough anger to prevent him from helping himself to a serving of "Gabe's famous clam sauce" loaded with garlic and freshly caught clams from the Great South Bay. Renee and Gabe had dug for them a few hours earlier.

It was a sight to see: Renee Tucker, who had previously needed coaxing into a pool, immersing half her body in the Great South Bay, and blindly pressing her pedicured feet against the muddy, sandy bottom, in search of clams. Gabe, the drummer, had apparently grown up in a small Long Island town not far from the Bay Shore ferry, and had spent his childhood catching blue point crabs and clamming. Somehow when he said, follow me, and waded waist deep into the dark mysterious water with a bucket hanging from his side like a messenger bag, Renee followed. It was like that trust game, where you fall back into someone else's arms, but on steroids.

"Who are you?" I yelled out, the bay gently lapping over my toes, "And what have you done with my best friend?"

I wasn't really that surprised to see Renee rising to the challenge, not wanting to look like an Upper East Side divorce attorney whose closest relationship with a clam was her standing Wednesday night date with a plate of spaghetti alle vongole at Elio's, in front of her young lover. At least five people I knew passed by and bore witness. I couldn't wait to hear how the girls working the register at the market would spin this saucy tale.

Gabe took her hand and led her through the water to an exposed sandbar. Another first, as I had never seen anyone lead Renee anywhere. Once there, he instructed her to step around, feeling for something hard with her feet a few inches below the surface.

"It should feel more like a baseball than a golf ball, if it's big enough for us to keep."

They cha-cha-slided through the shallow water—right foot let's stomp . . . left foot let's stomp.

"You OK?" Gabe asked with a sweet smile.

"Yeah, I'm digging this!" Renee responded, causing his smile to explode across his face. Hers too.

After a few minutes, her face lit up again. "I feel one!"

"OK, now reach down and dig it out with your hands."

She didn't stop to think. If she had, I doubt she would have gone through with it. The unknown and Renee didn't mix, but she reached down, dug her hand into the ground, and pulled out a clam.

"I got it, I got it," she sang, holding the shelled mollusk over her head like the prize that it was.

Gabe laughed. "Amazing—now we just need about thirty more!"

An hour or so later, they were back home with a bucketful. They both smelled like low tide, which smells an awful lot like a brinier version of garbage day in New York City. They headed straight to the outdoor shower.

"Is Matt still at work?" Gabe asked, soaping up his hands.

"Yes," she managed, praying it was true.

He took her nipple in his mouth. "Salty." He smiled before coating her breasts with his soapy hands. He moved his attention to her left ear; even under the running water, the sensation stirred the tiny hairs on her neck, sending shivers to every cell of her body. He planted tiny kisses between her breasts and continued to her belly, traveling farther and farther down her torso till she was trembling with desire. She tightened her thighs, in an attempt to take back control.

"Relax," he said.

She tried to let herself go. She really did. She put her hands on his head, directing his eyes toward hers.

"I'm worried that Matt will come home."

"I'll be quiet, if you can," he whispered, with a mischievous grin.

She wanted to let him. But she just couldn't.

"Stop!" she said, turning her back to him. She rinsed off, grabbed her towel, and slipped out and into the house.

Upstairs, she spent a long time in her room, trying to put some space between her and the uncomfortable interaction. She moisturized and powdered and slipped on a pretty white sundress. Downstairs, she found Gabe washing clams in the kitchen sink. He smiled when he saw her and rinsed off his hands.

"What happened back there?" he asked softly.

These millennials really know how to communicate.

"Nothing. I was worried about Matty coming home. He's honestly seen enough this year."

"But he works till the market closes, right? It didn't feel like that."

He paused, collecting his thoughts.

"I know that can be very intimate to a woman, and out there in broad daylight. I'm sorry. I should have asked you first."

I understood what he was saying. There are few things more intimate than that.

She stepped up to the sink and began scrubbing a clam as if she were prepping it for surgery.

"It's not that . . . I've never, I've never done that before."

"Wait, what? You never did it with your husband in the outdoor shower? How long have you had this house?"

Renee could have left it there. But she was feeling oddly open.

"Not that." She dropped the impeccably clean clam in the colander and looked Gabe right in the eye.

"I've never done *that* before," she said, motioning to her vagina, too embarrassed to even say the word.

"Oh," he said, echoing my sentiments exactly. I knew that Tuck and Renee's sex life was dull, but . . .

"Well, when I was young, I never felt close enough to someone to be that intimate, and Tuck didn't do that," she continued.

"What do you mean he 'didn't do that'?"

Renee blushed. She clearly couldn't believe she was having this conversation out loud. Though it seemed like she'd had it in her head many times before.

"When we first got together, he said, 'I just want you to know, I don't go down on girls. It grosses me out.'"

Her admission made me wonder if Lola's "screaming" was performative.

"That's what he said?" the drummer asked.

"Yes, that's what he said," Renee confirmed.

"And you married him?"

Renee laughed, shook her head, and changed the subject.

"I have a delicious Greek wine to go with this."

"That sounds perfect," he said, pulling her toward him and kissing her gently on the side of her neck.

seventeen

Lanai

On the seventh day of shiva, Ben noticed that the candle had finally burned out. He wondered what to do with it; it didn't feel right to just toss it. He thought about throwing it in the ocean so that it would become beach glass one day. I liked that idea.

That's great, baby, do that.

It felt like a nice way to mark the end of the week, and he figured he would replenish what we had collected over the years, like a carbon footprint of sorts—paying it forward to some kid in China searching for treasure on the shores of Yalong Bay.

Like most beach lovers, Ben and I took many a long walk looking down in search of shells and sand-turned glass. Bay Harbor sits somewhat in the middle of the island, so a beach walk always began with a simple question—east or west? Walking east, for us at least, was a more secluded, introspective journey. Once we traversed the first couple of inhabited towns, one where we knew some people, and one where we knew none, we would come upon a board-walked nature preserve called the Sunken Forest. We sometimes made the detour inland to walk through it, but just as often kept trudging across the sand. I picked up some of my greatest finds on that desolate stretch of beach, including sand dollars, shark teeth, and the rarest shades of beach glass—red and orange.

Traveling west was a whole different animal. In that direction, we could barely walk ten feet without stopping to schmooze. Collections of friends or acquaintances gathered along the shoreline, their beach chairs arranged in half-moon formations facing the ocean, holding court, playing Scrabble, or trying to get through a page in their books without interruption. Ben would stop to throw a football or play Kadima any chance he could. When it came to sports of any kind I was more an observer than a player. I was happiest plunking down next to whomever and infiltrating their conversation. These groups had been talking to each other ad nauseam day after day, summer after summer, making a passerby like me feel like a Vegas-worthy guest attraction. That was my favorite result of a beach walk, even though the only part of me that truly got any exercise was my mouth.

Ben turned his cell phone back on, lay down on the lanai, as we had taken to calling the porch since his fourth book, *Lanai*, came out, and listened, or half listened, to the endless stream of messages. When he got to the first from his agent, Elizabeth Barnes, he paused and poured a shot of vodka into his morning orange juice. He had never mentioned it, as we tended not to discuss the "after" part of my dying, but I knew he was dreading dealing with Elizabeth without me. She was tough, his agent, like a Waspy version of Judge Judy. It wasn't necessarily a bad thing, since both the writer and his editor were pushovers. She was known to be the best in the industry when it came to negotiations and had dedicated her life to her career.

"Publishing is my one true love," she had told Ben when selling him on representation. It was the warmest thing she ever said.

While he was a grown-ass man and she was nearing sixty and all of five feet two, Elizabeth scared Ben. We used to do once-twice-three-shoot for who would answer her calls, and when he lost he would sulk till I dealt with her anyway. I knew she cared for him, I was sure of it actually, but he was never convinced.

Now Elizabeth would be just the straight shooter that Ben needed. She didn't give a damn about how she came across, and this is not conjecture. She said it to me once after a publicist got annoyed that she sent an email to him in all caps.

She said, "I could care less what anyone thinks of me."

I remember it well, as I had the greatest urge to correct her with, "it's 'I couldn't care less,'" but refrained. I was scared of her too.

Even a brooding young widower with no game and a looming deadline would be no match for Elizabeth Barnes. He would have little choice but to answer her, no matter how much he dreaded their interactions. I remember only one time he felt otherwise: his proposal of our three-island tour.

"She loved the idea!" he'd stormed into our bedroom, shouting. He got himself together and added, "I'm pretty sure she was smiling!"

We jumped up and down on the bed in happiness chanting, "A three-island tour!"

The idea for the three-island tour—always sung instead of spoken to the tune of the theme song from *Gilligan's Island*—was mine. Our biggest success to date, *One Date in Berlin*, had already spent a year on the bestseller list, and Ben was suffering from an awful case of writer's block. I woke up one morning and proclaimed, "If the story isn't coming to you, let's go to the story." We put together a proposal for a series of books set on islands, which we intended to live on and breathe in for a month at a time, tacking my personal days and vacation time on to the standard winter break. It was a daring idea—and it worked.

After what felt like a high school group project in which one person suggests a topic and the other quickly disagrees, we finally, and delightedly, settled on our first stop—Lanai. *Settled* may have been the wrong word. The two of us were ecstatic. The success of Lanai was followed by Sicily, with the proposal for the third book in the series being due this past fall. With all that had been going on, the publisher (my boss), and Elizabeth had tentatively moved the delivery date to April, and when that never happened, to September. From the look of Ben, that was not going to happen either. It was a problem, especially if they made him return the advance, which was long spent.

Seeing her missed calls now, he knew he should call her back, and finished his drink to summon the liquid courage to do so. He listened to her message again—and deleted it. There was really no deleting Elizabeth—and of course, he knew that. She would find him, probably when he least expected it. The apprehension was enough to drive him to drink. And it did.

He topped off his glass, which rendered him unable to think clearly, let alone return a call from his formidable agent. With the past being far more palatable than the future, he lay down on the couch, closed his eyes, and thought about our time in Lanai.

Unlike Sicily, which we chose just because we were both dying to go there, the plot for the Lanai story precipitated our journey. I had seen it all coming together in his mind. It's funny being married to a writer. There are only short periods of time when they are all there with you. They may seem to pay attention as you are talking about this or that, but they are really off somewhere else, and having you pull them back into reality often leads to resentment. For a good part of the time, they are happiest elsewhere. I didn't have a problem with it, especially being Ben's editor, but I imagine other spouses might be less forgiving.

Lanai, the least inhabited of the Hawaiian Islands, was paradise, and I often found myself going back there in my mind as well, especially during chemo treatments. I would bring a book with me for the sessions, but it was hard to concentrate, and I would catch myself reading the same page over and over again. If I didn't love the book, I mean if it didn't grab me by the boots and I couldn't put it down, I would spend more time worrying that I should stop wasting my precious time than reading. Unlike most editors, who were quick to toss aside a title when they weren't crazy about it, due to the scarcity of time I had to actually read for pleasure, I was not a DNF kind of reader. I would finish a book if it killed me. I'm sure there's a joke there somewhere, but it's almost too easy.

After a while I started rereading my old favorites: *A Tree Grows in Brooklyn*, *To Kill a Mockingbird*, even *Alice in Wonderland*. I still ended up closing my eyes and daydreaming about Lanai.

There was one spot on the island that we visited often called the Garden of the Gods, a windy road lined with towers of rocks set in such perfect formations that it's hard to imagine that anyone created them but the gods themselves—ergo the name. On one end sat Shipwreck Beach—an eight-mile stretch of shore named for the hull of an old oil tanker that eerily rose above the waterline. There you can wade, but because of the current, swimming is not advised.

At the other end of the road, plus a short hike, sat Polihua Beach. The waves there were insane—huge, mesmerizing swells that even seasoned surfers didn't attempt. Images of those giant waves, rising and crashing and rising and crashing onto the flat narrow beach would put me in a trance when my mind needed to escape. And it needed to escape quite a lot.

We had rented a bright blue house outside of Lanai City—all eight hundred square feet of it, beachy and quaint. Given its relatively few visitors, it was easy, as a tourist, to stand out among the locals in Lanai. Unlike on Fire Island, where, I have to admit, renters are sometimes treated like second-class citizens, the people of Lanai were quite welcoming. Life was simple there, with Ben spending time on research at the pineapple plantation and me miraculously reading for pleasure, in between finishing up an edit that was due the week we were to return home.

We learned to paddleboard in Manele Bay, and I was surprised how quickly I took to it. I loved being on the calm clear waters, strengthening my core and gliding over the coral reefs. When we returned to Fire Island that summer, Ben surprised me with his and hers boards, but it wasn't the same. The waves of the Atlantic were much more daunting than in "our" cove in the Pacific. Try as I did, I couldn't get past the first break.

But in Hawaii I was righteous.

Most nights in Lanai, I would make a dinner of fresh fish and vegetables and we would eat out on the actual lanai. We would sip mai tais from scooped-out pineapples and play gin or Scrabble until our eyes got tired and it was time for bed. It was most definitely one of the most calm and peaceful times in my life.

The story of Lanai came together quickly for Ben, and when it did, he spent hour upon hour typing away on his laptop. His plot was a take on a famous Lanai legend—a tale of a beautiful young princess captured by a Hawaiian warrior and held captive in his fortress so that no one else could experience her beauty. One day, when the warrior was out warrioring, the princess drowned.

Heartbroken and unwilling to live without her, he leaped off the rocks to his death.

Ben modernized the story (to the 1940s at least), turning it into the tale of a pineapple plantation owner who courted a young Hollywood actress visiting the island and kept her captive on his estate, even coercing her to marry him. In his story, the actress faked her drowning and the plantation owner dove off the rocks to his death without knowing the truth—leaving the actress to inherit it all. She fell in love with a pineapple farmer who had always been kind to her, and the two of them lived happily ever after growing pineapples.

Loving to be all in, Ben ate so much pineapple while writing the book that the keys began to stick on his computer, slowing him down. It made me laugh when I would walk by and hear him griping about it.

At night, we would make love like the actress and the pineapple farmer, and Ben would narrate his moves straight from the book, in his most dramatic voice.

"'Her back arched as his hands traveled down her torso, reaching her hips. He sat back and drew her into him. She nuzzled her head into his chest, languishing in his tropical smell, his sweet taste. He lingered and teased and taunted until she couldn't take it any longer and quietly begged for him to take her.'"

I would go back and forth from squealing with laughter to squealing with desire.

Now, in the substitute lanai, Ben's phone rang again, and he answered it without thinking of the consequences. He was happy to hear it wasn't his agent, but definitely not thrilled by the voice of my Rabbi on the other end.

"Hello, Benjamin, you know your mailbox is full," she said, with the slightest hint of frustration. Ben heard a tone more akin to the wrath of God. While I had quickly considered this woman a friend, Ben never got past the notion that she was a rabbi. He thought of her as legit, holier than thou.

"You're gossiping with a woman of God?" he would ask when overhearing us chatting on the phone like BFFs.

I never could resist a good story.

I had originally thought the relationship would have been a comfort to Ben when I was gone. It was one reason I pursued it, but it never clicked for him like it did for me.

"Sorry. I turned my phone off for shiva," he said, hoping he had fulfilled some kind of commandment.

"That wasn't necessary," she said. "As far as I know, there is no mention of cell phones in the Torah." She laughed. He didn't. You could cut the awkwardness with a knife.

"So, I wanted to check in," she plowed on, "and to let you know that there is a wonderful custom to mark the last day of shiva that you may find comforting—taking a walk around the block of the shiva home."

Ben perked up at this. "I was looking for a way to mark it—so, that sounds nice."

"Good," she said.

"Can I ask what the religious reason is for this?"

I was surprised that he was asking, but also curious, as I had never heard of the ritual before either.

"One reason given is that on this walk, you accompany Julia's soul on its path to the afterlife."

Now I perked up.

The call ended with the Rabbi recommending a support group in the city and Ben pausing to pretend to make note of it. At least I thought he was pretending. I didn't check because I was still stuck on the "accompanying me to the afterlife" part of the conversation. I wasn't sure I was ready to go. Aside from the awful mental state of my husband, I really wanted to find out what happened with Renee and Gabe, and if Dylan and Matty ever get a condom. Plus, I was hoping to see my family one last time. Regardless, I did my best to lean in.

"Goodbye, Sally," I exclaimed, kissing her all over her face. "Goodbye, fireplace that kept us warm on chilly nights. Goodbye, exact spot where we got engaged."

Shep lumbered onto the porch.

"Goodbye, Shep," I said. "Thank you for keeping an eye on my guy."

Ben was attaching Sally's leash to her collar.

"Where are you off to?" Shep asked. "Game's on soon."

"I'm supposed to take a walk around the block—to signify the end of shiva. Did you do that?"

"Caroline wasn't Jewish, and I never really held up my end of things on that front."

"I think it's more for me than Julia. Wanna come?"

"It's for me!" I shouted. "It's time to say goodbye! Did you even listen to the explanation?"

"OK, why not?" Shep agreed.

Ben grabbed the glass canister that had once contained my candle, and the two left in silence. I followed, thinking it my big exit scene.

"Goodbye, house! I'll miss you!" I shouted as the screen door slammed behind us. We walked to the corner at the midway street and turned right ("Goodbye, ball field!"). Another right on the next block ("Goodbye, Mr. Moskowitz, sorry we named you the Killer of Joy when you complained that our music was too loud!") and headed for the beach ("Goodbye, deck that Martin Luther King made a speech from in the sixties!").

Once there, we stood silently gazing at the ocean, the dependable ebb and flow and ebb and flow and ebb and flow.

"Grief is tidal," Ben observed. "Calm one minute and crushing the next."

"Indeed," Shep agreed. "You gotta swim against the current, or it could take you away forever."

Ben stepped a few feet into the ocean and threw the glass canister into the water. We stood quietly and watched the waves transport it.

Ten minutes later, we were all right back where we started.

"Hello, house; hello, exact spot where we got engaged!" I called, entertaining only myself.

eighteen

The Ten O'Clock Ferry

The morning walk around the block didn't seem to have affected Ben in any way, and clearly, I was still here, but Shep looked more introspective than usual. It was obvious that he was sad—you could see it in his lackluster swing.

"What's up with him today?" Eddie asked Ben quietly.

"Hard morning, I guess." Ben explained, "We did this end-of-shiva thing—I think he's feeling like he didn't grieve correctly, or maybe enough."

"He grieved all right—me and some of the guys spent a week or two in and out of his place in the Village after Caroline died. I never saw a man cry so much. It was heartbreaking."

Rico butt in, as he does. "Where were his kids?"

"They switched off every other day at first—there's bad blood between the two sisters, you know?"

Of course he knew. It didn't matter whether you were a vault or held a secret like a wet bar of soap—the whole town had their theories about the two sisters, who were quite close until one summer many, many years ago, when it all went south.

Eddie continued. "Shep was so put off by their behavior that he threw them both out. He said, 'If you can't be here together, then don't come at all.' I think he thought it was an ultimatum, but it didn't work. The older one is still too hurt and the younger one, too selfish."

"He's hoping that they'll come in August," Ben volunteered.

"I'll believe it when I see it," Joel grunted.

August was just a few weeks away. I hoped they would come too, and that I would still be here to see it.

Everyone thought that when Shep and Caroline built the big house across the street, the sisters would make up and enjoy it together—but they never visited in the same month, not even for a weekend. For sure, people thought losing Caroline would unite them, but they took care of all the arrangements, and their father, by text, with very little personal interaction. It was well known that this division in their family was the biggest disappointment in both Caroline's and Shep's lives. I had no doubt it contributed to whatever it was that Shep was feeling today. I knew firsthand that life's wrongs stood a lot taller when you had little time left to right them—and he was not getting any younger.

My sister, Nora, and I were quite different, in looks and interests and even in our familial relationships, but I can't imagine any of our differences ever coming between us like that. The story I heard about the Silver sisters was a very basic one involving a love triangle with a hot lifeguard who amounted to little more in life than becoming a not-hot lifeguard.

Shep struck out and returned to the bench, putting a hard stop to the conversation, but I couldn't stop thinking about it. It always seemed to me like there must be more to the sister drama than I knew. Curiosity had definitely followed me to the afterlife.

We returned home from the game to a text message from my dad.

"Fuck," Ben said when he read it. "We have to clean up."

I didn't even have to ask. I knew my family would be there in the morning.

Renee stopped in from across the street to see if she could coax Ben away from his old friend for a few hours to listen to live music. He used the excuse of straightening up for my parents, who would indeed be on the 10:00 a.m. boat.

"I'm in!" I shouted, excited for so many reasons, not least of which was that watching them straighten up was not pleasant.

She had already asked Pam and Andie, but they couldn't get a sitter and Pam had read that loud drumming was bad for the baby's auditory development. Renee even invited Matty, but he didn't text back. While it wasn't particularly unusual for a sixteen-year-old boy to ignore his mother—she knew it was more than that.

She went on her own, as far as she knew, and as we walked into the young crowd she took a deep breath of relief. She was clearly thankful to be solo. Things aren't quite as embarrassing if there is no one there to bear witness. It was a concept I could relate to well, in my current state. I did a few moves of the Electric Slide and Cotton Eye Joe, just to prove the point.

Gabe saw her right away. His eyes widened as he stepped down from the stage, where he had been noodling around with some wires. I found him to be a little too hipster for my taste, with all of his woke introspection, but I understood the thrill of having him look at her the way he did. Especially after being tossed aside by Tuck, as she was. Her knees wobbled, and she pressed them together. I wondered if she was thinking about the scene in the shower. I would be. He kissed her gently on the lips—and she was immediately embarrassed by the public display of affection. She looked around the room to see if she knew anyone. She didn't. He led her to a table up front with a small sign on it that read FOR THE

BAND. A few people were already seated there, passing around a pitcher of margaritas. She was the only "girl" not wearing a crop top.

It had to feel beyond awkward sitting with a bunch of kids closer to Matty's age than her own. She obviously felt it as she did the math under the table on her fingers. I did it too. Matty was fourteen years younger than Gabe and she was thirteen years older. If she told the truth about her age she won by a year.

The music began, and Renee seemed thankful that she didn't need to make small talk. She followed the others' lead and stood by the stage, moving her hips from side to side to the loud beat. She liked the noise, she always liked noise. It somehow made her think more clearly. She caught a quick glimpse of herself in the mirror and saw a middle-aged woman standing in a flock of twentysomethings. She thought so clearly that she quietly made her way to the door.

At home she sat in her bed playing Wordle and contemplating the fact that solving the daily word game would once again be the most exciting part of her day. The house still smelled like garlic. Her phone buzzed as she typed in her standard five-letter first word: *TEARS*.

It was ironic, because I noticed she rarely shed any.

Where you at? Gabe asked.

She ignored it and studied the game. She had an *R*, an *A*, and a *T*. She placed down her next word. *QUART*. Nope. Just the order of the *ART* changed. Her phone buzzed again. It somehow sounded angrier than the first time.

Hello?

CHART, she thought as her phone vibrated yet again.

Are we good?

She knew she should answer, at the least; ghosting him wasn't nice. But she was too weak in her resolve to start a back-and-forth. She knew their pairing had a short shelf life, and she had laughed at Tuck's choice to rob the cradle too many times to do the same. Not to mention that she could barely look Matty in the eye all week.

It wasn't *CHART.*

She perused the available letters and played around with different combinations in her head.

Ok. I'm leaving on the 10:00 am ferry, but this is not goodbye. I really care about you.

She turned back to Wordle and typed in *APART.*

"Splendid!" the game responded.

She didn't feel splendid.

nineteen

Sitting on the Dock of the Bay

Early July brought a heat wave the likes of which I hadn't felt in years—not that I felt it now. The air was hot and heavy. Windless. Everyone seemed to be laboriously trudging through it, except for Ben. Dense with grief, he moved with it in perfect synchronicity.

I took a walk down to the bay and sat on the dock watching the kids in the water—learning to swim or just horsing around, their sunburned arms wrapped around brightly colored swim noodles, their heads bobbing up and down with the current. I had always had the same thought when watching similar scenes in the past—one day. The realization that that dream would not be achieved would have broken my heart a few months back, but now I sat firmly in the "it is what it is" mindset. It was a favorite saying of my mother's, and I cringed every time it left her lips. Nothing my mother did was what it was—unless it was exactly what she wanted. Ironically, the phrase had now become my death mantra.

I was surprised to see Matty and Dylan whip by me and dive in, racing to the floating dock as they probably had countless times before. The contrast between their behavior now and the last time I saw them together made me laugh. I noted they seemed more comfortable acting like kids than contemplating adulthood.

It may have been the first time they had been together since the incident on the dunes. Dylan was working nights at the ferry terminal while Matty was delivering groceries during the day. Dylan would never say no to a night shift, and the overtime money that came with it, while Matty had other motivations aside from his finances for working a summer job.

Being a delivery boy at the market was a rite of passage. Matty was honored to be one of the chosen few whom Big Les tapped on the shoulder and said, "Hey, kid, want to work here?" The tasks were divided according to the sexual norms of the 1950s. The chosen girls stacked the shelves and checked out groceries, while the boys mostly did deliveries or, on very busy days, helped behind the deli counter. Though only day-trippers and renters gave them their sandwich orders. It took years to learn how to make a sandwich to rival Little Les's.

Dylan, on the other hand, was working for every bit of her spending money at UC San Diego. Her goal was to earn enough to last till next summer so that she could just be a student and study and have fun. The fun part made me worry. Between her strict father and growing up on this isolated island, she seemed a bit starved for it. I was honestly happy about her and Matty's plan to lose their virginity together. At least she wasn't thinking like one of those girls that gets to college, goes wild, and burns out. Though, between the lack of time, place, and prophylactic, who knew if it would ever happen for them? I hoped it would before I left. I'm not particularly partial to a cliffhanger.

Apparently, Dylan had spent the morning completing online registration for her fall term. When she shut her computer, she felt a weird mixture of panic and excitement. She embraced the latter and used the Find My Friends app to surprise Matty. She found him sweating over a cart full of groceries a few blocks from her house. She helped him quickly deliver his load and convinced him to take a quick break to go jump in the bay.

That first slap of the cold, dark water brought them right back. Dylan reached the dock ahead of Matty, climbed on, and held out her hand for him. She was a faster swimmer, yes, but more than that, she never hesitated at the start. Her leap was a part of her last stride while Matty always paused and hung back for one, and two, and even three seconds more. By the time he jumped in, Dylan was three lengths ahead. Dylan was always three lengths ahead. It may have been why she was so consumed with the thought of being behind.

"I'll get you next time," he said, reaching for her hand, hoisting himself up and sprawling out on the floating square dock beside her.

I doubted that would ever happen.

Matty may have been a star on the ball field, but Dylan was practically half-fish. When they were young, you could see her coaxing him to ride the waves. He would still be standing at the edge timing his entry while she had already cut through the third break. Legend is she swam before she walked. She would take off from the safety of her parents' blanket, crawling full speed ahead to the ocean at just ten months. Jake taught her to swim soon after, and her mother nicknamed her the Little Mermaid. The nickname stuck, but her mother did not. She took off when Dylan was just a toddler.

"This summer bites, Matty. We hardly see each other."

"Maybe I can ride the ferry over with you tonight and help you work."

"My dad will never allow that."

"What's he gonna do, throw me overboard?"

Neither commented on the possibility. The truth was, Jake had barely made eye contact with Dylan over the past few days, and she was beginning to worry she would leave for school with them in a bad place. She was not about to ask him for a favor—especially one involving Matty.

Jake had silently handed her a book the morning after the now legendary night. (I'd already overheard the girls at the register whispering about it.) The look Jake gave Dylan during the exchange was the closest they had come to discussing the incident. She held his gaze, preparing herself for some embarrassing and archaic manual on sex education. But the book, titled *The Fragile Ecosystem of the Barrier Beach*, mortified her more.

"You'll have a day off soon, and we can spend it together," Dylan promised Matty.

"Well, at this rate, it's a good thing you only want to do it once," Matty joked.

Dylan didn't think it was funny.

"We'll figure something out," he assured her, reeling back in his joke.

"You still have to get a condom, you know. Don't forget!"

"Believe me, I haven't forgotten."

The conversation made me wonder about their determination. As far as I was aware, neither seemed to be trying very hard to put their plan into action.

A group of kids wearing arm floats or life vests climbed the ladder to the dock and surrounded the two teenage sunbathers, putting an end to their R-rated conversation.

Matty and Dylan sat up and watched them longingly as they laughed and swayed their linked arms back and forth and back and forth to the shouts of one, two, three, before jumping back in to the bay.

"I have to get back to the store," Matty said, his tone in great contrast to the gaggle of giggling children.

"I'm gonna stay here for a bit," Dylan said, adding, "Don't forget to ask for off for my birthday."

"I already did," Matty managed, before sliding off the dock without so much as a splash.

Dylan lay on her belly for a bit, dangling her hand off the dock in the dark bay, a pensive look on her face. Two kids climbed the ladder, stormed past her, and cannonballed off the back of the dock, outside of the confines of the swim cradle.

"You're gonna get in trouble," Dylan preached knowingly, as the lifeguards blew their whistles.

In my head, I imagined her cannonballing off the back of the dock with them, as opposed to warning them. It would have been a better ending.

twenty

Incoming

The first summer after we bought the house, we were excited to invite guests, myself more than Ben, I may add. There was more than one instance when he kicked me under the table as whomever we were sitting with in the city pronounced, "I've never been to Fire Island," usually with a bucket of hope in their eyes. The kick was to stop me from responding, "You have to come visit us this summer, then!"

We had a full house nearly every weekend of our first summer as homeowners. We hadn't put down roots yet, and we filled our calendar with sincere and greatly anticipated invitations. By year two, we cringed as those same guests began hinting at the next summer's invite as early as October. By year three, Ben scribbled the words *NO GUESTS* in red Sharpie over half the weekends on our calendar. By year four, he wrote his version of "The Rime of the Ancient Mariner."

There are good guests, and bad guests, but the best
guests are no guests.

He wanted to have it needlepointed and framed and hung on the wall over our entranceway.

"We'll lose all our friends!" I protested.

"Or rule out the humorless ones," he responded with a hopeful smirk.

We are not ogres or ingrates, but the truth is, most guests don't know how to behave. They arrive full of potential, bearing gifts of food and wine and, if we are really lucky, a case of toilet paper, but things quickly sour. They overstay their welcome (two nights tops), use up all the good sunblock, don't help themselves or help in general, and forget to shut the screen door and wipe the sand from their feet when entering the house.

My family, especially my mom, who adheres to the old "we're not guests we're family" adage, were the worst offenders. They'd arrive empty-handed and hungry, no matter what ferry they made. And my mother, regardless of how much she complained about the short walk to our house, always wore inappropriate shoes. The belief that "a lady should always wear heels" was a pillar of her personal brand of insanity.

Now Ben pulled the wagon to the ferry at a sloth-like pace to meet my sister and my parents. Unlike him, I was happy they were coming. While my relationship with my mom was fraught with typical mother-daughter stuff, teenage blowouts over ridiculous things like my bra strap showing or her constant cry of "Don't forget lipstick!" every time I left the house, I didn't feel badly about any of it. I was a good daughter, and there was no doubt she was a proud mother. She loved bragging about my accomplishments and Ben's. She replaced her coffee table books with the novels I had edited and told anyone who would listen, "My daughter is married to the bestselling author Benjamin Morse," in a haughty voice that she could turn on and off in an instant. My sister, Nora, and I called it her Highland Manor tone in reference to the elocution lessons she took at the fancy boarding school she was sent off to as a teenager. Apparently, her younger self hadn't gotten along with her own mother very well either. She insisted it was on account of her mother being a classic narcissist—there was lots of pot-calling-the-kettle-black action between my mother and my grandmother.

Generally, I think the classic narcissist label is thrown around too liberally, but in my mother and grandmother's case, it was spot-on. Hopefully, it would prevent her from looking inward too much after I passed. I would hate for her to dwell on the short-comings of our relationship for the rest of her life. I certainly never did. Though I appreciated that my relationships with my dad and my sister were much simpler.

Even at Ben's slow pace, we reached the ferry early. Ben walked out to the edge of the dock and sat down, his legs swinging back and forth above the water like a kid. Two swans were doing a lap around the perimeter of the basin. I waited with anticipation to watch them effortlessly glide in unison over the wake of the ferry when it arrived. Ben took a deep cleansing breath to counter the distant sight of the boat cutting through the morning fog. I wondered about the future of his relationship with my family—if that obligation died with me or not.

The boat arrived, and three strangers staggered off. My mother, makeup free and wearing tennis shoes, my sister, pulling a giant Yeti cooler with another strapped to her back, and my dad, who also looked like he had aged ten years since the funeral. While Ben stood between them for a group hug, I reminded myself they would be OK, that they had one another. He slid the backpack from my sister's shoulder and grabbed the cooler. The insanity of my father not even noticing that my sister was carrying everything wasn't lost on either of us.

As the ferry pulled away, Renee raced up on her bike, tossed it against the fence, and ran out on the dock. She had obviously had a change of heart regarding the drummer. It was too late. She watched as the boat got smaller and smaller until it disappeared into the fog. Then she sat down on the bench, alone, and buried her face in her hands.

"I got you an iced coffee at the market," Gabe said, tapping her on the shoulder and handing it to her like it was the plan all along. She looked up at him and released a pent-up sob.

"Don't," he said, pulling her to him for an embrace. When he released her, she looked into his eyes.

"What happened to the ten o'clock boat?"

"You weren't on it."

She shook off her obvious emotion, embarrassed by the spectacle of it. "Wanna come back to the house, stay with me for a few days?"

I wondered if Gabe knew what a big deal this was for her. He seemed to be oddly insightful. He answered by scooping her up into his arms and kissing her passionately. Her knees shook again, and she pressed them against his legs to steady them. The kiss clearly moved her more. She couldn't get enough of him.

"Are you sure?" he asked, when they came up for air.

"No. Not at all," she said, with a shy smile.

"You know, being sure is overrated."

She didn't. But she was suddenly willing to find out.

twenty-one

Mementos

The walk back to the house from the ferry dock was even slower than the walk there, and with the added depressing element of people diverting their eyes as we passed—their collective grief was palpable. As much as it may have hurt my family, I was thankful that Ben had escaped to the beach. If this is what they looked like after the week of shiva, I couldn't imagine how Ben would have fared. Maybe they were better when they had an audience. I'm sure my mother was.

"I have to freshen up," my mom said when we arrived, giving Sally an obligatory pat on the head before heading straight for my bedroom. She closed the door behind her, locked it, and sat down on my side of the bed. I wondered about the depths of a mother's love, of a mother's grief, and again felt thankful that I hadn't left a child behind.

My nightstand was untouched since last summer, except for a pair of Shep's reading glasses. She opened a novel I had been reading and studied it as if it were the holy grail. In reality, it had been a painfully slow read, and I had uncharacteristically given up on it at chapter six, where it was earmarked. She slipped it in her purse while I uselessly protested.

"That book was a bore. Take something else!"

I hoped every one of my belongings would not be held on to with misguided nostalgia. I had tossed or donated a lot of stuff in the city over the past few months so that Ben wouldn't have to bother with it, but everything here at the beach was just as we left it back when our lives were picture-perfect.

She picked up an old family photo of us that sat framed on my nightstand next to one of Sally as a pup and another of Ben and me the summer that we started dating. It was a photo of my family when we were young on Saint Bart's, before it became the bougie place to go. The shot was very Slim Aarons, and I treasured it.

Every Christmas, my parents would rent a villa on Saint Bart's, where we proceeded to make some of my happiest childhood memories—except, that is, for our arrival. To get to Saint Bart's, you had to first fly to Anguilla and then charter a small plane to navigate one of the shortest runways in the world, nestled between two mountains. I found the famously harrowing landings thrilling but can still hear the piercing cries from my sister, who always thought we were going to crash. She would hold my hand so tightly I thought my fingers would fall off. The same happened when we got shots at the pediatrician or when the scary monkeys came on-screen during *The Wizard of Oz*. It worried me, even then, that she wasn't brave on her own.

In the picture we are around thirteen and nine and standing poolside, looking over at our parents, who were deep in a game of backgammon. Our skin is tanned, and our hair stiff and sticky from the lemons we squeezed on daily, ridiculously hoping for highlights in our monochromatic black locks. In the photo, Nora holds her right fist against her chest, clutching a piece of red beach glass smoothed to perfection and abstractly shaped like a heart. I had been the one who found it on the beach earlier that day. I handed her the heart-shaped treasure and said, "This is for you, Nora. It has magic in it. Hold it tight when you're scared and I'm not around."

She clutched that little piece of glass in her little fist for most of the day, as if taking in its powers, and cried when she lost it at the end of the trip.

My mother placed the photo back on the nightstand and opened my top drawer. I had actually seen her do this before. Not one to respect boundaries, she thought nothing of going through my closet or dresser like a camp counselor during morning inspection. I had even caught her refolding things on occasion.

She pulled out an old silk scarf of mine and buried her nose in it. It was interesting to me, how people grasp on to scent after someone passes. I had never much thought of it before. I guess it's the last possible sensory connection. I doubt it still smelled like me, if it ever had. I couldn't remember the last time I wore it. It was one of those wardrobe pieces that went to the beach to die.

She shoved the barely worn scarf in her bag with the book and left the bedroom. She seemed to have gotten what she came for. I wasn't surprised; my mother always had a thing for things—something tangible of mine to hold on to would help her to grieve.

"Where's Nora?" she asked my dad and Ben, who were unloading a massive amount of leftovers from the shiva, mostly from the aforementioned Upper West Side trifecta of Zabar's, Fairway, and Citarella. Shep had made himself scarce for the visit, but I imagined he would be thrilled the next time he opened the fridge. The selections from the "Brisket Brigade" had been dwindling.

"She went to the beach," Ben answered. "She should be back soon."

I spotted Nora a few blocks east, her bright yellow sweatshirt peeking out from the morning fog as if it were the sun itself. I reached her mid-conversation. She was perched on a cut of sand, looking out over the ocean on the empty beach, talking out loud—to me. It felt more like a confession than a conversation. As if the endless sea in front of her was her church and I was her priest. This wasn't surprising to me. The vastness of the ocean is humbling, and its color a reflection of the heavens above. I felt humbled as well, and still no closer to entering the "world to come" as my Rabbi friend had suggested I eventually would.

I sat down beside her and rubbed my hand up and down her back. She flinched when I did, but I was pretty sure it was just a coincidence.

She sat at the shoreline, the salt from both the ocean and her tears stinging her wounds. The fog was so thick, and her tears so heavy that if someone approached, she wouldn't see them until they were on top of her. I hoped, for her sake, that no one would spring up.

"I miss you too much," Nora cried. "I'm so sorry this happened to you. I wish it was me. Not you. You're so good." She sobbed uncontrollably.

I uselessly argued against her points, but I knew I would have felt the same if the tables were turned.

"I can't stand not being able to talk to you," she continued. "You should have seen Mom trying to keep her hair still when we sat up top on the ferry. It's no fun, witnessing her crazy anymore, without you to tell." She smiled in the middle of her tears, disproving her point. She was too upset to recognize it.

"You can talk to me," I cried. "You just did!" I knew she

couldn't hear me, but for the first time, I wondered if someone else could, when the tide pulled out and something red caught my eye. The Rabbi had told me there are many signs during the first month after death, and to tell my loved ones to look out for them. I hadn't, because it was just too hard to have those conversations.

Nora saw it too and wiped her eyes clear to focus. She concentrated intently as she stood at the water's edge and waited for the tide to descend again. When it did, her eyes darted along the shoreline until she landed on the bright red treasure. She scooped it up with the sand around it and spread her fingers like a sieve, releasing all but a piece of red sea glass, starkly reminiscent of the piece I had gifted her in Saint Bart's.

"You can hear me!" she cried, her painful tears now mixing with joyous ones.

"Thank you, thank you, Julia, thank you!" she cried out in relief.

"Be brave," I replied, adding, "I'm so sorry, Nora. So sorry for the bumpy ride."

The fog lifted from both the sky and our spirits as we walked back to the house. Nora clutched the piece of red sea glass in her closed fist just as she had when we were kids. The whole exercise, as corny and dramatic as it was, felt transcendent. I knew she would get through this, and hoped she would talk to me with complete abandon forever.

And then there was my dad.

Everyone seemed to have their own agenda for the visit, and it was no surprise that my dad's centered around Ben. I walked in to them sitting on the lanai, deep in conversation.

"The thing is, son, you are all we have of her."

I wondered if he had said that for Ben or for himself. Ben was always one to fall for Jewish guilt, and my dad was always one to know what was best for his children, Ben included. It was actually the perfect thing to tie them together—pieces of me.

"I expect you for Sunday brunches in the city as often as possible, please."

"Of course," Ben said, before hugging him, awkwardly at first because they typically went for the handshake or fist bump, and even more awkwardly after, because neither could bear to let go.

I was relieved that my dad was insisting they stay close. At least I would know Ben would eat well on Sundays.

My mom made a brief mention of the ferry schedule, and Ben jumped at the chance to steer them to an early departure. He announced the before- and after-dinner ferry times and threw in a half-assed invitation to stay for the later boat.

"We have enough food—that's for sure," he offered.

"If I never see a pastrami sandwich again, it will be too soon," my dad proclaimed, not wanting to overstay his welcome, I imagined. Besides, it seemed like everyone had gotten what they needed from the visit—myself included.

Something inside me held me back from accompanying them to the boat for the big goodbye. I worried it would mess with the closure I was already feeling. When I watched them walk down the block, away from me, I felt a calmness that I hadn't since I'd passed. I went back to the beach and sat on the stairs, searching for dolphins.

twenty-two

Bang the Drum Slowly

Matty stood in the kitchen, emptying the dishwasher at a volume and with a vengeance usually reserved for passive-aggressively punishing a housework-averse spouse. He dumped the silverware into the drawer in one fell swoop, causing a cacophony of clanking. Renee raced down the stairs, alarmed by the commotion. A look of satisfaction crossed his face. He was obviously aware that the drummer was back and angry at his mother for it. I understood, but personally, I was loving the whole May–December romance. It was my favorite plot twist of the summer, and I had many different endings in mind.

Just as it wasn't an accident that Renee chose Tuck, it wasn't an accident that Renee became a divorce attorney. Both choices directly resulted from her childhood. Renee's mother, like Renee, was prom queen, but unlike Renee, was not crowned most likely to succeed. In fact, when Renee won both titles her senior year of high school, her mother went on and on, bragging about the first, with little mention of the second. For Renee it summed up everything that was wrong with her mother. She vowed not to end up like her.

Renee's mother's definition of success was to marry well, and that had been her own number one goal in college. After a grand total of six dates with Renee's dad, she became pregnant. She swore it wasn't her intention, but she also swore that she was a natural redhead—so there was that. She dropped out of school, married, and had Renee.

By the time Renee was old enough to know what was going on, it became quite clear that her dad was not faithful to her mom. While it was obvious to Renee, her mom seemed oblivious. Her life revolved around her weekly activities: mah-jongg on Mondays, tennis on Tuesdays, a manicure on Wednesdays, volunteering at the Scarsdale Historical Society on Thursdays, and her weekly hair appointment on Fridays. Renee had never seen her mother with wet hair, aside from when she had accompanied her to the beauty salon—where it was washed, coiffed to perfection, and shellacked to last the week. When they visited their summer home on Fire Island, her Pucci kerchief remained in place for the entire ferry ride and most of the weekend. Much like my own mother.

Sometime during Renee's junior year of high school, she and her mom set out on a college tour. As usual, Renee was beyond prepared. She had mapped out every liberal arts school on the eastern seaboard that matched her criteria, set up interviews at all of her top choices, and created a folder filled with directions, schedules, and which questions to ask at which schools in order to stand out. Just before they got to the parkway, she realized she had left the whole thing at home. Her mom didn't want to go back, but Renee had insisted. When she ran upstairs to grab the prized folder, she passed by her parents' open bedroom door and froze. Inside, her father was screwing her mother's best friend, their neighbor, Judy Skylar, doggy style. She only knew it was doggy style from the black-and-white illustrations in the copy of *The Joy of Sex* that she and Judy Skylar's daughter, Jilly, used to sneak down from the top row of their bookshelf when no one was home. It wasn't easy to retrieve and even harder to put back in the exact same spot. Renee had to stand on top of the banister and scale the shelves to reach it while Jilly Skylar held her right leg steady so she wouldn't fall. They had both decided that the doggy position—number ninety-five in the book—didn't look very attractive. There was no eye contact, and the woman in the illustration's breasts hung down like two eggplants. It had looked that way in real life too.

For a brief moment, everyone involved in the unfortunate encounter froze and stared silently. Determined to continue with her plan, Renee squeezed her eyes shut, trying to erase what she had seen, and ran to her room for the folder. She visited four colleges, asked all the right questions, and didn't mention a thing about what she had witnessed until she and her mom were on the way back home.

At a diner in Tivoli, New York, she admitted, "Mom. When I ran back for my folder, Daddy was home."

"OK," her mother said, followed by, "I think I'm going to get the grapefruit. It sounds refreshing."

When Renee relayed the story to me, years and years later, the two of us sitting on the beach before sunset with a glass of wine, she was visibly shaken. The words got caught in her throat, just as they had all those years before.

Renee took a deep breath and told her mom what she had seen.

"Mom, when I went back to the house, Daddy was in your bed with Judy Skylar."

The server chose that moment to come take their orders.

"I'll have the Grand Slam with pancakes and extra sausage,"

her mother said, switching from the grapefruit without missing a beat.

She ate the whole thing in silence, then went to the bathroom and threw it all up. She never said another word about it until Renee's dad came home from work, a few weeks later, and told them he was leaving. He packed his bags and moved out, which didn't take long because he literally moved next door. In the end, he couldn't keep up with the three houses, the two in Scarsdale and their summer place on Fire Island. They sold Renee's childhood home and the beach house and moved to a walk-up apartment in town, where her mom got a job answering phones at a local insurance agency. Her mother was pretty stoic about the whole thing. In fact, Renee said that the only time she saw her cry was when she had to do her own hair.

Years later, her mother married the owner of that insurance company. He had asked her right in the office. She said yes and used the receptionist's phone one last time—to resecure her standing appointment at the beauty salon.

Renee had missed the house on Fire Island more than she had missed her dad.

The divorce was tough on Renee. For one thing, she got into all the colleges she had applied to, but with her father's income listed on her financial aid forms, she didn't get the help she needed to attend. She called the schools and explained that he was no longer supporting her, but they all said there was nothing they could do at that late juncture. She ended up at a state school, where she did very well, and swore she would never depend on, or trust, a man again. And she didn't, through law school and afterward, until she met Tuck Tucker. Dull, reliable Tuck Tucker, whose loyal and steady demeanor assured her she was unlikely ever to catch him dogging her neighbor.

I could see that Renee truly loved Tuck, though it surprised me. Even after she told me what had happened, I was careful not to speak too badly about him, in case she took him back. I kind of felt like she knew how everyone felt about him, anyway. They were always invited to the big parties that people threw every summer, but when we would attend smaller intimate get-togethers, it was rare for them to be included. People couldn't tolerate being trapped in a small setting with Tuck Tucker. It was hard for me to get Ben to go out to eat with them, even though Renee was one of my closest friends.

"Consider it a character study," I would tell Ben. In the end, it turned out to be more of a lack of character study.

Now Renee entered the kitchen with a joke.

"I really appreciate that you're helping out, but can you empty that any louder?"

"I'm sorry. Were you sleeping?" Matty asked, with biting sarcasm.

Renee blushed, a skill she seemed to be perfecting lately, and reached out to help with the dishwasher. Avoiding eye contact.

"How long is this guy gonna be hanging around?" Matty asked.

"I don't know. I haven't really thought it through."

It was probably the first time she had ever uttered that statement in her life. Poor Matty. It's hard to see your mother and father as real people and not just your parents.

"Well, let me know when you figure it out, please—I'm going to work."

"Wait, Matty." She grabbed his arm, and he recoiled. Her eyes widened, and she blinked away tears.

"Want to take a bike ride tomorrow to Sunken Forest? Just the two of us?"

"Tomorrow's Dylan's birthday."

He left without so much as a shrug goodbye.

Renee grabbed a mug, fumbled with a Keurig pod, and then went to the refrigerator for milk. On it, under a magnet that read, *Fire Island, Blissfully Unaware*, sat an old photo of the two of us. She pulled it off the fridge and took in the image. We were sitting on the dock of the bay watching the sunset. I was smiling at the camera, but she was looking at me. She spoke to the photo as if I were there.

"It's not fair, Jules, why does Tuck get to live his life without judgment and I have to be the perfect mom?"

It wasn't really true, as far as the judgment goes. It was quite clear that Matty had lost what little respect he had for his father and that Renee was just now treading into that territory. I wished I could tell her to communicate with him better. It wasn't like her not to say what she was feeling. I wondered if she even knew herself.

She stared at the photo for a bit before the tears finally came.

"I don't know what to do. I miss you so much. I never felt like this before. Not even when my marriage ended. It's hard to breathe." She sobbed, surprising herself with the power of her emotions. By the time the drummer found her, she was curled up in a ball all-out ugly crying.

"Maybe you should go," she managed. "I have"—sob—"to put"—sob—"Matty first."

Gabe got down on the floor next to her and rubbed her back.

"Now?" he asked.

She curled her body into his, and I could see the pain release from her eyes. He wrapped his arms around her and held her close.

"Maybe tomorrow," she said, drying her tears on his shirt.

twenty-three

Dylan's Birthday

On the morning of Dylan's birthday, Matty met Dylan on the beach to begin their annual four-mile run and 182-step climb to the top of the Fire Island Lighthouse. Once there, the tradition continued with Dylan reading her yearly birthday letter from her mother. She received postcards from her mom from different places throughout the year—all saying very little, but on her birthday, she always got a long letter. It was usually a few pages of advice, mostly feminine stuff that her mother deemed age-appropriate, and it always contained a fresh hundred-dollar bill. Dylan never shared what it said with Matty and always did the same thing. She pocketed the money and tore the letter into a million little pieces, tossing them like confetti from the gallery platform of the lighthouse. It was the only time that she littered. Today she folded the letter up and put it back in her pocket.

When Dylan was about three, her mom literally ran off to join the circus. It was one of those things that if Ben had written it in one of his novels, I may have called it unbelievable and taken a blue pencil to it.

She wasn't an acrobat, or a clown. In fact, she was neither flexible nor funny—she was a bookkeeper.

The story began a few years before when Dylan's mother, Melissa, who originally hailed from a landlocked town in upstate New York, took a summer job at Rachel's Restaurant & Bakery, a staple in town serving up cookies, cakes, and brownies. There she met Jake, a strong handsome guy who worked on the ferry dock and was exceedingly fond of Rachel's world-famous crumb cake topped with mountains of sweet, but not too sweet, cinnamon crumble. He would eat it from the top down, which always made Melissa laugh. She soon fell in love with both Jake and Fire Island.

Jake, thrilled to find a girl who never wanted to leave, quickly married her. By the following summer, Dylan was born and Melissa was happy, at first. She still helped out at the bakery on some nights and was excited to spend the winter alone with Jake and their baby, but when the summer people left and the bakery and most everything else shut for the season, staying home all day with an infant proved too much for her. What she imagined as an adventure was in reality isolating and depressing, and by the time Jake returned home at night, Melissa was often in tears. She had suffered from seasonal affective disorder before—although she didn't know the name for it. Add in the remote lifestyle and a sprinkling of postpartum symptoms and she was clinically depressed. At least that is what the shrink who Jake took her to off-island had said.

The doctor suggested she come weekly, and Jake would bring her, watching over Dylan in the waiting room while Melissa was inside. He was good at caring for the baby. It was easy to tend to her needs. Just follow a schedule: a bottle, a clean diaper, a bath—it didn't feel much different from taking care of the ferries.

Methodically checking off a list of tasks and then doing it all over again the next day.

Melissa was prescribed antidepressants, and by the time the summer people arrived, she seemed better. But as soon as they left again, and the season changed, her sadness came back. This time, it seemed worse. On some days, she couldn't get out of bed, and Jake would strap Dylan into the BabyBjörn and take her to work with him, but it was hard. Melissa was always sad.

The doctor thought she needed something of her own and suggested she take an online class. She had always been good with numbers, so she enrolled in bookkeeping. At the end of the course, the teacher gave out a list of employment opportunities. Number three on the list caught her eye. A traveling circus with offices out of Long Island, close to the Bay Shore ferry terminal. Jake encouraged her to go for it, anything to see a smile on her face again.

Melissa applied and got the job, though there was a hitch. The office on Long Island was really just the circus owner's house; the job was on the road. In the few days between getting the job and learning of this caveat, Melissa was happier than she had ever been. And so Jake was as well. When she learned of the travel requirement, she was heartbroken. They decided she would go for one season, and between him and his mom, who lived across the bay, they would manage—as long as she was back by May, when high-season kicked in on Fire Island. After that, she would have something great on her résumé and could find work closer to home. Maybe even with the ferry company, whose current bookkeeper was nearing retirement.

Two months in, she sent a postcard from Cawker City, Kansas—home of the world's largest ball of twine. It said she had fallen in love with life on the road and would not be coming back.

"I'm not good for Dylan, anyway," she wrote. "She is better off with you. Please tell her I will always love her."

There was no word from her for years. In that time Jake became mom, dad, and teacher to Dylan. They spent their days playing in the surf, fishing off the bay and sanding boats. He taught her the difference between a stratus cloud and a cumulus, a new moon and a harvest moon, a piping plover and a sandpiper. So much of who she was now, and what she loved, came from being brought up by her dad. In the winters, when it snowed, Jake would pull her in a toboggan to the little yellow school bus that drove down the beach. In the summers, she would go to the local day camp, then ride the afternoon ferry boats, wiping down the benches and collecting tickets. And though she never wore a dress and her hair was usually a bit of a mess, she was a happy little girl with a happy childhood—filled with the security of her father's love.

There was no divorce, and no formal custody agreement. They all just lived that way until her sixth birthday.

Now, Dylan and Matty walked the 182 steps down from the lighthouse and headed for the first town—Kismet—where they continued their annual tradition with a big breakfast at the Kismet Inn.

Matty broke the silence. "Wanna share pancakes and waffles? 'Cause I can't decide."

"Sure," she said. Pancakes and waffles would usually get more of a rise out of her.

"Dyl, can I ask what the letter said?"

"Yeah, OK," she answered, but fell back into silence.

Matty poked her and smiled. "What did the letter say?"

"Did I ever tell you about my sixth birthday?"

He shook his head, and I inched closer so as not to miss a word.

"My dad took off the whole day, and we went out on the boat. We docked at a waterside restaurant for lunch. I remember feeling so cool, being one of those people who arrive by boat, you know what I mean?"

We both did. There was a whole world of boat people on the Great South Bay. I had only gotten a taste of it a few times, but it seemed like a very fun alternate universe. They would gather their boats in groups around sandbars or on uninhabited islets and plop down beach chairs and drink beers. When visiting Fire Island they would dock for lunch or dinner at the local restaurants—just like Dylan was describing doing on the mainland.

She continued, explaining how she and Jake had spent the rest of her sixth birthday fishing in the ocean, and they caught a big snapper for dinner. And how when they arrived home, sunburned and beat, her mother was standing in front of the house with a tall lanky acrobat named Earl, who she said turned her life upside down. She was carrying one of those big round Tupperware cake holders.

I had gotten one of those cake holders as a shower gift, and it was now sitting on a shelf at Housing Works on Columbus Avenue along with a waffle maker and a juicer. I had cleaned out the kitchen, imagining that never-used plastic cake holder accompanying Ben on every move he made for the rest of his days.

Melissa quickly informed Jake that she and Earl wanted to marry and that she would need a divorce. He was fine with it, but then she said she thought it was time that Dylan lived with her, with them—on the road. She said that now that she was a happy woman, she would be a good mother.

Dylan was sitting at the Kismet Inn, rolling her paper napkin between her fingers, like a rosary. I could tell that it wasn't the sullen mood she had anticipated on her seventeenth birthday, especially on one of Matty's few days off. Matty clearly felt badly for pushing her to talk. Especially on her birthday. She had to finish the story though. It was too late to stop.

"She sat me down and apologized for having left," Dylan continued. "She said, 'A girl needs a mother more than a father,' and, 'I know it seems as if I abandoned you, but I needed to leave here in order to come back as a capable, fulfilled person.'"

It sounded like her mother had memorized the part in that old movie, *Kramer vs. Kramer*, where Meryl Streep begs the judge for custody of her son.

"She asked me if I would want to live with her—to travel all over the country and see new things instead of living on this little island all the time. She said there were other kids and a mobile school, and she made it sound so awesome. Back then, I had barely left Fire Island besides going to my grandma's in Islip. And it did sound exciting. I mean, anything would, let alone a traveling circus. But I explained that I couldn't leave my dad. That he would miss me too much. She said that I could come here every summer to be with him. I thought about it for a few minutes, I really did. And then she gave me a birthday present. It was a pink tutu with layers of tulle and a rainbow of butterflies sewn on it."

Matty laughed at the thought of Dylan in a tutu.

"I thought it was a joke too. But then she asked me to try it on. I did. I was still dirty from the day. You know: fish guts under my nails, sand deep in my hair that even a long shower wouldn't get at. I pulled it on, wanting to please her, but when I did, I burst into tears. 'I can't leave my dad,' I cried.

"'You can. It's our turn to be together,' she said. 'Let's have some cake.'

"We went into the kitchen, where skinny Earl was sitting at the table drinking a glass of water. My dad was standing at the sink. My mother went into the cabinet and took out four plates, and then four forks from the drawer, as if she still lived there. I remember thinking she had a lot of nerve going into our stuff like that. It really bothered me. And then she opened up the Tupperware and announced that she had baked a cake, just like the recipe from Rachel's. It was vanilla cake with chocolate frosting. My dad finally spoke. He said, 'Dylan doesn't like vanilla cake with chocolate frosting. She likes chocolate cake with vanilla frosting. If you'd been here, you would know that.'

"He left and went upstairs, and I sat at the table with them and ate the cake, even though I didn't like it."

Dylan continued telling the story in such detail that I felt like I was there. I tried to think back to what I remembered from being six years old and came up with nothing. My guess was that the whole event was traumatic and therefore she remembered it vividly.

"Dale from the post office called a few days later saying she had a certified letter for my dad. It was a request for custody from a big law firm that the circus used. My dad was quiet for a few days after that. He barely spoke until he sat me down and told me that my mom wanted custody and that if I wanted to go and live with her, he wouldn't be mad. I thought he didn't want me anymore. I remember his exact words, 'Maybe it would be good for you to have a woman around. To take you dress shopping and to have a pretty pink room with a flowery blanket."

Melissa had shown Dylan a picture of the little room she had set up for her in her trailer. She must have shown it to Jake, too. She told her dad that she hated pink and didn't want to go. She begged. He wiped tears from his eyes. She had never seen him cry before. He hired a big lawyer too, who sent Melissa a certified letter saying that she had deserted them and he would take her to court. And she backed off, just like that.

"In the end, I figured she didn't want me that bad after all."

"Wow. I can't believe you never told me any of that, Dyl. I'm sorry."

"It's OK. I guess I always thought you had the perfect family, and I didn't want you to feel bad for me."

"Not anymore."

"Guess not. At least we can know better, you know, with our own families one day."

"I hope. So what did the letter say, and why didn't you tear it up like always?"

"It basically says since I'm leaving home that now it's up to me and her what kind of relationship we have. And she said she would love to meet me at college drop-off—and help decorate my room. She said we could go to Urban Outfitters and get all the latest stuff, her treat."

"That's nice."

"Do you think my dad would feel badly?"

"About not decorating and going shopping at Urban Outfitters? I doubt it."

"I don't know. I just want to fit in."

"Dylan, you're going to the best marine biology program in the country, and I bet you'll know more than some of your professors. I wouldn't worry about fitting in."

"That's not what I mean. Like with the city kids, you know how I have to ask you what the hell they're talking about sometimes?"

"That hasn't happened since we were, like, twelve."

"Well, I'm still insecure from it."

The waitress came over with a big piece of chocolate cake with vanilla frosting—the kind Dylan liked.

Dylan blew out the candles and instead of making a wish she said, "I love you, Matty."

At least I thought it was instead of making a wish.

"I love you too, Dyl," he said, putting his hand on top of hers.

"No, really, you will always be family," she promised.

"Thanks, you will too."

I wondered about that the entire walk home. If her mother would help her pick out bedding and posters and those fairy lights that the kids hang in their dorm rooms now. If Melissa would duplicitously post pictures of the finished product on social media like all the other moms do with captions like *Dylan's a freshman!* and *Where have the years gone?!* I wondered how different Dylan would have been if she had grown up with a mother. Would she have polished her nails and straightened her hair, or would she be just as she was right now in spite of it?

It would be nice to think of them really becoming family one day, but I doubted that would ever happen. I wasn't even so sure that Dylan would be back the following summer. I sometimes thought she was just marking time until she escaped.

twenty-four

Be My Baby

I returned home from the birthday breakfast ahead of Matty and Dylan. I had no interest in stopping to ogle the smattering of naked sunbathers at Lighthouse Beach, as I knew they would. The mile-long length of sandy shore was once a designated nude beach until some conservatives, motivated by the area's proximity to the lighthouse, a popular family attraction, found the concept appalling and went to court to change the law. It was a bummer for the nudists, especially on an island where "to each his own" may as well be the official motto. If you go au naturel there now, you risk a five-grand fine and a six-month stint in jail. Quite a hefty price for sunning in the buff.

Visiting Lighthouse Beach was a Fire Island rite of passage. For most kids, it promised their first look at a pair of breasts that didn't belong to their mother. I had no doubt that these two particularly feral kids had managed to sneak away to check out the situation by the time they were ten. Renee once told me that when Matty and Dylan were seven and eight, she and Jake had spent hours driving around looking for them one cold November afternoon. It was the last day that the Bay Harbor water was on (if you live there year-round you either need your own water well or access to the adjacent town's line). Renee and Tuck had come out to close up the house. It was late for them. They usually closed by early October, but that particular year had been a busy one, both socially and work-wise. The minute they disembarked, Matty had headed straight to Dylan's house, and when Renee went over to fetch him in time to make the last boat home, Jake had no idea where they'd run off to.

Renee and Jake had a brief personal history. They had once made out as teenagers, but neither of them spoke of it. In fact, Renee wondered if Jake even remembered. He never indicated that he did, and being that she was quite the looker—especially at sixteen, when the incident had occurred—it kind of bugged her. When he opened the passenger-seat door for her to jump in his truck, Jake blushed in a funny way that made her think he had remembered their kissing all along, though it could have been embarrassment from the big mess of odd junk he had to push from the seat to make room for her.

After looking everywhere for them (Jake calm, Renee panicked), Matty and Dylan were found playing capture the flag atop a giant heap of garbage at the dump two towns away. They smelled so badly that Renee and Jake had to hang their faces out the window like dogs on the way back to make the last ferry. Jake parked his truck by the boat and boarded with them to steer the boat across the bay. They made the kids sit up top, even though it was forty degrees out—more to air them out than as some form of corporal punishment for wandering off and playing in a garbage dump. It was an endless series of shenanigans like this, bringing up a spirited kid like Dylan. From what I heard over the years, she once refused to leave an abandoned baby seal on the beach for three days, she saved a giant buck whose head got caught in a garbage pail cover, and tried to catch lightning in glass after watching the movie *Sweet Home Alabama*. The first two examples were in the off-season, but Matty was present for the lightning debacle. They were lucky to be alive to tell the tale. I wondered what Jake would think of her and Matty's virginity-losing pact. To me it seemed benign in comparison to all of her other schemes, but I'm not the single dad of a teenage daughter.

As I reached Bay Harbor, I passed Pam and Andie sitting on the beach. Pam was consumed with the final chapters of a beach read, while Andie was passed out under the umbrella, next to baby Oliver. They both lightly snored in sweet synchronicity. My guess was that Andie had been on baby duty the night before, and that this was a well-deserved nap. Pam was a big reader though; like me there was nothing that could come between her and finishing a book—not even total exhaustion.

A few blocks down I found Ben, sitting in a chair by the ocean. Our song, "Be My Baby" by the Ronettes, was blasting from his earbuds so loudly I could hear it on my approach. At first I thought it was sweet, and even danced around his chair a bit, like old times, but I soon realized that he must have been listening to it on repeat all morning. Even under his Wayfarers, I recognized the comatose look in his tear-stained eyes. This auditory torture wasn't new for him; I had heard him filling the morning silence with my old phone messages more than once. He had kept a handful from before I was sick, and every one from after. He listened to the before ones on repeat, simple messages from a busy, happy life.

"Thinking about cooking tonight—want to pick up everything I need?"

"Hi, baby, meet me and Sally at the dog park by the museum. Love you!"

"Hi, baby, the reservation's at eight. Want to meet me earlier for a drink?"

"Hi, baby, I think you should switch chapters nine and eleven. Take a look."

And his apparent favorite from the multitude of times he played it, just "It's me, Jules," followed by a small fit of laughter for my unnecessary introduction. "Call me back."

If this were the nineties, he would have already worn through the answering machine tape.

Playing "Be My Baby" and doing a few jokingly sexy dance moves was traditionally the easiest way to get Ben out of his chair. I tried now—really embracing the saying "dance like no one is watching"—you know, because no one was watching. The song hooked you in from its famous first beat.

BUMP Bump-bump bump. BUMP bump-bump bump.

The first time we danced to "Be My Baby" was about two weeks after "meeting" on Fire Island. We had already squeezed in six dates, including the Foo Fighters at the Beacon, *Sweeney Todd* on Broadway, and a Yankee game where Ben got to show off his press access. We watched the action from George Steinbrenner's old box—though the word *box* was a misnomer—it was more the size of a shipping container. It held many years' worth of memorabilia, chairs shaped like leather baseball gloves, and an odd selection of B-list celebrities of the day—reality-show players like a runner-up on *American Idol* and the then–*Apprentice* star, Donald Trump.

Ben admitted he was happier sitting in the nosebleed seats eating hot dogs and drinking beer than hobnobbing with the rich and almost famous. I was happy to hear that.

For date number seven, I chose one of my favorite restaurants—a little Italian place in the West Village called Palma. We were still in that phase where each story was new and each touch electric. After two and a half hours sitting at the tiny table soaking up every last bit of marinara and every last word from each other's mouths, "Be My Baby" came on overhead. It was definitely a song of my parents' generation, but I had always loved it too.

Ben stood as the incomparable intro registered in his mind and unexpectedly pulled me from my seat. The combination of a couple of bottles of vino, his old soul contemplating the possibility of new love, and the fact that we were the last ones left at the restaurant caused him to uncharacteristically let loose. He danced in a funny way, one minute waving his arms around, the next comedically pulling me close, but his eyes never strayed from mine.

That night, along with the ethereal voice of Ronnie Spector, he vowed, "*Oh, since the day I saw you, I have been waiting for you, you know I will adore you, till eternity.*"

He was right about that.

When the song ended, we couldn't even wait for the check. He threw down all the cash in his wallet, more than enough, and we jumped in a cab—madly kissing the entire way to my apartment. I swatted his hands off me in the lobby—embarrassed by the watchful eye of my doorman, Jermaine, who had made it his personal business to screen my dates since I had moved into the studio apartment downtown. Jermaine would go as far as signaling his approval or disapproval when buzzing up a guy with cryptic weather-themed messages that had no correlation to the actual conditions outside.

"It's a beautiful night tonight, Julia," for someone who met his approval, even in the dead of winter, or "Big storm coming, don't forget an umbrella," during a drought in May, for someone who did not.

I kept my distance in the elevator too—cameras—but barely

made it down the hall without ripping his clothes off. I dumped out my bag on the carpet, searching for my keys, and kicked my belongings into the apartment as I opened the door. We made love for the very first time on the floor of my studio, scarcely making it inside. It was quick, hot, and desperate—not at all like Erin O'Malley and Patrick O'Reilly on the fields of Tipperary. That came later when we finally made it the ten feet over to my Murphy bed. It remained open for the entirety of the weekend.

And "Be My Baby" became our song.

Ever since, the tune always got him up from his seat, whether from the stereo in our living room or on our honeymoon in Rome, when we randomly heard it performed by a group of street musicians on the Spanish Steps. We stood and danced around the Piazza di Spagna, our hearts beating along to its famous drumbeat.

BUMP bump-bump bump, BUMP bump-bump bump.

Ben pulled his sunglasses down and wiped his eyes. I sunk into the sand next to him, concerned. I hoped that one day he would smile again when he heard our song, smile at the memory of us dancing to it, but that day was surely not today. I was pretty certain it wouldn't be tomorrow or the next day either.

"Are you using the sunblock from last summer? You should check if it's expired," I said, noticing that the redness of his eyes matched his sunburned cheeks.

He pressed Play again. This time a pained, almost guttural sigh escaped his lips, overriding the *BUMP bump-bump bump* of the music.

"This is not productive," I added.

I can't express how badly I did not want to have the sound of that song eternally marred by this memory. I closed my eyes and thought back to happy times we had heard it together. When I opened them, Shep was setting up his chair next to Ben's.

I loved this man more and more each day.

"What up, son?" he asked, always adding a hint of humor, this time in the form of his youthful greeting. "Did you get up at the crack of dawn to come down here to cry?"

I wondered the same thing. He had little privacy back at the house. He seemed to make a big point of crying in the shower. Not a terrible place to let it out, all things considered.

"What's it to you?"

Boy, he was in a mood.

"Just asking."

Shep waited a bit before saying, "You're gonna have to get into some sort of routine, you know."

"I have a routine," Ben insisted.

"Waking up and suffering does not constitute a routine."

Ben shook his head, thought for a bit, and then threw Shep a bone. "It does seem like you're way better than I am."

"Well, I have a few months on you, and besides, I'm mourning Caroline and what was, while you're mourning Julia, what was, and what should have been."

"I feel like I have nothing, nothing. What do I have?"

"Well, for one thing, you have a magnificent head of hair!" Shep ruffled his hands through it.

Ben didn't find it amusing.

"Saw Joel this morning, he said that Goldilocks fellow broke in to his house last night. Made pancakes."

"Hm. Any damage?"

"No. But he used up all their syrup."

Ben didn't even crack a smile.

They both looked east to see a famously annoying couple, the Kerchaikens, on their daily exercise walk. The Kerchaikens weren't ballplayers or tennis players. They were a paunchy, rather boring pair who walked, or more aptly strolled, all twelve blocks from one end of town to the other under the guise of exercise. My kind side would say "to each his own," but they acted like they were marathon runners on account of it. Aside from that, Shep held on to an old grudge with Mr. Kerchaiken with the vengeance of Taylor Swift after a breakup.

"Please don't let them stop, please don't let them stop, please don't let them stop."

Yes, Ben said that out loud, three times. It was clearly one of those days when he presented as getting worse, not better. At least he was aware of it.

Ben developed an issue with small talk quickly after my diagnosis. I was beginning to wonder if he would ever embrace chatting again. He used to be relatively fond of it, especially when it involved sports. Not with the Kerchaikens though; he never enjoyed talking to them. On the nights that we ventured into town for a scoop of ice cream—him, Moose Tracks, me Graham Central Station—they always seemed to be on line. Mr. Kerchaiken was the kind of guy who started a conversation with, "Did you hear about this?" or "Did you hear about that?" regarding a multitude of things we didn't care to hear about.

The Kerchaikens made their move, angling from the shoreline to our chairs. The sand had formed a cliff-like wall between the ocean and the beach, making Ben and Shep difficult to access. Ben especially hoped it would deter them, but they were clearly determined to make a condolence stop-by.

The beach configures differently throughout the summer. In June it is often flat and wide, but in late August and early September things can get funky. Sometimes tide pools form: shallow lakes in the sand carrying foam and sea life and a host of children swimming and boogie boarding and catching errant fish with nothing more than nets or beach pails—screaming in delight over what they may remember as the best day in their young lives.

Walls of sand, like the one that appeared today, are fun as well, albeit briefly. I love the feeling of standing at the edge, pointing my toes over the side, and leaning back to slide down the humble cliff on my heels. I counted it as another gift from the island that tickled the kid in me.

The way up, though, is always clumsy and awkward.

After a few failed attempts, the Kerchaikens pulled each other up.

"Fuck," Ben mumbled, I thought quite audibly.

"I got this," Shep, the self-proclaimed King of the Conversation Stopper, promised.

Mrs. Kerchaiken spoke first. "How are you doing, Benjamin?" She paused and added in a consolatory tone, "And you, Shep? Such tragedy."

"I'm doing OK, thanks." Shep smiled at them mischievously. "But you see that rock over there?" he continued. "The big one that looks like only the ocean could move it."

They did and nodded.

"Ben wants to bash in our skulls with it and then strap it to his back and drown himself."

"We should be on our way," Mr. Kerchaiken responded. The Mrs. was visibly shaken.

"Thanks, Shep." Ben smiled before putting his earphones back in his ears.

BUMP, bump-bump bump. BUMP bump-bump bump.

twenty-five

To Town!

The summer continued in a two-steps-forward, three-steps-back kind of manner, with Ben enjoying playing ball, sometimes, but lying in my closet in tears, inhaling the scent of my sweaters at others. Matty had gotten no further in his quest for a rubber. And each of Shep's daughters canceled their visits. They said they would come individually. Shep said he only wanted them together, and no one backed down. Family is often ridiculous.

The only one who was truly happy was Renee. The drummer was still in the picture, and from the look of her, she was having sex, good sex and plenty of it.

"That guy's hanging around an awful lot," Ben had commented one morning while he and Matty were on deck at the game. "Do you think it will continue in the city after the summer?"

"I don't think so," Matty contemplated. "I've never even seen him wear shoes."

Ben laughed, though I didn't think Matty meant it as a joke.

"You know, if it gets to be too much, Shep's offer to bunk with us is good for me too."

That night, when Renee announced "we" will be staying out for all of August, Matty gave up. He showed up across the street a few hours later with a duffel bag and his mitt.

The meal choices were dwindling, but Shep put in a bit more energy since it was Matty's first night. He made a fresh salad and some garlic bread and defrosted Elissa Cron's five-meat lasagna—no one could figure out what the fifth meat was, which was why it was a late taker. The bread was the biggest hit.

Neither Shep nor Ben put much effort into their dinner conversation since becoming partners in grief, but with Matty at the table, their usual routine of lamenting and languishing felt tiresome. Shep did the honor of breaking the ice with a hatchet as opposed to a pick.

"So, your mother's still banging the drummer?"

"Shep! You need a seven-second delay, like on television," Ben exclaimed.

"Oh please. He was caught necking with Dylan in the dunes. No need to watch his virgin ears."

"I'm sure he still has virgin ears. You do, right?" Ben asked.

"Yeah—for now. How does everyone know?"

"Come on, Matty, how does everyone know that Moe Schwartz has hemorrhoids or that Kelly Kramer is a screamer? Everyone knows everything in this town."

Like I told you—bungalow colony.

"You better be careful, Matty," Ben warned. "Jake Finley's only daughter."

"That's an understatement. I'd think twice before deflowering that girl," Shep piped in.

Matty clearly didn't get the archaic lingo. Ben rolled his eyes and brought it at least to this century.

"He means popping her cherry."

"You mean taking her v-card?" Matty asked.

"Never heard that one," Ben admitted.

"Whatever you call it nowadays, I'm pretty sure the phrase 'Don't knock her up' still applies—you better get a hold of a banana slicker or two first."

Between the popping cherries and the banana slickers, it sounded more like they were sharing a recipe for fruit salad than encouraging safe sex. I wished they would just speak to the poor kid in English. In the end, Matty took care of that himself.

"About that . . . do either of you have a condom?"

I could almost see the words sink into their brains and release in the most welcome sound I'd heard in months, joyous and hysterical laughter. It was the kind of laughter that begets more laughter until your stomach hurts and your eyes water with happy tears. After what felt like minutes, Ben managed an apology.

"I'm sorry, Matty, it's been so long since I laughed . . ." He broke down again but got himself together. Tears were now pouring down Shep's cheeks, but Matty wasn't even slightly amused.

"Sorry, Matt, but really, look who you are asking for a condom," Ben offered.

Shep barely squeaked out "The widower fornicators," which started them both up again. Shep finally regained control, sipped his glass of water, and stated, "I don't think there will be many rubbers in my future."

"Yeah," Ben agreed, adding, "The Brisket Brigade probably doesn't have one good egg between them."

They laughed some more, but stopped as Matty asked earnestly, "Really? What am I supposed to do? I can't exactly buy one at the market, and I can't swipe one 'cause they're behind the counter."

"That's true. Miss Sullivan hasn't left that counter since 1998," Shep noted, adding, "the Ex-Lax brownie incident."

They all grimaced in unison, remembering it.

"Can't you get one in town?" Ben suggested. Matty had already thought that through.

"No way. Jake would find out in under an hour. 'Matthew Tucker bought condoms at Ocean Beach Trading.'"

"He'll be castrated before he gets to use it. You know who probably has one?" Shep asked.

"Don't even say it!" Matty countered. "I can barely look at that guy. Every time I see him my mind goes right to my fifth-grade holiday concert where we sang 'Little Drummer Boy.' It must be some kind of coping mechanism. I had the opening solo, you know, 'Come, they told me, pa rum pum pum pum.'"

Ben loved Christmas music, literally knew every word to every Christmas song, from Mariah Carey to the Chipmunks. It's one of those contradictory things about him that makes him who he is. The chance to sing a Christmas carol in July lit him right up.

"'A newborn king to see pa rum pum pum pum.'"

Matty loosened up too. "You got it."

And he smiled as Shep stood up and bellowed, "'Our finest gifts we bring, pa rum pum pum pum.'"

They all laughed and crooned together, "'To lay before the king, pa rum pum pum pum, rum pum pum pum, rum pum pum pum.'"

Inspired by the Christmas spirit, I imagine, Shep proudly announced, "I'll do it! I'll get the rubber in town!"

Ben quickly put a pin in it. "You're going to walk into the Ocean Beach market and ask for a condom?"

"Yup. What's the big deal, Scrooge?"

"You really understand the repercussions of this?"

"Maybe word will get out that I am interested in the premenopausal set!"

Their faces reflected their doubt. Shep reaffirmed his resolve.

"I got this. Battle conditions! I'll get in, do my best, and get out."

He placed his plate on the ground for Sally, then raised his hand in the air like Napoleon leading the troops to Waterloo.

"To town!"

The three men jumped on their bikes and rode off, with Shep leading them in their new battle hymn as they pa-rum-pum-pum-pummed all the way there.

twenty-six

Whack-a-Mole

It was a Monday night, when town is usually desolate, and tonight was no exception. Matty and Ben sat on the bench outside of OB Trading while Shep did the deed. The weather was unseasonably cool, and none of them had thought to grab a sweatshirt. They sat closer than usual on account of it. The physical intimacy seemed to beget emotional intimacy.

"So, is this like your first love, or is it just a sex thing?"

"I don't know. To be honest, this is all Dylan's idea. I mean, we really only started messing around last summer 'cause we had covered every other inch of this place."

"That's kind of funny."

"I guess."

Ben paused. His expression got serious.

"I know Dylan is pretty headstrong, I mean, is this what you want too?"

Matty responded just how he did when Dylan asked him. "Yeah, sure."

Ben may be onto something, I thought. Matty wasn't very convincing.

"Do you have any questions? I mean, I know you're not tight with your dad right now."

"Nah, I'm good. I've seen porn."

"Yeah, it's not really like it is in the movies, Matty. Don't expect to be moving heaven and earth."

Matty was listening intently, now. Seeing Ben as a father figure definitely tugged at my heart. I hoped he still had the chance, or took the chance, I should say, to become a dad. I worried he would never get there again. He continued with his version of a sex talk, and as with most things, there were plenty of sports references thrown in.

"Later on, maybe, but the first time, the first time is pretty rudimentary, not a lot of moaning and groaning . . . and you won't need much time. . . . It's kind of like, keep your eye on the ball, make contact, and boom! Maybe one moan."

This from the man who wrote . . .

> Erin lay spent at day's end, thinking back to making love to Patrick in the fields, their breath fast, their flesh warm and wet. She slipped her hand beneath her stockings and moved her fingers as he had until she climaxed, burying her face into the ground as if to inject the sound of her ecstasy into the earth.

Shep walked out with three bananas—and as far as I could see, no condoms.

"Banana?" he offered the guys.

They looked at him blankly.

"I couldn't do it. Maybe a drink will help. Let's go to Housers."

Housers sat just around the bend from the Ocean Beach market and mostly attracted locals on a weeknight. We had spent many an evening there drinking tequila, playing darts or pool, and dancing to eighties songs on their old jukebox. Tonight felt different. For starters, I didn't recognize anyone except for the staff, and there seemed to be a shady element hanging around.

The three of them slid into one of the few booths as a familiar salty face came over to take their order. The conversation between the waiter and Shep was priceless.

"What can I get you?"

"Three shots of tequila."

"Not for him."

"What, he's eighteen."

"He's not eighteen, *and* the drinking age is twenty-one."

"Twenty-one? When did that happen?"

"1984." The waiter tickled Matty under his chin, adding, "Decades before his mother wheeled her cute little baby boy off the Bay Harbor ferry."

Ben smiled, as did Shep and the waiter. Matty did not.

"I remember that day." Shep beamed. "You were such a cute baby, Matty. Caroline would push you up and down the block in your pram like you were her grandchild."

Matty buried his head as Ben took control.

"Bring us two each and a cola for him."

When the drinks arrived, Shep held one up to toast. "To young love!"

"It's not really like that," Matty explained. "And besides, look at my parents. I don't even believe in that crazy-in-love shit anymore."

"You may be better off," Ben piped in, in a voice more similar to Eeyore's than his own.

Shep wasn't having it. "You don't really mean that, Ben."

"Well, I never want to feel like this again."

"You may want to rethink that, because your life is gonna suck with that attitude. I'm just passing time till I can be with Caroline again, but you have a ways to go. You can't just pass forty-odd years of time."

As the drinks were placed on the table, Shep ordered another round.

The waiter looked at him skeptically but nodded in agreement as Ben pronounced, "All that better-to-have-loved-and-lost nonsense feels like a crock."

He dramatically drank his shot and headed for the dartboard.

"Don't listen to him, son." Shep discreetly passed a shot to Matty and took one himself. "Even your scorned mother has gotten back on the horse." He held up his shot glass hopefully.

"I'm not drinking to that," Matty lamented.

"Go ahead and drink yours to misery, but I'm drinking mine to your mother banging the drummer." Shep drank his shot, slammed it on the table, and got up.

Matty mumbled and drank his as well. He winced at the taste and placed the empty glass back across the table. As time passed, the shot glasses increased by threes to a dozen, plus a couple of bottles of beer, and I wondered how they would make it home. Especially Matty, who was now asleep with his head flat on the table. Ben and Shep were playing darts with some equally liquored-up, bad-ass day-trippers sporting an abundance of tattoos and seventies-style facial hair. Shep, who needed to steady one hand with the other to even hit the board, somehow managed a bull's-eye. He and Ben reacted like they had defeated Russia for Olympic gold. On Shep's way down from his victory jump, he reached up to his big bad-ass opponent and swiped the red baseball hat off his half-bald head. It was a big mistake—HUGE, I would say. The bald day-tripper went nuts, grabbed Shep's arm and blasted him. He did not seem to care that he was getting into it with an old man.

"You can fuck with my friends, you can fuck with my wife, but never, ever, fuck with my hat."

Ben had no choice but to get between them—though his choice of words was questionable. He came back with, "So, where's your wife?"

A childish grin took hold of his face until the angry bald man let go of Shep, whose eyes were now popping from his head, and went for Ben. I worried Ben would go full-on Mike Tyson on the guy, especially since his jaw and fists had been clenched since the day of my diagnosis. I wondered if he could even feel physical pain in his current numb condition. While the release of a good punch may have done him good, his opponent was massive, and I had no desire to see him in the afterlife just yet. Luckily, he wiggled from Red Hat Guy's grip.

"Let's go!" Shep yelled, grabbing Matty by the collar with one hand and the lone beer left on the table with the other.

They bolted from the bar. The bad-ass day-trippers followed but lost interest as soon as they saw my guys jump on their bikes.

The three of them hightailed it home, adrenaline overriding fear. It had been a long time since Ben or Shep had found themselves in that youthful position of facing down a fight, and I didn't imagine there were many playground brawls at Matty's posh prep school. They were all feeling pretty brave and brazen. When they realized they had surely escaped, they slowed down to catch their breath, and allowed themselves to laugh with relief before riding off in silent, albeit wobbly, retrospection.

Ben's face was especially joyful and seeing him happy—seeing the twinkle I had fallen for reignited in his eyes—it lit me up too. Matty's face went from giddy to queasy. His drinking experience was negligible and had probably comprised a few beers at high school house parties and glasses of watered-down wine at his local

Chinese restaurant in the city, known for not carding minors. Three or four shots of tequila followed by a beer or two were surely over his limit.

Shep was leading the way, humming a few rounds of *pa rum pum pum pum*. He was downright chipper. If he didn't think there would be an occasion for condoms in his future, I doubted he'd imagined partaking in a good old bar fight. He pulled the lone beer from his coat pocket, popped off the cap with his teeth like a boss, and looked back at the other two, holding the bottle in the air in victory. He turned back around just at the point where the midway street ended and didn't have the time to right himself. I yelled, "Watch out!" as his bike hit the fence, catapulting him over it and into the Kerchaikens' vegetable garden. Of course no one heard my warning, except possibly the Kerchaikens. The lights in their house quickly switched on and I thought back to their last interaction with Ben and Shep on the beach. The widower card would surely not double as a get-out-of-jail-free card here.

Matty and Ben jumped off their bikes and peered over the fence at Shep, sprawled out among Mrs. Kerchaiken's prized tomatoes.

"Let's get him out before anyone notices!" Ben quietly instructed Matty, who looked like he would be little help. It was too late anyway. Mr. and Mrs. Kerchaiken appeared on the sidewalk: bathrobed, barefoot, and simmering with anger.

Ben whispered to Matty, way too loud, "Oh Jesus, of all people."

Matty was clueless as to the origin of Ben's reaction. I was not. If you remember, there was bad blood between Shep and the Kerchaikens.

Mr. Kerchaiken put his phone to his ear and slowly pronounced, "Bay Harbor Security?"

Of course, he had them on speed dial.

With the stakes raised, Ben and Matty got themselves together and tried, unsuccessfully, to pull Shep out of the garden. "No need to call security over this. I'm sure they've got their hands full with that Goldilocks Intruder."

"Good try, Ben. I'm calling."

"It's true," Matty added. "You shouldn't bother them over this."

Mr. Kerchaiken ignored their pleas and spoke into the phone while Ben and Matty attempted to retrieve Shep.

"We'll be out of your way in a minute," Ben pleaded.

"We'll see about that." Mr. Kerchaiken grinned sinisterly as his wife nervously begged them to be careful of her tomatoes. They both heeded her warning and stepped gingerly.

"If I am not mistaken," Mr. Kerchaiken admonished, "this is the last straw with Mr. Silver and a bicycle."

The threat got Shep's attention, and not in a helpful way. He stood up on his own and protested.

"That was ten years ago! Give it up, Kerchaiken."

Shep had famously ridden Kerchaiken's Schwinn into the Great South Bay after a poker game went south. He reiterated his decade-old complaint of "He cheated!" while inadvertently crushing a tomato under his left foot. Mrs. Kerchaiken's rising concern turned to panic.

"Careful . . . my tomatoes!"

There was really no avoiding them. Shep lifted up his foot cautiously but landed on one and then another. With each brutal crush, Mrs. Kerchaiken became more and more hysterical. "My tomatoes! My tomatoes!"

Matty and Ben tried their best to control Shep, but when Matty joked, "He's like a human whack-a-mole!" the two of them completely lost it.

Shep hesitated, I imagined trying his damnedest to pass on the joke, but as was usually the case with Shep, landing the punch line overrode any thread of human decency. He stood up straight, pressed his feet together, and jumped from tomato to tomato to tomato. Each landing yielded a shriek from Mrs. Kerchaiken, which was hard to hear over Ben and Matty, who were now lying on the ground in hysterics. They were laughing so hard that they couldn't breathe, and Matty's complexion grew greener and greener. Three Bay Harbor Security guys showed up just as the scene accelerated to bedlam. One of them crunched a piece of the now-broken beer bottle under his shoe. He picked it up and examined it.

"Are you drinking?" he asked Shep.

"Are you buying?" Shep answered back, without missing a beat.

I was so glad that Ben had mourned with these guys instead of my great-uncle Morris and my cousin Shirley. Who's to say that shiva need be such a sober affair.

Two of the guards, visibly pissed at Shep's lack of respect, climbed the fence and physically lifted him over it.

"Which one is his bike?" the third guard asked.

"Oh, come on. Don't take his bike!" Ben pleaded.

"Not so funny now, huh?" Mr. Kerchaiken piped in.

One of the three guards had been in Bay Harbor for years and wasn't a fan of the Kerchaikens either. They called security for every little thing, and while this certainly wasn't a little thing—especially with the whack-a-mole escalation—it was evident that they could have handled it in an easier fashion from the start. Now, given the condition of Mrs. Kerchaiken's crop, he had no choice but to take action.

"Sorry, Shep. You know this is your third strike with a bicycle," he commiserated.

"That first one was 'cause he cheated," Shep protested, to no avail. The men held Shep by the arms. He made a feeble attempt to break free and go after his wheels, but he was no match for two guys half his age with security-guard egos.

"We'll bring him home. You get the bike," one instructed the others.

Ben stayed behind in an effort to help Mrs. Kerchaiken fix her garden. Still drunk, he kept trying to stick two halves of a tomato back together. He pulled off a leaf from another plant and smelled it.

"Is this basil? Maybe you can make a nice sauce." He laughed, still holding on to that joy.

As the remaining security guard walked off with Shep's bike, Mr. Kerchaiken smiled with satisfaction. Matty steadied himself, his gaze running from Kerchaiken's pompous expression to Shep looking back longingly at his bike while being led from the scene. Matty mustered up whatever gumption he could find and began rambling in protest.

"You know what, Mr. Kerchaiken? One dollar for six bags of groceries is not a good tip!" His slurred words came out jumbled, and Mr. Kerchaiken asked him to repeat them. Matty got right up in his face to do so. He gathered his insult in his head again, but this time, all that came out was vomit.

Five shots of tequila and the remnants of Elissa Cron's five-meat lasagna splattered all over Mr. Kerchaiken's bare feet as the Mrs. looked on in tears.

Shep was ecstatic—"Thanks, kid!"

Matty beamed back at him with a big, proud, puke-faced smile.

twenty-seven

The Hangover

The next day, Matty and Ben were sprawled out on the bleachers, hungover. It definitely took their standings down a few notches when the teams were being made—they both looked useless. Shep, on the other hand, was fine. Though he was quick to brag.

"I haven't been that drunk since 1983, when I fell asleep mid-Slurpee at a 7-Eleven!"

He sat next to Matty and commended him again for both his aim and his timing when tossing his cookies the night before.

"That was great last night, son—really—I'd be hard-pressed to think of a time that I was more proud."

Two tennis guys walked over. Their outfits alone—collared shirts with matching shorts by old-time tennis designers like Sergio Tacchini and Lacoste—made a striking contrast with the attire of the softball players. Shep was wearing a threadbare Eastern Airlines T-shirt circa 1979, and Ben, a threadbare *Born in the U.S.A.* tour shirt circa 1984. I had taken it out of his rotation, and it made me laugh that he must have dug it out from the giveaway pile that was never quite given away, like a consolation prize for my passing.

The man in Tacchini called out, "Hey, Shep! Catch!" and threw a tomato at him. Shep instinctively reached out his glove and caught it. He opened his mitt to take a look.

"Very funny," he responded with ire.

Ben sat up and inched closer to the conversation. He was in no shape to defend this guy again but, considering the small stature of the two tennis guys and the backup on the field, he wasn't worried. Besides, throwing the tomato was probably the extent of the torment they were capable of.

"We're here on official business, to discuss the rules with you guys," Tacchini Man continued.

Shep still needed backup. On his best day the old man wasn't a big fan of diplomacy.

The nastier of the two tennis guys, the one in the alligator shirt, added, "After losing your bike last night, maybe you should consider playing by the rules."

"I'll get my bike back."

The whole lot of them sounded more like ten-year-olds on a playground than grown men with receding hairlines and mortgages.

"That's not what I hear," the Lacoste player shot back.

Shep whipped the tomato back at them. "Catch!"

They both moved out of the way. Ben put his hand on Shep's shoulder. "No need to live up to your reputation," he whispered with a laugh.

Shep smiled and took a symbolic step back as Ben stepped in. Half the team had now gathered around.

"OK, boys, what is it you came over here to say?" Ben asked.

"Oh, Benjamin, I heard about Julia's passing. I am so sorry for your loss."

Ben acknowledged the words with a simple nod, while Shep

got back into the mix. "What about my loss? Throwing a tomato at me!"

Ben placed his hand back on Shep's shoulder and continued, "Thank you, Sid, let's finish this up. We have a game to play."

"OK, well, we think we should continue with the same three-strike rule we had before the new net went up."

The rule was: over the net once, out for the game; twice, out for three weeks; third time, out for the season.

Ben agreed, adding, "That's fine—it will never happen with that tall net, anyway."

Or will it? I thought, appreciating the foreshadowing.

They all dispersed and went off to play their games.

That afternoon, we walked in to the phone ringing. Ben braced himself and grabbed it. This time it was Shep's oldest daughter, Beatrix, looking for her dad. Somehow, word of last night's shenanigans had gotten all the way to Ohio, where she taught English lit at Kenyon College. When Shep hadn't answered his house phone or his cell, which was home dead in a drawer somewhere, she called the market and asked for Little Les. They had grown up together, and while Little Les felt for the old guy, his allegiance lay with Beatrix.

Shep usually had more patience for Bea than his younger daughter, Veronica, who now lived in Palo Alto, the wife of a tech giant and a stay-at-home mom of twin teenage girls. But today he wasn't taking it and told her so.

"I played a lousy game today, Beatrix, and am in no mood to be lectured like a child."

It always amazed me how much their moods correlated with

how well they played ball that day, though, dealing with his daughters was never Shep's strong suit. It hadn't always been like that, especially with Bea. When she was young, the two were thick as thieves. Bea adored her dad and would do anything Shep suggested just to be with him. Tossing a ball, fishing in the bay, mixing and delivering him the perfect martini, memorizing the words to his favorite poem, "Gunga Din"—anything to spend time with her father. It was pretty obvious that he favored her over Veronica. Also, Bea looked a lot like Shep's own mother, with her dark hair, olive skin, and full, round figure—and while it was clear from early on that most people preferred to look at long and lithe Veronica, Shep preferred looking at Bea. Being with her warmed his heart.

Veronica looked more like Caroline's side of the family: the British side. She had strawberry-blond hair and fair skin like her mother. And like her mother, she burned easily, so taking her along fishing or to play ball or just to go to the beach had always involved coating her from head to toe in sunblock. That kind of meticulous preparation was not Shep's jam—in fact, the one time he attempted it he missed so many spots that the kid came home looking like a stick of cherry fruit-striped gum. Beatrix, with her easily-tanned skin and overall sturdiness, was relatively indestructible. Except, as it turned out, for her heart.

The only connection the two sisters maintained during their adult years was through conversations with their mother. After the inciting incident had occurred with the lifeguard, Caroline didn't dare mention Veronica's name to Beatrix, but as the years went on curiosity poked holes in the anger for each sister, at least allowing them to tolerate hearing about the other. That was basically the extent of their interaction, if you could even call it that.

When Caroline had died suddenly over the winter, Shep thought the two would put their differences aside, but they couldn't. Devastated by the entire situation, he put his foot down, saying, "I was never sure why your mother stood for your bullshit, but I will not. Don't come back until you can be real sisters again."

And so far they had listened.

twenty-eight

The Dreaded Trike

Apparently, word of last night's incident had traveled all the way to Palo Alto as well, and Veronica did what she usually did when faced with a problem—she threw money at it. She called Steve at the hardware store—whom it was rumored she once had a thing with—and bought a souped-up tricycle for her father. I like to believe she thought she was doing the right thing, but the notion was hard to swallow.

The next day, Big Les asked Matty to make a delivery that no one would want to make. He said it real casually. "I need you to walk over to the hardware store in town and pick up a trike for Shep."

Big Les knew it was not a casual request.

"Sorry, kid. He needs a way to get around, and I figure it's better coming from you than from Corey."

That was for sure.

An hour later Matty wheeled the trike up the ramp to our house, a big fake smile plastered on his face for encouragement. Shep silently wheeled it back down and parked it at the baseball field to be stolen. It was back up on our deck within the hour, this time with Shep's name written in Sharpie beneath the saddle.

The trike wasn't the only unwelcome surprise of the day.

An ominous cloud hovered over the island, and it felt very much like a warning. Of what, I had no idea, until an hour later when Ben's agent, the infamous Elizabeth Barnes, was standing on our porch rapping her knuckles on the door with the strength of someone ten times her size. She was wearing lipstick and a colorful shirt. I had never seen her in makeup or in anything but muted earth tones. I found it unnerving.

"I wish you had told me you were coming."

That was Ben's actual greeting.

"Why, so you could tell me not to?" she said, with a hint of warmth.

Ben noticed the change in her tone and her apparel and agreed with my assessment. Unnerving.

"No, because if I knew you were coming, I would have asked you to bring condoms."

He didn't even bother to explain his odd request. She thought it a joke and snickered.

"OK, then. How about I freshen up and then you take me to town for lunch?" she suggested.

"Do you ride a bike?"

"Not since I was twelve. Can't we walk?"

"I guess."

Walking to town, unless you lived near the border, was just not done. Walking on the beach—great—but the sidewalks of Bay Harbor were made for riding. Personally, I find the trek by foot to be quite tedious, with bikers alarmingly ringing their bells on their approach until you move aside, or the stress-inducing vroom of the random golf cart following too close behind you. The latter always made me feel like Cary Grant being chased by that crop duster in *North by Northwest.*

For Ben to walk to town with Elizabeth would mean filling fifteen minutes or more with small talk. At least at lunch there would be the distraction of the ordering and the chewing, and he could down a stiff drink—or three. His new favorite pastime.

"She's not at all like you described her," Shep noted.

Ben had described her as a real battle-ax—a term that Shep would immediately understand and that Ben enjoyed using. He loved throwing dated idioms into his writing, and I spent a lot of time suggesting he edit them out. I often saw him jotting down Shep's random jargon like it was literary gold. I was always trying to get him to use more youthful words like *dope* or *basic* while he lit up when Shep said "How are things in Glocca Morra?" instead of hello.

Ben and I didn't usually argue about work, and made great efforts not to do "business" after hours, but once we had such a big fight over his insistence that a modern-day character say *anyhoo* instead of *anyhow* that I slept on the couch. He was born in the wrong era—which I have to admit was a great part of his success. Mine too, actually. I think I subconsciously gravitated to young authors to mix things up and ended up discovering some fabulous, career-making debuts.

"She seems to really care about you," Shep stated, while she was still out of earshot.

"She only cares about fifteen percent of me."

"She came all the way here, that's very—motherly," he said, for lack of a better word.

"She came all the way here because of my imminent deadline. And she is most definitely not motherly. She's tough, tough as the day is long—and the day is fucking long."

Shep laughed and agreed, "The day *is* fucking long."

As much as this day was turning out to be an eventful one, the entire summer was like the antithesis of the saying "time flies when you're having fun." Seriously, July, that I used to say lasted all of four minutes, had lasted four hundred thousand million. On some days, when there was no ball game to break things up, I could swear the clock was going backward. Those days were the worst. Sometimes, even with Matty and Shep nudging him to get outside, Ben just laid in the dark for hours.

It was quite the opposite of his schedule in summers past, when his morning paddleboard ride ran into the ball game, which ran into lunch and the beach and happy hour and an outdoor shower and dinner, and the two of us dancing around the living room to dance tunes from artists like Flo Rida and Deee-Lite, until it began all over again the next morning. Ben hadn't belted "Groove Is in the Heart," let alone touched his paddleboard since he got here. I wasn't unhappy about the latter. Paddleboarding in the ocean definitely required a will to live that, for now, seemed to have escaped him. I was very worried about his writing though, or more aptly, his lack thereof.

Time, as with most else lately, was not on his side.

Elizabeth returned from the bathroom with the additions of a sun hat and more lipstick. Shep was suddenly very interested in her—and it wasn't because of this new look she was sporting.

"Shep Silver," he announced, reaching his hand out to shake hers. "You shouldn't walk to town; it's really not done," he added in a strangely enthusiastic tone. "Take my trike. It's easy to ride!"

Ben jumped in—to save himself.

"I was going to put Elizabeth on the four o'clock ferry. I can't ride my bike back and the trike."

Ben could ride two regular bikes, FYI, sitting on one and

steering the other along next to him. It was a skill I had only seen demonstrated on Fire Island, and even then, only by a coordinated few. It was really hot.

Shep piped in. "I was counting on that. Leave it in town somewhere—anywhere."

"It's just a bicycle with three wheels instead of two. Why is it such a big deal?"

"Because. I'm tired of being infantilized. The other day a girl at the market asked me if I needed help bringing my grocery bag to my bike. Age prejudice is a real thing, you know."

It was hard to tell if Ben was caving or just losing patience. Either way, Shep succeeded.

"OK, fine—but I can't keep doing this for you. Veronica called before with a preemptive warning—she said to cut it out."

"She called here?" He grimaced. "I'm surprised she remembered the number."

Ben locked up his bike at the edge of town and instructed Elizabeth to leave Shep's on the sidewalk.

"Won't someone take it?" she asked.

"One can only hope."

She looped her arm around Ben's elbow and while it wasn't quite motherly as Shep had suggested, it was most definitely sweet. They walked through town like bookends, and I began to worry that she had become a pushover. At this juncture a pushover was the last thing he needed in an agent.

"How are you?" she asked.

"I'm fine," he lied.

It was a dumb question that was asked of him so many times since I passed that it even made me want to scream. Just once I wish he would tell the truth, saying something like, "Every day is worse than the last." But he never did. She asked again, "No, really, how are you?" She dragged out the word *how* like it had six syllables.

He just shrugged.

He got a table at the next place they passed, the Skipper and the Swan. It was his least favorite restaurant in town, but her motherly transformation was beginning to unnerve him, and if he didn't get her arm off his soon, he thought he may lose his cool entirely.

Be nice, I tried to remind him. *It will be easier to get your deadline extended*.

He seemed to have heard me—or at least to remember what I would say to do in this situation. When she rested her hand on his at the table, he let her leave it there for a full five seconds before lifting it to call for the server and order a bottle of sauvignon blanc—her favorite.

After a few large sips he came right out and asked her.

"What's going on, Elizabeth? You seem—different."

"You can call me Liz," she said.

"No, thank you—seriously, what gives? What did you do with my tough and demanding agent whom I had grown to love?"

"Did you?" she asked.

"I guess I did," he admitted.

She laughed. "It's Julia's fault actually. I was at the shiva and—"

Ben interrupted, "Sorry about that."

"It's OK. I was glad you were at large. You would have hated it. Remember that time at the Texas Book Festival when everyone wanted a piece of you and you escaped to a gay bar down the street? It was like that, but heartbreaking."

Ben nodded aimlessly. Between my family's visit and this little interlude, he was already nearing his limit on patience and kindness. Liz continued.

"Everyone was saying nice things and recalling loving anecdotes about Julia. It got me thinking, what would people say about me after I died? It was my Alfred Nobel moment."

We both laughed.

In 1888 Alfred Nobel's brother Ludwig died of a heart attack and one of the French papers mistook him for Alfred, and wrote a brutal obituary. Alfred had invented dynamite and manufactured explosives, so they labeled him the merchant of death and called him a war profiteer. Desperate to change his image—and therefore his future obituary—he created and funded the Nobel Prize, for which his name would forever be remembered.

Ergo, Elizabeth's Alfred Nobel moment.

"I realized that no one would have anything good to say about me after I die."

"That's not true," Ben piped in.

"Really, what would you say about me?"

Ben laughed. "I would say Elizabeth Barnes—"

"Liz!" she interrupted.

"OK, Liz Barnes came out to Fire Island after my wife passed and held my hand."

She smiled. "Thanks. As nice as I am trying to be, Ben, we still have to talk about your future."

"You could have called me on the phone for that."

"Yes, I could have—if you would ever answer."

He smiled and got his thoughts together to answer her now. Apparently Ben had been thinking about his future more than I realized.

"You're not going to like this, but sometimes I wonder if it would be best for me to bag the whole novelist thing and go back on the road for the newspaper again. I loved being a sportswriter when I had nothing to hold me close to home, and reporting on what's going on in a ball game would be a hell of a lot easier on my broken heart than dreaming up stories."

He smiled at her, channeling the boyish charm. "What do you think, Liz?"

She laughed and spoke like the old Elizabeth. He actually appreciated the lack of BS and ass-kissing that had been everyone's MO with him for months. It was getting to be a bit much.

"I bet we could get you your own column now," she said, in a tentative but surprisingly supportive tone.

His eyes widened with hope. It was short-lived.

"How close are you with book three?" she asked.

He downed the rest of his wine—in vino veritas—and spoke calmly.

"I don't even have the island."

"I can get you another six months, but unless you want to return your hefty advance, I can't get you out of it, Benjamin, I'm sorry."

Between apartment renovations and the cost of my private room on the fancy floor of Sloan Kettering, our savings were depleted. He couldn't afford to give back the hefty advance he had received for the third book.

She put her hand back on top of his and brought back the new, softer Liz voice.

"And we have to discuss another editor."

Ben visibly flinched.

"I'll have it for you in six months," he conceded. "But no editor and no proposal. I'm just gonna turn in the completed manuscript. Can you arrange that for me?" he asked, still without a clue what he'd be writing about.

"Probably, considering the circumstances. But please, just start. Maybe try and embrace the pain instead of fighting it; it may be cathartic."

They walked to the four-o'clock boat, where the new arrivals happily disembarked. The crew released the rope to let Elizabeth and the others on. Before she left she reached up for Ben's shoulders, pulled them down toward her, and kissed him gently on the top of his head. When he stood back up straight she was gone. He watched her ascend onto the ferry.

And when he returned home, the trike was sitting right back in front of our house again.

twenty-nine

Sicily

In the days after Elizabeth (Liz) had graced us with her newfangled maternal presence, Ben woke up with the sun (his best time to write) and sat on the "lanai" (his best place to write) and came up with nothing. He pulled up the list of islands we had thought up, when still in Sicily, on his phone.

Corfu
Saint Bart's
Galapagos
Venice
Cuba

Without me along for the ride, each one felt less appealing than the next. He closed the computer and lay down on the couch to think. I prayed he would come up with somewhere inspiring for the third installment of the three-book deal. Thinking back, he hadn't even come up with Sicily; it had been my idea.

We were watching *The Godfather* on a rainy afternoon at the point right before Michael's young Sicilian wife gets blown up in the car. We watched (or half watched) the *Godfather* trilogy often, as background noise, and would always look up from whatever else we were doing to perform our favorite lines in unison.

"'Sunday, Monday, Tuesday, Saturday,'" we said, right on cue.

And that's when it hit me. "Sicily!" I proclaimed, with a confident resolve.

Ben's entire face had lit up. He'd responded in his best Marlon Brando, "You have made me an offer I can't refuse," before diving onto my end of the couch and kissing me all over my face.

We popped open a bottle of prosecco that had been sitting in our fridge for ages and ordered in a Sicilian-style pie and a Caesar salad to celebrate. By the time the delivery guy arrived with our food, we had already purchased two one-way tickets to Italy.

We would spend Christmas in Catania.

Most people advise getting in and out of Catania quickly, but Ben was never one to listen to most people. An idea was clearly brewing because, by the time we landed, he told me he needed a full day at a place called the Museo Storico dello Sbarco (translation: the Museum of the Landing). I knew better than to ask why. Questions were not welcome during the time Ben was coming up with a story—not from his wife and definitely not from his editor. Those times, before he got the basic plot points down in his mind, were the loneliest times of our marriage. He had no use for me and, honestly, if I even asked him to pass the olive oil, he could lose his train of thought and never get it back. When he was living in his head like that, there was little room for much else.

I had paired this trip with my ten-year sabbatical and was very excited to recharge and catch up on my personal reading. I had a TBR list as big as the Duomo.

Ben spent the entirety of our first day immersed in World War

II Sicily at the Museo Storico dello Sbarco. I could see his wheels turning as we sat in our bed that night, mapping out the rest of our journey. Unlike Lanai, where Ben had outlined much of the story and found a beautiful Airbnb for us to stay at in advance, Sicily was an open book—literally. We didn't know where we would end up, but Ben assured me he would know when we got there.

By the time he had left the museum, he had his main character, an American named Jack Koslowsky. Jack had left behind the love of his life, his fiancée, Lucy Dubois, back in Louisiana, in order to fight the Nazis. Neither Jack nor Lucy knew she was pregnant when he shipped off. Jack was gravely injured during the invasion of Sicily and left for dead. A farmer, who was also hiding a young Jewish woman in his barn, subsequently saved him. The woman nursed Jack back to health, but not before the two had fallen in love.

"Wow," I'd said, so turned on by his thought process, which he rarely revealed to me as it played out like that. We made love that night, I imagined like Jack Koslowsky and the beautiful Jewish stowaway in a bombed-out barn in a little town called ________.

The next day, we set out on our journey to discover the location of that little town.

Our first stop was Taormina, the jewel of Sicily, where we splurged and booked a suite overlooking the Ionian Sea at an old monastery turned five-star hotel. If Taormina were a painting, it would be the *Mona Lisa*—beautiful, but hard to see through all the tourists. Within minutes of our arrival, I knew this would not be the place that Jack Koslowsky would settle, but I didn't care. It was magnificent.

"Please tell me we can stay here for a few days," I said, concerned we would leave before I got to try the eight flavors of gelato and the signature lava scrub at the spa—courtesy of Mount Etna. We could see the active volcano in the distance from our window.

Ben pointed it out. "Absolutely—we are going to climb that tomorrow!"

At the top of Mount Etna, the guide spewed countless facts about the active volcano in front of us, as well as volcanoes in general. Ben listened intently, but only scribbled down one note.

> In 2010, a volcano in Iceland stopped air travel in Europe for 7 days.

"I got it, Jules, I really got it," he boasted proudly on the way back down the mountain.

"Are we still looking for Jack Koslowsky's farm?"

"We are," he said. "I'll let you know when we find it."

On our last morning in Taormina, we sat at breakfast on the terrace of the hotel's restaurant, taking it all in. Ben was staring out at the garden, where cacti grew to be the size of palm trees, and palm trees the size of oaks, but I found myself lost in the table across from us. The fabulously chic couple seated there looked like they would fit in on any riviera. The wife possessed that casual European style, wearing a stunning combination of white and camel, accented by her gold watch and jewelry—all Bulgari. Of course, there was an oversize pair of sunglasses perched on top of her head. The husband wore a pale pink button-down tucked into perfectly creased jeans with a Gucci belt and Ferragamo loafers. I pictured Ben in the pink shirt and laughed. But what really got me was their child: a well-behaved boy of around ten, also impeccably dressed, keeping himself busy on his phone as his parents read the London *Times* in between bites of orange fennel salad and poached egg.

I was going to miss the orange fennel salad. I wondered if it was a staple everywhere in Sicily or just in Taormina.

I whispered to Ben, "Look how bored that poor kid is. It makes me think we should have two, you know, so they can entertain each other."

His face dropped as he glanced at the table I was referring to.

"Two? I'm not even so sure about one anymore," he quickly joked.

My face did more than drop. I imagine it distorted on impact. I didn't find it funny.

Of course, being married for a while then, we'd had the general conversation about wanting at least one child, but as far as the timing of it went, we were a little lax. It always felt like a discussion for another day, and then another day, and another still. Until right then and there, when I realized that the discussion was not based on *when* but on *if.* Joking or not, his comment really landed with a punch, as Ben would say.

I didn't even have to explain myself. The look on my face turned out to be enough. He backpedaled.

"But if you still want one, of course, I'm still willing."

I knew Ben would do anything for me. But was that how I wanted this to go down? Either way, this was not the place to discuss it. The fancy people on the restaurant's terrace were barely even speaking to one another, let alone having heated heart-to-hearts about the single most important decision in life.

"Now is not the time," I said.

"I agree!" he concurred with marked relief. "Our life is so perfect right now, why would we complicate it with a baby?"

"I meant now is not the time to discuss it."

This time, it was his face that epically distorted.

After breakfast, we checked out and hit the road for our next destination, Siracusa. I thought about bringing parenthood up again in the car, but if you have ever driven in Sicily, you know that full attention is necessary. The roads are curvy, the speed limit lax, and the other drivers showed a tendency to be casual about the traffic rules. Besides, it really wasn't fair to broach such a serious discussion when he was in the thinking phase of his novel. I decided to wait.

We arrived in Siracusa by lunchtime, threw down our bags in the less than superior hotel and left in search of pressed prosciutto and mozzarella sandwiches. We found the perfect iteration at the far end of the famous Mercato di Ortigia. We sat by the water and ate it while watching Sicilian teenagers and tourists sunbathe on the rocks and jump from the cliffs to the sea. Don't tell Little Les, but it was the best sandwich I'd ever eaten.

The food in Siracusa was generally a little briny for my taste, but, if I steered clear of anchovies, sublime. I had never even liked olives before arriving there; suddenly I couldn't get enough of them. But even they weren't reason enough to stay. Besides, Delia Ephron had already covered Siracusa beautifully in her novel of the same name.

We slept that night on top of the covers in a too-hot room, checked out early, and headed toward Licata, the town where young Jack Koslowsky had landed in the allied invasion of 1943. There, Ben spent a lot of time sitting at the water's edge, taking it all in.

A few towns later, after stopping in Modena for chocolate and Noto for risotto, we arrived at the Villa Athena in Agrigento before dusk. We sat on our terrace, sipping prosecco while the sun set on the Valley of the Temples, causing the fifth- and sixth-century Greek ruins to glow in shades of red and orange and pink. As the sky turned dark, the two temples were lit like a Hollywood movie set. It was hard to choose which was better, act one or act two.

The next day, for act three, we went to see the ruins up close. We learned that besides creating these architectural masterpieces, the Greeks were also responsible for introducing a population of Girgenti goats to the area. So called after the former name of the city of Agrigento, the goats could be traced back to sometime around 700 BC. Famous for their long beards and twisty horns, there were tons of them in the forties, when Jack would have lived in the valley—though now they're protected from extinction by a handful of local farmers.

After writing down every bit of info he heard on the subject, Ben asked me, "Would you be OK staying in Agrigento for a while?"

"Sure, it's beautiful."

"Good, because the farmer lost his only son in the war and taught Jack Koslowsky all he knew about raising Girgenti goats."

We rented an Airbnb right off the Piazza Perron, Agrigento's charming town square, right between the requisite church and theater. The streets were lined with Brazilian pepper trees and olive trees with actual olives dangling from their branches. If you could stand the slightly bitter taste, you could actually walk and snack.

I spent my mornings lounging around at home or at the adjacent Avenue Cafe, while Ben spent his with his new friend, the goat farmer. Most afternoons, we would sit in the piazza enjoying a late lunch as the town came alive. The energy was fantastic: Children racing each other home from school. Men hugging hello like long-lost brothers, thinking nothing of resting their arms around each other's shoulders.

The women were cooler and harder to figure out. They wore tight jeans, sexy blouses, and black high-heeled boots. They kissed each other's cheeks—"Ciao!"—"Ciao!"—and told entire stories with their hands and their eyes.

The week we were set to return home Ben turned in his proposal.

Sicily

By Benjamin Morse

A story of two brothers named Jack, neither of whom knew the other existed.

When Jack Koslowsky shipped off in the summer of '42, he had no idea that his fiancée was pregnant with his child. A casualty of the invasion of Sicily, he was left for dead in the battlefield. Jack had no other family and named his fiancée next of kin. She was notified, and their child was born without a father. She named him Jack Koslowsky, in his honor. After days of lying abandoned on the ground where he had been shot, Jack was discovered by an old goat farmer. He carried him to his wagon, covered him with straw, and took him home to his farm, where he was also harboring a young Jewish refugee, Fanca Sigal. Together, they nursed Jack back to health. The farmer's only son died in the war, and Jack stepped in to help him on the land. Eventually, Jack and Fanca fell in love. Fanca, too, became pregnant, and the two married after the war and raised their son, Jack Jr., on the farm in Sicily.

Fifty years later, Jack's American son comes to Sicily in an attempt to heal his ailing marriage and to see where the father he never knew had lost his life. The unhappy couple got stuck in Agrigento due to the eruption of a volcano in Iceland that grounded all air travel. There they hear of another man named Jack Koslowsky, a second-generation goat farmer with similar looks to the American. When one son meets the other, the past is unveiled and new and old connections are ignited.

I loved it. Elizabeth and our team loved it too. Which was a good thing, because truth was Ben was so into the story that he had it half written already.

We sat at our usual table and toasted Ben's success. On one side of us, the men ate seafood couscous and drank wine out of water glasses, happily arguing. The women sat at another table, holding babies and holding court—the words from their lively conversations bounced off the limestone gates. There was so much love all around—palpable love.

As a father lifted his cherubic toddler up from the ground and doused his face in kisses, Ben proclaimed, "Maybe, one little baby wouldn't be all that bad." He doused me in kisses as well, and I burst into tears, surprising even myself. I was so happy.

We started trying while still in Sicily, and Ben even attempted to get me to try on the airplane home, but I chickened out. We tried in Manhattan, we tried on Fire Island, and by the end of that summer when we had passed the "nothing to worry about until you've been trying for six months" mark, I started to worry. I made an appointment with my gynecologist for the first week in September to discuss it, but by the time it came I knew I was pregnant. I was bloated, exhausted, had to pee every two minutes, and was constipated as hell. When the plus sign appeared on the pregnancy test I was very relieved. Ben, on the other hand, looked panicked.

thirty

New York City

I was excited for Dr. Finkelstein to deliver our baby, just as he had delivered me. He was a kind man whose warm heart could only be topped by his warm hands—an important attribute in a gynecologist. I had been seeing him since my mother first took me for birth control before college. I was a virgin at the time, but she insisted that my condition, as she called it, wouldn't last long, and she didn't want me showing up back home "preggers," adding in her off-brand humor that there are better ways to gain the freshman fifteen. As per usual, there was no arguing with her, and I left with a three-month supply of birth control pills, which I didn't touch until my sophomore year.

Dr. Finkelstein was nearing retirement, and if we were to have a second child, I would probably have to go to his associate, but at least this time it would be him. He was old-school, and when I called him with a UTI or yeast infection over the years, he would always say, "Don't worry, honey," and he was right, as I would feel better the minute he said it. It was funny because if anyone else called me honey, I would shoot them the feminist death stare, but from him it soothed me. I think it's a gynecologist thing.

It was a beautiful day. "Not a cloud in the sky," I said, as we walked through Central Park toward the doctor's Fifth Avenue office.

Ben looked up. "Just like on September eleventh," he pointed out. An unoriginal comment, as everyone always said that, and a huge downer of an observation on such a special day.

He had pissed me off for the third time since breakfast. In all fairness, the first time was because I thought he was chewing too loudly. Along with the baby, I was carrying a short fuse, though it now felt warranted. Another sign of his parental apathy: Ben claimed to be downplaying his excitement until the official appointment, unlike my mother, who had been sending me pictures of cribs and baby bedding and beautiful outfits from the windows of French baby boutiques like Bonpoint and Jacadi daily. For the first time maybe ever, I liked my mom's attitude better. The baby would always be on the best dressed list with my mother as its grandma, that was certain. It was just the kind of controlling thing that would have driven me crazy in the past, but this time, I was eating it up. I couldn't wait to wrap him or her in a baby blanket from NakedCashmere, no matter how absurd the cost.

As in many ob-gyn offices of their generation, Dr. Finkelstein's smiling wife stood guard at the reception desk. Her toy poodles, Salt and Pepper, sat at her feet, yet she was still happy to show me the latest pictures of them—and the grandkids—in that order. After dispensing with the niceties and introducing Ben, whose books she and the nurse were both big fans of, they instructed me to leave a urine sample in the back bathroom. I did so and then joined Ben, whose heavy frame was sunk deep into the down-filled cushions of the beige waiting room couch. He was staring straight ahead at the exceedingly pregnant woman sitting across from us.

I sat down next to him and got lost in the latest issue of *People* magazine. His left leg bounced anxiously on the floor until I placed my hand on his knee and left it there. The motion had already made me nauseous, and I had to push blaming him for it from my mind. I wanted this first appointment to be perfect. I picked up the copy of *What to Expect When You're Expecting* from the side table, opened it to the page marked vaginal tearing, and handed it to him as payback for the nausea. He read it and swallowed hard. I felt vindicated.

They soon called us into the doctor's personal office, and we sat in the two velvet-covered armchairs opposite his desk to wait for him. The shades were tilted open with a beautiful view of Central Park peeking through. We watched silently as the slats in the blinds sliced through the images of the people passing by, causing them to look like abstract art.

The doctor arrived and announced, "You're indeed pregnant!" with a big smile on his face. We both stood up to greet him. He shook Ben's hand first and then gave me a somewhat awkward hug.

"Full circle!" he added, beaming. I guessed it wasn't often that he delivered the baby of a baby he'd delivered.

We talked for a bit about how far along he thought I was and how often I was to see him. He calculated the due date and answered a few of our rookie questions. The first being, "When can we hear the heartbeat?"

The answer to that was usually at around eight weeks, and Ben, who was much more in it by then, accompanied me to that appointment as well, eager to hear our baby. We again walked through Central Park, this time debating the baby name of the day—his pick, Venus or Serena if it was a girl and Rafael or Roger if it was a boy—he was suddenly on a tennis kick. I was still stuck on Henry or Haddie—both for Nana Hannah, but didn't even bother. There was plenty of time and, in the end, after all the pushing and the possible tearing, which he still couldn't discuss without turning green, I knew I would win.

We both agreed on not finding out the sex and had even spent the prior weekend playing around with paint colors for the nursery with names like Soothing Sage and Earthy Orange.

We arrived at the office, and it was hard to tell who was more excited—me, Ben, or the doctor.

"I hope we can hear it," Dr. Finkelstein warned. "It's still early, so no promises."

Ben stood by my side as the doctor turned on the ultrasound machine and spread the warm jelly on my belly. He placed the doppler on my stomach, and before long we heard the most magnificent sound, our baby's heartbeat. It was fast, like a train. The doctor reached for the monitor, to turn it toward us like you see in the movies and stopped dead in his tracks. His expression completely changed.

"Is there something wrong with the baby?" I asked, immediately panicked.

"No. The baby looks fine," he said. He smiled at me with the kindest smile and added, "Get dressed and I'll meet you both back in my office."

He explained that the sonogram showed a shadow on one of my ovaries, but he needed more information. He suggested another, more detailed sonogram be performed at the hospital by a radiologist. It was a Monday, and we were set to leave for Florida that Wednesday to visit Ben's mom. I told him so and waited for him to say some version of his "Don't worry, honey," like he had when I had a yeast infection or UTI, but he didn't.

"That's not a problem," he said instead. "Let's see if we can get you in this afternoon."

Even with the alarms going off in my head, I matched his kind smile. I could pretend everything was OK too—at least for a few more hours.

Ben, though, hadn't even sat down in the velvet armchair across from the doctor. He was standing with his back against the door, frozen in fear.

You already know the ending, so I will explain it as simply as possible. The second sonogram showed a large mass around my ovary, consistent with a malignancy. Surgery confirmed that I had ovarian cancer and that it had metastasized to my intestine and my liver. The surgeon removed everything she could, and there was no choice but to terminate the pregnancy. Everyone in my family insisted that I could beat it, and while I agreed to aggressive treatment, I knew in my heart that it was too far gone.

Ovarian cancer is not really silent like people say; it whispers subtle clues like my bloated belly, how frequently I had to pee, the constipation, the exhaustion, the back pain. The signs were all there, muted betrayals that I couldn't hear over the pregnancy, or hadn't even noticed before.

As soon as I vocalized my lack of hope to Ben, he unfroze. He refused to give up and spent the entire time I had left searching for ways to save me. He was so scared by the idea of losing me that we never discussed what would happen when he did. I believe it's one of the reasons I am still hanging around here now.

thirty-one

Accountable

Dylan texted Matty from the ticket booth in Bay Shore with fair warning.

Tuck is on the 12:00 ferry!

Matty didn't even realize he had said it out loud and looked up to find ten men staring up at him.

Matty and Renee were on better terms now, but she agreed that he could keep staying over at our place for the rest of August. He had heard his mother crying herself to sleep enough times over the past year to appreciate the perpetual smile on her face, even if the way it got there made him want to retch.

Now he faced a predicament. Why was his father surprising them? And should he let him be the one surprised? There was a good reason Matty always texted, knocked, and yelled "I'm here!" before venturing into his house across the street these days. Even I entered with caution. Part of him wanted his father to experience the same humiliation he had inflicted on him and his mother. In that way, the drummer was the perfect pawn.

As if reading his mind, Ben said, "You know what, Matty? You are not the adult here. This is not your problem."

More good advice from my man. I was proud. The other guys agreed, piping in with "give him a taste of his own medicine" and such. They all held a grudge. There were plenty of men who couldn't play ball well and came out all season and tried, just because they enjoyed it. The regulars were usually pretty nice about it. Only Tuck would barely show all year and then insist on playing in the Homeowners' Game. Plus, they all deeply cared for Renee—some of them had known her forever.

Just as the last inning of the game was wrapping up, Tuck appeared. He was dressed like a Hamptonite in Moscot frames, a Canali linen shirt, and Tod's driving loafers. The contrast between him and the guys on the field was comical. Everyone noticed, but of course Shep went for the joke.

"Pardon me, sir, would you have any Grey Poupon?"

Matty held in his laughter and hugged his dad hello. As much as he didn't want to be involved in the upcoming drama, he was clearly in the best position to steer the boat.

"Is Mom home?" Tuck asked, ignoring Shep.

The look on Matty's face confirmed that he didn't know how to answer. Ben stepped in.

"Why don't you come visit with us first—game's nearly done and Little Les sent over some turkey sandwiches for lunch."

I know I'm making Les sound like Emeril Lagasse but no one could resist his turkey sandwiches. A few summers ago, he was helicoptered off the island for a medical emergency. The surgeon, known as the premier in his field, asked, "I have operated on rock stars, top athletes, even kings. I got more phone calls about you today than any of them. What do you do?"

To which Little Les answered, "I make a good sandwich."

Tuck couldn't resist either.

The four men sat around the porch table eating the local delicacies right off the paper they were wrapped in. A bag of chips lay open between them, just a few inches from an empty bowl. It made me cringe. How hard would it be to pour them in?

Matty kicked Ben under the table and excused himself to go to the bathroom. As soon as he was out of sight, Ben did the dirty deed.

"So, Tuck. What is it you want to see Renee about?"

"Umm. I don't know, really. I ummm . . ."

Shep lost patience with him, if he ever had any to begin with. "Spit it out, man."

"I miss my family. I think I made a mistake."

Ben and Shep both sat back in their chairs. Shep opened his mouth to speak, but Ben grabbed his forearm to stop him.

"I got this."

Shep reluctantly agreed.

"Renee is seeing someone—he's kind of living in the house with her."

Tuck's face dropped in shock, until Ben added, "Matty has been staying here."

The shock turned to anger. "What? She can't do that. That's not fair to Matty."

Matty caught the last line on his return. Apparently it was the final straw. He held nothing back and didn't care that Shep and Ben bore witness. Everything he'd been thinking for the year rolled off his tongue like a steamroller.

It began with a reaction to Tuck's comment "that's not fair to Matty" and continued until the poor kid was folded into a ball on the couch, crying, with his father rubbing his back and begging his forgiveness. Tuck took full blame, which both surprised me and made me happy, though he kept mixing up the words *affect* and *effect*, which made me want to strangle him.

In the end, Ben agreed to help Tuck craft a letter to Renee, Cyrano style, and Matty agreed to give it to her.

It went like this:

Dear Renee,

I don't know where your head is right now, but I have to tell you where mine is. I miss my family and I would do anything to get back what we had. I made an awful mistake and with each passing day I regret what I've done—to you, to us, and to Matthew—more and more. You did not deserve the pain I caused, and I would give anything for the chance to spend the rest of my life making it up to you. I understand you may need time to process this. I hope you do. I will be back to watch Matt play in the Homeowners' Game. If you could find some time to talk, then I'd be grateful.

With love,
Tuck

I watched Renee read the letter that night, quietly sitting at her kitchen table. Her face was blank afterward. She didn't cry or laugh or tear it up. She put it in the pocket of her robe, grabbed a pint of ice cream and two spoons, and headed back upstairs to her young lover.

thirty-two

High Tide

In between softball, and mourning, and sitting at the beach staring at the ocean, and drinking Scotch like it was water, and watching old home movies of Shep and Caroline on Shep's 35-millimeter projector that was somehow still up in *our* attic, the "boys" spent the greater part of August trying to get rid of the trike. It became a sport—and not one they were lettering in. The damn bike always came back.

Today it was the garbage man's turn to return it. Shep had convinced Matty to ride it straight into the dump the night before.

"I was told this belongs to you?" The man rolled in the bike—thinking he would be greeted with joy and appreciation.

Shep grimaced. Ben thanked him. Then the silverware klepto, Lisa Marlin-Cohen-Fitzpatrick, showed up with another pie.

Ben, tired of her making moves on him, said it as clearly as he could. "I don't like pie."

"I do!" said the garbage man.

"Look, Ben, you made a match," Shep joked.

I laughed, alone as usual, and wondered, again, where was Caroline? I didn't feel any closer to leaving than I had on day one, and Ben didn't seem any better, really. Nothing was moving forward, until late that night, when the tide quite literally turned.

At around 2:00 a.m. Dylan banged on Matty's window. Everyone was only half-asleep—in anticipation. Matty pulled open the shade and motioned for her to go around back so he could let her in. They were both very excited for the big night, and no, it had nothing to do with their virginity.

Dylan had come up with a plan to push the trike out to sea at high tide, in the middle of the night when no one would be watching. Matty questioned the environmental effect of it, but Dylan insisted that it would sink out at sea, and between the tires and the metal, create a much welcomed artificial reef.

Matty didn't think it would work, but she promised it would. She had once seen a couple of cidiots (as her dad referred to them) mis-navigate the tides and lose their brand-new Range Rover to the ocean during the off-season. It got caught on some rocks and they had no choice but to abandon ship—or car, as the case may be. When the water rose over the wheels it took the sturdily built machine out to sea like it was nothing more than a piece of driftwood. Dylan had watched in awe with her dad from the wooden stairs that descend from the end of each block.

"More proof that city folk have no place here in the winter," Jake had said.

The locals who drive on a daily or weekly basis (only in the off-season) are über-aware of the tide schedule.

In order to have a car on Fire Island, you have to live there for a year straight, and living there for a year straight proves quite difficult without a car. It's a purposeful catch-22 to ensure that too many people don't get car permits.

Another fun literary fact: Joseph Heller, who wrote the book *Catch-22*, also summered on Fire Island.

Dylan and Matty hovered over Ben, Shep, and Sally the dog, all asleep in our king-size bed.

Dylan whispered, "It's a little weird how they sleep in the same bed, no?"

"Maybe it's weirder for them to sleep alone," Matty responded, speaking straight from his old soul. He gently shook Ben. "Wake up. It's high tide."

Shep must have been sleeping with one eye open, because he sat up before Ben did.

"I'm coming too."

Even in the dark, Shep could sense their apprehension.

"What? It's my bike."

Ben sat up and mumbled under his breath, "*Now* it's your bike?"

We all laughed.

The four of them lifted the bike in the air at the foot of the stairs and carried it up and over, placing it down on the sand. Wheeling it to the shoreline wasn't too hard, but getting it into the ocean turned out to be difficult. Every time they thought they had caught a good wave, it took the bike out and then brought it back in again. In the end, Matty and Dylan had to steer it past the first break to really get it out there. We all sat on the sand and watched silently as the moonlit ocean took it away. Eventually, it just disappeared. Shep was the first to break the silence.

"Vivian and Beatrix are gonna be pissed about this," he said with a big smile.

"Maybe they'll bond over it," Ben joked.

"Fat chance." Shep turned to the kids. "I'm gonna get you that condom to pay you back for this."

"Matty!" Dylan screamed. "I said no friends!"

Matty jumped up and took off, with Dylan quick on his tail.

"Look at that. She thinks of us as friends," Shep proudly proclaimed.

We watched as Matty ran serpentine up and down the beach with Dylan chasing close behind. They were both laughing, and it made us laugh too. It always feels good to be around youth. Even when you're dead, their energy is catching.

"I'm going to Gay Bingo next Tuesday night at Cherry's in the Grove with Pam and Andie. I'll pick one up for them there," Ben told Shep.

Cherry's is a bar on the east end of the island in one of the two towns that make up the storied gay enclave, Cherry Grove and the Pines. They had been hosting Gay Bingo there once a week for ages. Led by a resident drag queen, attending always makes for a fun change of pace from the Groundhog Day–like existence of Bay Harbor. We usually headed down there a couple of times a summer with Pam and Andie to have dinner, go dancing, or play bingo.

"In this woke-up day and age you're still allowed to say Gay Bingo? That's crazy," Shep observed.

"It's woke, not woke up, and yes, that's what Pam and Andie call it, and that's what it's called, Gay Bingo," Ben explained, adding, "but you're not supposed to say crazy anymore."

"But you can say Gay Bingo? That's lame."

"You shouldn't say lame."

"I just shouldn't speak."

Ben stood and helped Shep to his feet. "Now that's an idea I can get behind."

Shep laughed. "Let's get some sleep. I want to play ball in the morning."

As they headed home, I listened to their repartee and was again thankful for their unusual friendship.

"Gay Bingo at Cherry's?" Shep shook his head in disbelief.

"I'm just going because I promised Julia."

"That made the cut? No promise to keep the dog off the couch or to phone your mother every Sunday. . . . I promise I will go to Gay Bingo?"

"Not exactly. She said something about me promising to laugh, and it somehow morphed into that. I haven't felt up for it all summer, but with one Tuesday night left, I'm kind of out of time."

Shep slapped Ben on the back. "Well, don't go picking up some sugar daddy. There's no room in our bed."

Ben snorted.

"Made you laugh," Shep boasted as Ben conceded. "See, Julia was right. It's working already."

thirty-three

The Grove

As we stepped off the water taxi in Cherry Grove, two drag queens stepped on, quickly signaling that we were not in Kansas anymore. We were, in fact, somewhere more equivalent to Oz—somewhere fabulous.

While it's always magical to arrive by boat anywhere on Fire Island, it feels a little extra stepping off a water taxi at Cherry Grove. The vibe encompasses both the current definition of the word *gay*—homosexual—and the dated one: lighthearted and carefree. Every time I visit, I feel envious of the board-walked community of beautiful homes and stylishly dressed people who seem, to me, to do everything at a higher level.

We headed over to Cherry's on the Bay, where the back deck was hopping—as is usually the case on bingo night, and every other night too. Groups of friends sat with drinks and bingo boards, ready to go. Strings of cherry-red lights reflected off the walls and off the patrons' faces, creating a vibe that was part Moulin Rouge, part red-light district, and part vaudeville. I knew it wasn't Pam, Andie, or Ben's scene, but I loved it, I always had. I never imagined I would have the chance to be here again.

We sat at a table for four, but our server was quick to point out that we were three.

"A threesome! What can I get you?"

Even the servers were in on the schtick.

"What kind of beer is on tap?" Ben inquired.

"Heineken."

Ben nodded and raised one finger. Andie added, "I can start with a beer—make it two."

The server winked and joked, "Two Heinies on top? Perfect. And you, Blanche?"

Pam responded with her usual, "A glass of chardonnay, please."

The drinks arrived as the voice of "God" introduced the "Bingo Bitch" of the evening. "Let's give it up for the Queen of Soul—Ms. Urethra Franklin."

Everyone applauded as the empty seat, mine, seemed to scream my absence.

"Are you ready to jam?" Urethra called out, before breaking out into a rowdy rendition of "(You Make Me Feel Like) a Natural Woman."

The crowd cheered, some more than others, and from that moment on I think we all realized this was a bad idea. Ben was not ready for this kind of revelry. It was painful to look at him. He was pale and glassy-eyed.

Andie tapped the server as he passed and shouted, "Three shots of tequila too, please, and some of those soft pretzels to soak it up."

Even the server, without having a clue about the situation, could sense the struggle.

As the song ended and bingo began, we all hoped that Ben's competitive spirit would pull him out of his funk, but he was barely even paying attention.

"Anyone got some lube to get the balls rolling?" Urethra joked, before calling out her first number. "N your butt thirty-seven!"

Andie pointed out N37 on Ben's board and he reluctantly slid it open.

By the time the first game ended with—"G fifty-four, to the meat rack to score"—Pam needed a break.

"I'm gonna go pee," she announced, before running off.

Urethra began another game with "May the odds be in your favor, and the balls be in your mouth."

It made Ben chuckle, and I hoped he would turn his mood around. My hope was short-lived. Pam returned from the bathroom with an old friend.

"Andie, look who I found—remember Josie Miller, from First Boston?"

I knew her too. We had met briefly at Pam and Andie's wedding. She fixed my dress in the bathroom—the fabric had gotten caught in the zipper with me inside it. Two other women in the bathroom had witnessed my distress and gone about their business, but she had stopped to help. I was immediately taken by her kindness and her beauty: short cropped hair and dark eyes with impeccable brows and pale pink lips. It had been about five years, but she looked the same.

Andie stood to kiss her hello.

"Josie, this is our good friend Ben."

"Nice to meet you." She smiled, and Ben mumbled something unintelligible in return, before stiffening up like a board.

"Josie is visiting friends," Pam informed us, before motioning to the empty chair for her to join us.

Ben looked her over, and I knew he was sizing up her "gayness." His eyes traveled from her crisp white blouse to her loosely cropped jeans before focusing in on her tan suede Birkenstock sandals. He looked at the feet of two women canoodling at the next table and focused in on their Birkenstock sandals as well; he visibly breathed a sigh of relief, ignoring the fact that every straight woman and their mother owns a pair too.

"I come this time every summer," Josie explained, as she sat.

Ben smiled like a human being and nodded.

"I feel awful that we lost touch," Pam remarked. "Last time we spoke you were engaged to that British guy."

Ben's smile immediately disappeared, and he went from not paying attention to the game to playing as if his life depended on it.

"OOOOOOOOOOOH—sixty-nine."

Ben had O69.

"What was his name?" Pam asks Josie.

"Reginald Lord."

"And wasn't he, like, actual royalty? Wasn't it Lord Reginald Lord?"

"G fitty—like my titty!"

Ben had G50.

"Something like that," Josie confirmed. "He was a baronet. And it's long over. Turns out Sir Lord was a bit more racist than he let on."

"That's awful, Josie, I'm sorry."

"Don't be—glad I found out before the wedding. I would have had to go all Harry and Meghan on them."

"N and out and N and out 17!"

Ben had N17.

"Are you still in finance?" Pam asked.

"Wow, we really lost touch. I'm not. I opened a cupcake company."

"Oh my God, you're Josie-cakes?"

"I am."

I knew this story. To get through the breakup, Josie had started baking chocolate and vanilla cupcakes filled with cream, somewhat like the Hostess cakes we ate as kids—but with adult flavored fillings like coffee and amaretto and Grand Marnier. She would bring them to work every day. They were so popular that the hedge fund she worked at approached her to start up a business. I read an article about it—out loud to Ben, bragging about how she was that girl who fixed my dress at the wedding. I didn't know if he hadn't been listening then or wasn't now. His eyes looked dead, like he had completely checked out.

Urethra Franklin called out, "B fifty-two—bang, bang, bang on the door, baby!"

Andie looked down at Ben's board and yelled with the force of ten cis men, "Bingo!! Ben's got bingo!"

All eyes turned to Ben as the hoopla surrounding the crowning of the bingo winner began. Ben was in complete shock. Urethra approached our table to check his numbers while beginning a number of her own. She belted, "*You got to think—think about what you're trying to do to me . . . Think, think . . .* "

By the time she got to our table—and the chorus, "*Freedom, freedom, freedom, freedom*"—Ben took her up on the suggestion and fled the scene.

"Where you going, papi chula?" she yelled out after him. "You gonna end up in the meat rack!"

Urethra danced and sang around our table—as Pam jumped down Andie's throat.

"What the hell, Andie, why did you do that?"

Josie looked thoroughly confused. She watched them fight like it was Wimbledon.

"I'm sorry—he had bingo!"

"Couldn't you see he was barely hanging on?"

"Urethra said B fifty-two. He had B fifty-two. I shouted bingo. It was my natural competitive instinct." She put her head in her hands. "For fuck's sake, Pam, I'm sorry, but I told you it was too soon for him to come here."

"It wouldn't have been if you'd have used your head."

Josie was clearly mortified, Urethra entertained.

"Should I go after him?" Andie asked.

"No. Let him walk it off. He'll come back when he's ready. Just try to think from now on."

Urethra piped in like a Greek chorus, "You gotta think!"

"I should think? You're the one who brought Josie over here and sat her down in Julia's seat."

"Think!" Urethra crooned before moving on.

"Am I sitting in someone's seat?" Josie asked nervously.

"Ben's wife Julia died of cancer just six weeks ago," Pam said quietly. "We all had this tradition to come to Gay Bingo once a summer. That's her seat . . . figuratively speaking."

Josie bolted to her feet. They both reached out for her shoulders to coax her back down.

"It's fine, Josie, I'm sorry. Obviously, this has nothing to do with you and," she continued, turning to Andie, "I'm sorry, baby. I know you didn't mean for this to happen."

Andie nodded. "I'm sorry too." She leaned in to kiss Pam sweetly on the lips. Pam smiled back lovingly.

"We really don't know what to do for him. He's a wreck, and we always feel like we're doing or saying the wrong thing," Pam explained to Josie.

"I'm sure you're not. It takes time."

We all sat in silence for a minute, a sullen and quiet table in a sea of gay.

"Do you want to order a drink?" Andie broke it and asked.

"I think I should go in case he comes back," said Josie. "Besides, I'm still hungover from last night—I'm gonna grab some Tylenol at the store and head back to my friend's place."

Pam stood and hugged her goodbye. "Let's not lose touch again," Josie said.

"Definitely not, and follow me on social media—lots of pictures of our baby."

"Follow me too—lots of pictures of cupcakes!"

"I will."

Pam and Andie both raised their hands for more shots as I followed Josie out in search of Benjamin. I found him at Cherry Grove Sundries, a bright shop that's part hardware store, part drugstore, and part rainbow emporium. Ben milled about, both embarrassed and curious. He waited until the store was empty and approached the guy at the register. A giant pump vat of lube sat on the counter like hand sanitizer.

"Do you have condoms?" he asked.

"Of course. What size?"

He was painfully uncomfortable. "What size? I don't know."

"Do you want to see a chart, or should I eye it for you?"

"No, it's not for me. Um, I guess, small."

"OK, small, we have—"

The phone rang, interrupting his explanation. The campy shopkeeper held up a one-sec finger and answered, "Cherry Grove Sundries . . . Because I told you, I don't want to invite him. . . . 'Cause he's a bitch, and I don't want to."

Ben was rocking back and forth—heel, toe, heel, toe, heel, toe. I couldn't decide if it was out of impatience or anxiety. Josie entered the shop, and even though she was standing directly under a 24-carat-gold penis-shaped pool float, its head comically pointing at hers, Ben didn't notice. She grabbed a bottle of Tylenol, approached the counter, and awkwardly greeted him.

"Hi again," she said.

"Hey," he responded.

Quite the conversationalist, my husband.

They couldn't help but listen as the man at the register continued. "Not her, the one that looks like Bianca Del Rio and does that horrible Dolly Parton imitation."

They shared a smile, and Josie attempted conversation.

"I know that was weird in there for you. I'm so sorry about your wife."

I felt oddly thankful when Ben answered like a normal person. "Thank you. I probably shouldn't have come, but I am trying to get back into ordinary life—and what better place to start than the Grove?"

Josie laughed. "Well, I guess maybe it's better to take baby steps," she offered.

"Maybe. I did kind of jump right in the deep end."

"I think it's brave you even get up in the morning."

Finally, a person who says the right thing. Hallelujah!

The man at the register hung up the phone and placed two colorful beach pails filled with condoms down on the counter, size SMALL written boldly on each.

"Here you go. Hubba bubba or tutti fruity?"

Ben died, right then and there, and Josie's mouth hung so low I worried a fly would swoop in. He looked from her shocked face to the blaring size SMALL written on the buckets and died a second and third death. The man behind the counter seemed clueless.

"Come on, doll, it's a simple choice. Do you like a hot pink cock or a purple one?"

Fourth death.

Ben turned to explain to Josie, but only caught the back of her flying out the door. He went after her, catching a glimpse of her heading down the windy boardwalk path to the beach. She was fast, and by the time he reached her, he was out of breath.

He yelled out, "Josie, wait, please!"

She kept walking. He kept following.

"Stop. Please let me explain."

She stopped and trudged back to him, but not for an explanation.

"You have nothing to explain to me, but I think you should inform your friends that they can stop worrying about you!"

"They're not for me."

"Whatever." She turned and raced in the direction she'd been going.

"I swear! I was getting them for this kid back in Bay Harbor."

She couldn't let it go, shouting back toward him, "Because there are no condoms back in Bay Harbor?"

Ben ran to catch up with her. She was still trudging along. He kept up with her anger-fueled pace, explaining in a pleading tone, "Well, there are, but it's a small town, and the kid wants to lose his virginity with the ferry captain's daughter. If you saw the ferry captain, you would totally believe me—even I have to look up at him."

Josie took a few more steps, each landing a little lighter than the last. The moonlight briefly caught her smile. He saw it too and smiled as well, relieved.

"You believe me?" he asked hopefully.

"I guess. I'm sorry. It was really none of my business, anyway. I don't know why I got so upset."

"That's OK. I don't know why I had such a need to defend myself."

She began to laugh, and Ben joined her.

"That was pretty funny?" he offered.

"Now it is."

After a beat, Ben admitted, "Well, I was promised a laugh tonight, so thank you. It was good to meet you."

"You too."

They were both still walking in the same direction on an empty beach. After a few more awkward in-pace steps, they couldn't help but laugh again. Ben explained, "I'm gonna walk back home from here."

"Me too."

"Aren't you staying in the other direction?"

"No, Point O'Woods, believe it or not. I just spent the day with some friends in the Grove."

Point O'Woods and the Grove were polar opposites in nearly every way imaginable. Point of Woods was a gated community where you needed an actual key and a decades-old Waspy pedigree to get in or out, whereas in the Grove, you just need to be out.

"I'll walk with you for a little—till I get to my friend's street," she said.

"OK . . . sure."

Ben and Josie and I walked along in the moonlight. They stayed about a foot apart, but somewhat in sync. They were silent, but it was a graceful silence. In another time, years from now I imagined, Ben might have thought it romantic. Right now it seemed obvious that the only one crushing on the smart, sweet, beautiful Josie was me. Time and space seemed to blur, and neither of them realized they had gone too far until the clouds shifted and Ben noticed the American flag that waves like a beacon from Keith Fogerty's deck, signaling that he was close to home.

"You forgot to stop at your friend's block," he said.

"Oh my. I did."

"It must've been the dynamic conversation."

They both laughed until Ben admitted, "You were probably worried I would drown myself."

"The thought entered my mind."

"I'll walk you back."

"But then I'd have to walk you back, and we'd be out here all night."

"Come to my house. I'll give you a bike and you can ride back."

She paused and dismissed the idea, but Ben insisted, nudging her toward the steps to our street.

"Come on—they're calling for rain. Julia would want you to use it."

She gave in. As they walked the last steps to our house she asked, "Julia is your wife?"

"Yes."

"That's a beautiful name."

"She was the most beautiful woman I'd ever known, and somehow *she* was enamored with *me*."

Josie laughed.

"Why are you laughing?" He stood sideways, pulled in his gut and made a couple of bodybuilder poses.

She laughed more. I did too. It was the first time in ages I'd heard him talk about me other than reporting on my doctors' appointments and chemo sessions. I was happy to hear him remembering me as his beautiful healthy wife.

Josie waited outside our house, fidgeting in the dark, until Ben showed up again with my bike in tow. The streetlight caught the top of her head, creating the illusion of a halo. Thunder rumbled in the distance. It was all very dramatic.

When she saw the baby seat, she lit up—making the obvious

assumption. With a big smile, she said, "Oh, I didn't know you had kids!"

I could see the vomit rise in Ben's throat. He swallowed hard and shook his head. She looked equally, if not more, nauseated by his response. He tilted the handlebar toward her, and she accepted it.

"You sure about this? I feel funny taking it," she said.

"Don't, no one's using it anyway."

They both paused to take that in too.

"I'll bring it back before I go. My friend has one of those tandems, so it will be a simple exchange."

"Whatever you want. Just remember I'm the house near the ball field."

He pointed to the place where the four corners met.

"It was nice meeting you, Ben." She smiled her beautiful smile and lightened the mood with "Please tell your friend I'm sorry I foiled his deflowering!"

Ben rallied and met her tone. "I will definitely let him know the entire story! Nice meeting you too, Josie."

He flipped on her bike light—my bike light—and waved as she rode off into the night.

thirty-four

Redemption

Some men mature with age. Others, like Shep, seem to perpetually navigate life through the lens of a twelve-year-old boy. In that way, Shep was the youngest in the house. Late that night, when Ben was sound asleep, Shep woke up, stirred by the sound of the rain tapping on the skylight. Shep loved the rain. He considered it an invitation. He entertained the offer, grabbing a flashlight and a slicker, and left the bedroom to check it out.

He journeyed toward the room Matty was staying in and shined his flashlight on the seventies-era digital clock on Matty's nightstand—the kind where the numbers flip. It had come with the house back when Shep and Caroline bought it. There were a few such treasures still hanging around, like that clock. My favorites were a white Fitz and Floyd ashtray that looked like a diaphragm and a set of Portuguese porcelain corn plates with the name of the famous old New York department store, Bonwit Teller, stamped on the back.

The clock read 2:00 a.m. Shep moved the beam of light onto Matty's sleeping face, but Matty didn't budge—so he shook him.

"Matty, wake up."

Matty opened his eyes and cringed from the light.

"You all right?" Shep asked.

"Aside from the blindness." Matty sat up and rubbed his eyes. "Are you wearing a raincoat?"

"Yes. Want to go for a ride?"

"Are you still drunk from dinner?"

"Maybe a little."

Matty looked at the clock.

"It's two in the morning, and it sounds like it's pouring out, and besides—one of us is not supposed to be riding."

"Well, it's two in the morning and pouring out, so no one will see either of us."

"You're half right. They won't see me."

Matty rolled back over and closed his eyes tight.

"Come on. Get up." Shep shook him again. "There'll be plenty of time to sleep in the grave."

I laughed. Falser words had never been spoken.

Matty didn't budge. I could hear the rain picking up.

"I bet the sidewalks are like rivers, Matty. You know there's nothing better than riding your bike in the rain."

Shep was right. There was nothing better. Some of my happiest memories of Fire Island were not from the beach or the ball field or the bay, but from getting caught in a storm coming back from town. I would laugh the entire way as the rain soaked my clothes and beat down on my face—feeling like a kid again. If you know, you know.

Matty knew.

Minutes later, Shep was pulling Ben's bike from the shed with Matty right behind him. The rainwater had already begun collecting on the sidewalks, but they were both old pros. They peddled hard on the approach, lifting their feet in the air at the deepest spots and coasting as far as the previous pedal would take them. Huge smiles were plastered on both of their faces. Mine too. They had to wipe their eyes to see. Shep began to sing an old army tune, though as far as I knew he had never been in the army. Word was he was a peacenik activist back in the day. Fire Island was a real haven for those types. Still, he crooned a George Cohan song like he was ready to enlist. I was surprised by how much these guys liked to sing.

"'Over there, over there, send the word, send the word over there. That the Yanks are coming, the Yanks are coming'—come on, Matty—sing!"

Matty tried to join in.

"'Over there, over there, *nannannan, nannannan*, over there!'"

They continued singing and laughing and cruising through the puddles, as the rain poured down on their delighted faces.

But, while we chose to go out in the rain, someone else sinisterly took cover from it.

Pam and Andie lived in one of the original old two-story cottages that lined the first few streets of Bay Harbor. They were sound asleep in their bed, with baby Oliver asleep in a bassinet next to them, when—*BOOM*—Pam awoke to what sounded like a door slamming open. She jolted straight up.

"Andie, did you hear that?"

"It's just the rain. Go back to sleep."

There was no way she was dismissing the loud boom. She shook Andie's shoulder.

"I'm gonna go check. It sounds like the wind blew the door open."

"We'll close it in the morning."

It had been a long night, their first hiring a babysitter, and they had both been overserved at Cherry's.

"But a deer could get in, or a raccoon—what if it's that three-bears bandit?"

"The Goldilocks Interloper? Maybe she'll leave us breakfast."

"I'll go," Pam said, not really meaning it.

"No, I'll do it."

"Thanks, honey."

Andie begrudgingly got up and headed downstairs, surprised to see that the door was indeed wide open. She shut it and turned to see a light coming from the kitchen. She thought she had closed up before they went to bed, but they hadn't partied like that since before Pam was pregnant, so she wasn't really sure.

A large, dark-haired man with a crew cut (the complete opposite of Goldilocks) stood at the sink washing his hands. He reached up and dried them on Pam's new curtains. Just last week Andie had splattered grease on them and Pam had threatened divorce.

"Oh no, not the curtains," Andie pleaded, with little thought.

"Who the hell are you?" the man shouted, grinding his teeth as if he were strung out on drugs. Andie wasn't as afraid as she should have been. Looks and attitude aside, she was still assuming it was the Goldilocks Interloper, who had been billed more as a menace than a threat.

"This is my house," Andie answered.

"This is *my* house," the seemingly strung-out man insisted.

Andie, still not afraid, tried reason.

"Listen, it's dark out, and raining. You got the wrong house, bud."

The stranger sat down at the kitchen table. Andie grabbed a box of cookies from the cabinet and handed them to him.

"Take these if you're hungry."

With a somewhat appreciative look, the man took the box, before mumbling something resembling, "Thank you, OK, bye."

Relief flooded Andie's face. She exhaled and waited for the intruder to stand up and leave. But the man looked up from his chair and yelled.

"I said BYE!"

She was now officially afraid. She ran out of the kitchen and back upstairs as the man rested his head on the table.

"Call nine-one-one, call nine-one-one! There's a man in the kitchen. He's very angry. He thinks this is his house."

"Is it the Goldilocks Interloper? What a misleading name."

"Well he didn't name himself—just call nine-one-one!"

She left, closing the door behind her, and headed back down to monitor the guy. A quick peek in the kitchen revealed that the uninvited guest was still resting his head on the table. Upstairs, Pam was having a hell of a time on the phone with the police.

"There is no house number. It's two houses in from Midway. On 'A' street, please hurry. No, not the Blancs' house, closer toward the bay, not the beach."

It wasn't uncommon, even for the authorities, to have no idea which house you were referring to. Every attempt at directions came with confusing descriptions of flowerpots and door colors and third-house-from-the-left or the right or nearer to the beach or to the bay. There's a bizarre house numbering system in that there is none. People would walk up to my house weekly asking for some person or another who didn't live there.

Andie returned as Pam hung up the phone.

"Are they coming?"

"I hope. They seem so confused."

"Then call Bay Harbor Security, call the Ocean Beach Police, keep calling till someone comes. I think this guy is on something—and it's not porridge."

She ran back down to the kitchen, where the man was still sitting at the table, now rocking.

This time, he saw Andie and bolted from his seat, yelling, "I told you to get out of my house!"

"I told you, this is my house—it's time for you to leave, before this turns into something."

The man stood right up to Andie. "It's time for *you* to leave, before this turns into something."

"I'll give you a minute," she managed, as she slowly backed out of the kitchen. She opened the front door all the way, turned on every light, and ran back up the stairs. Pam was now on the phone with Bay Harbor Security. Andie grabbed it.

"What is taking you so long? Come now, or something bad is going to happen. . . . We don't have a house number . . . 'cause there's no mail here. Why would we need to know? OK, yes, I see that now but please, 'A' street, the door's wide open, all the lights are on!"

The two women pushed the dresser in front of the door and sat on the floor, their backs pressed up against it with all of their strength. They could hear shouting downstairs and hoped the police had arrived. It got quieter, and they could hear footsteps race up the stairs. The doorknob turned, and they pushed back onto the dresser with all of their might, until they heard a familiar voice.

"Girls! You OK?" Shep Silver called out.

The two women burst out in tears of relief. They pulled the dresser out of the way, opened the door, and threw their arms around their savior.

"There's a huge man downstairs!"

"He wasn't that huge. I chased him out with a baseball bat."

Andie hugged Shep again as Pam declared, "I'll never yell at you about keeping that bat in the umbrella stand again!"

Pam scooped up Oliver, even though he was asleep, and they covered him in kisses as Matty escorted two police officers upstairs with their too little, too late pronouncement.

"Did someone call nine-one-one?"

thirty-five

The Return of Dignity

It was a long night, and all three men slept in later than usual on account of it. Matty and Shep didn't even attempt to come in quietly upon their return from their big adventure. They ran right into our bedroom and told Ben the entire story of what may have been the most action-packed night in Bay Harbor history. Despite the more than sixty years between them, I swear they both looked the same age as they relayed what had occurred, like two kids on an adrenaline high. Ben only interrupted to ask them to slow down. When they were through, having heard himself describe chasing a big angry man out into the street with a bat out loud like that, Shep sat down on the bed to catch his breath.

"Oh boy," he said. "That was intense."

It was as if he had just realized what had happened.

"Pour him a Scotch," Ben told Matty.

"Make it a double," Shep added.

When they finally got to bed, it was after four, so when people congregated outside the house at 9:00 a.m., it was only Sally who heard them.

She barked at the door and then ran to each bedroom, licking their faces and hands till they stirred.

A small crowd had gathered by then, including Pam, Andie, Big Les (who I had never seen this far from the store!), a bunch of the ballplayers, the two policemen from the night before, and the security guys who had confiscated Shep's bike. Apparently, two other officers had caught the perpetrator as Shep chased him from the house and he was in police custody. And while he wasn't the Goldilocks Interloper, news of the lockup would surely discourage future break-ins.

Matty, Ben, and Shep came out in whatever they had slept in to investigate the ruckus.

"What's the big hoopla about?" Shep asked.

"It's for you," Andie was the first to volunteer. "You're a hero, Shep!"

The small crowd clapped and cheered, before parting for one of the security guards to wheel Shep's old bike through.

"Here you go, Shep. If you can handle what you did last night, we all agree that you can definitely handle a two-wheeler."

Shep grimaced at him nonetheless. There was no way he was giving the guard the satisfaction of a smile. Though he was indeed happy. He took his bike and walked it up the ramp—grinning from ear to ear for Ben and Matty. They smiled back in kind. It was most definitely a happy ending.

The policemen explained that they had caught the man in question, a day-tripper who had missed the last boat and who, as Andie had thought, was strung out on something. He was, indeed, more menacing than some guy with the munchies a.k.a. a modern-day Goldilocks. Though by the time he dried out in the cell at the police station in town, he couldn't even remember what he had done. Soon everyone went on their way, except for Pam, Andie, and baby Oliver, who wanted a few moments alone with Shep.

Matty was holding up the bike while Shep was inspecting it.

"Need a hand with that?" Andie asked.

"No, we got it."

She choked up. "I wanted to thank you again, Shep. I don't know what would have happened if you didn't—"

Shep interrupted, "Forget about it. Nothing happened."

"Yes, well, OK, but regardless, we want you to come by tomorrow night for a big steak dinner . . . to thank you," Pam offered.

Two monarch butterflies on their yearly migration appeared, dancing in between them as they spoke. September was indeed just around the corner.

"Sure, we could use some meat and potatoes. Can I bring Ben and the kid?" Shep asked.

"Yes, yes. Of course."

Andie looked around. "You still staying over here, Shep?"

"Yeah, why? You think it's strange?"

"No—maybe."

"Get the WD-40 from the shed," Shep instructed Matty.

Andie took the handlebars from him.

"Let me ask you something," Shep expounded. "You ever have a guy stop you and ask you for directions?"

"Yeah, of course."

"And sometimes, if the directions are hard to explain, you ever just say to the guy, 'Follow me and I'll show you the way'?"

"Yeah, I've done that."

"Same thing here."

She smiled and nodded in understanding as Matty returned with the WD-40.

"On second thought—we have to take a rain check. My daughter Bea is coming for Labor Day weekend."

"She is?" Matty asked, surprised.

"Yup. Soon as I call her and tell her to."

thirty-six

Beatrix

Beatrix Silver arrived on the 7:00 a.m. boat and was in our kitchen making her mother's famous frittata before the boys even woke. As I watched her wipe down the counter like a pro, I felt a sense of relief—as sexist as it may sound; I was happy to have a live woman in the house. I was sure she would at least use plates and maybe, after she scrubbed the counters clean, locate the source of the rancid stench that had all three sniffing, then grimacing, whenever they entered the house. I was not surprised. I had seen each of these guys reach under their beds and put on a pair of dirty socks on more than one occasion.

The smell of the frittata overrode all, and it was clear from their faces as they descended from the bedrooms that the residents of our former Love Shack were happy to have a live woman around as well. Shep wrapped his eldest daughter in his arms, stepped back to inspect her, as parents do, and then wrapped her up again.

After breakfast, the two of them took a long walk on the beach.

"Do you think he'll go home now?" Matty asked after they left.

Ben laughed. "I guess."

Matty's face held an odd expression, and Ben read it as concern. "Don't worry, you're still welcome to stay."

"Thanks. I'm worried about more than that. School starts next week, and it doesn't seem like the barefoot drummer is hitting the road anytime soon."

"Still no shoes?"

"Still no shoes."

"Well, that's a good sign—hard to walk barefoot in the big city."

"My dad's coming to watch the big game tomorrow—so we'll see what happens with him and my mom."

There had been no word of the apology letter since Tuck's last visit. I was the only one who even knew that Renee had read it.

"Are you hoping they'll get back together?"

"All I'm hoping is to survive the next two years and then get into a good college somewhere far away."

I wasn't surprised he said that. Many kids I knew in high school whose parents divorced got as far away as they could when it was time for college. Collateral damage runs deep when these things aren't handled well, and this divorce was most definitely not handled well.

Bea and Shep returned in time for batting practice. And Renee, who had taken her usual spot on the stands, *New York Times* in tow, jumped from the bleachers at the first sight of her old friend Bea. They embraced and separated to get a good look at each other before embracing again. Underneath a spattering of fine lines and errant grays were the same two kids who spent their childhood summers painting shells and playing walkie-talkie hide-and-seek up and down the streets of Bay Harbor.

I was eager to hear what Renee had to say to one of her oldest friends. I knew they hadn't stayed in close touch over the years. Renee was not the greatest keeper of girlfriends; she claimed she didn't have much use for more than one or two at a time. But she clearly loved Bea, and that hadn't changed.

"God, how long has it been?" Bea asked.

"Well, I saw you at your mom's funeral."

"I wasn't really all there then. I'm so sorry about Julia; I know how close you were."

"Thank you. She was my adult version of you—my summer sister—come sit." She added, "Matty's on deck."

They climbed back up into the bleachers, and I copped a squat next to them, eager to be in on their catching up.

"So—word is you're seeing someone," Bea said.

"I don't know if I would say that. But I did meet a really nice guy who is the polar opposite of Tuck."

"In what way?"

"In every way you could imagine."

"You seem smitten," Bea observed with a mischievous smile.

Renee turned red—red as a tomato, and I knew right then and there that she had let herself go with Gabe. If I were around, there is no doubt she would have spilled all the tawdry details to me, like a kid descending from her first roller-coaster ride. I recognized the look on her face before Beatrix even asked the question. I remember a time, at the beginning of mine and Ben's relationship, when I felt closer to him, sexually, than I had ever felt to anyone before. Truly naked. We would make love so intimately that I would find myself daydreaming about it the next day with that same look on my face. I'd be at work, in the middle of a meeting, and feel my cheeks redden with warmth.

Tuck Tucker had little chance of winning her back now.

Renee got herself together.

"I'm not sure about that, but I will say that in the short time I've known him he's taught me how to slow down and be in the moment. Yesterday we spent the day on the beach and came home around three, sunburned and sandy. We showered and climbed onto my bed for a nap. I swear it was my first nap since I was a little kid. And even then I wasn't a big napper. It was perfection."

I was a big fan of that post-beach nap when you lie down on top of your covers, sunburned and squeaky clean and drift off till dinnertime. People are always touting the disco nap and the catnap, but I'm telling you—this is *the* nap. It just needs a catchy name.

"Well, I can't wait to meet this guy—he sounds like just what you need right now. Bring him to dinner at my dad's house tonight? Eight o'clock?"

"I'd love to!"

Renee reached out for another hug. "So happy to see you, Bea."

"Me too—I'm so happy to be here."

thirty-seven

Bea's Secret

That afternoon, Bea helped get Shep set up back home, before cooking a big paella dinner over at their house. She used Caroline's recipe, and it tasted like a memory to anyone who'd had it before. Besides Ben, a bunch of her old friends came, Little Les and Darcy, Eddie, Rico, Steve from the hardware store, Pam and Andie, and Renee and the drummer—who, I hate to say, was wearing shoes. And not just flip-flops—the guy was wearing high-tops, fully laced. He seemed to always be touching Renee, his hand on the small of her back or a finger gently twirling her hair. They were definitely in that stage where you can't keep your hands off each other, or at least he was, which must have felt so good for Renee—to be wanted like that after what had happened with Tuck.

I watched Ben mix his own drink at the bar cart. He used to make quite an effort fixing a cocktail—even fancied himself an amateur mixologist—always whipping up something new for me to try. Lately, he barely bothered retrieving an ice cube. Now as he mixed bourbon, triple sec, and even some simple syrup and a lime, I smiled. It was a step in the right direction. I could tell that people weren't treating him quite as tentatively as they had been, and I considered that a good thing too. I'm sure he did, as well. Two months is a long time to be under a microscope.

Everyone helped with the dishes until Shep kicked them out to get some sleep before the big game. Ben went home and grabbed Sally for a walk on the beach. She found a stray tennis ball and nudged at him till he gave in. He sat on the bottom stair, tossing it, hoping a good game of fetch would tire her out.

"You gonna be OK tonight, Ben, all alone in that big bed?" Bea called out from the top step.

I hoped her question came from a place of caring and not a yearning to let down her hair, slip from her dress, and stand naked and timorous like Fanca Sigal in the loving gaze of Jack Koslowsky in the Sicilian moonlight.

"I'll manage." Ben laughed.

Truth was, Shep had already instructed him to sleep in the middle and put pillows next to him on either side to curb the loneliness. Bea came down the steps and stood on the beach, feeling its cold surface beneath her bare feet and digging in. I could tell it felt good. She was a real Fire Island girl, happiest with sand between her toes.

"Thank you for taking care of my dad."

"That paella was thanks enough. Much better than Shep's Frank and Bean Surprise."

"And you slept in a bed with him, so you know what the surprise is!"

They both laughed, until Bea got serious.

"Seriously though. It meant a lot to us, knowing he wasn't alone."

I wondered who "us" was. I imagined it was her and her sister, which made me wonder if there was still something left of their bond, for Bea to include her in the thank-you like that.

"He honestly has been taking care of me. Though I've eaten enough hot dog surprise to last a lifetime. Have you always been such a good cook?"

"When you live in a small college town with few decent restaurants, you have little choice. Plus, I love making my mom's recipes. Makes me feel like she's still here."

"It really was delicious."

"I wanted to make something special. Too bad Matty couldn't make it."

"He has to hang out with people his own age once in a while—it's been a tough summer for him."

"Renee taking up with that drummer—who would have thunk?"

"I forgot you two know each other."

"Yes, we go way back, though we lost touch when her folks got divorced and sold the house. I couldn't believe it when she bought across from my parents."

"Small world."

"Small Fire Island world, for sure."

Sally returned with the tennis ball and dropped it at Beatrix's feet. Bea threw it and then took a seat next to Ben on the stairs.

"The stars are beautiful tonight," she said.

Ben rested his elbows on the step behind him and looked up. "They really are." He took a beat. "I just began to notice them again."

I was surprised he was being so open, but not unhappy about it. He'd been repressing so much, I worried he may suffocate. As much as watching him cry in my sweaters was painful, at least it was a release.

"I can't even imagine what the past year was like for you, and for Julia. I mean, did you even have a chance to grieve the baby?"

"Not really. Julia's illness rode right over that. It was like baptism by fire—we went right into saving Julia mode."

He was right. He went from starting a family to burying one in an instant.

Then he said something that shocked me.

"I have a lot of guilt about the baby. You know, I didn't really want a family. I liked the life we had together and didn't see where a baby would fit into it. When we lost him, I was devastated and felt maybe it was my fault. It was like I didn't want him enough until I realized I couldn't have him."

His words were just what I didn't know I needed to hear. I never really expressed my true feelings on the subject and didn't even realize that I was still holding on to them. I was angry at him for his initial apathy, and taking that anger to the grave was really an awful feeling. Especially since my love for Ben and his for me was truly my greatest gift in life. As he spoke I felt that anger drift from my heart like a swirl of smoke from a campfire.

"It was a boy?" Bea asked.

"It was a boy," Ben echoed.

"I know how you feel—about not wanting a baby until you realize you can't have them. I sort of lost a child too, a girl, though through much different circumstances."

"I'm sorry," he said, noting that once again his heartache implored others to spill theirs.

"Do you know what happened between me and Veronica?"

"Just how that lifeguard Logan Chase got between you. He's still here you know—tends bar at the Old Pelican and seems to drink up his tip money. She may have done you a favor."

"There's a lot more to the story than that. No one really knows all of it, especially now that my mom's gone."

She took a beat before asking, "Want to hear it?" It was clear she wanted to tell it.

"Sure," he said, patting her on the knee for encouragement.

"It's a long story," she warned.

"I don't know if you know this, but my first novel was seven hundred pages."

"I know, I read it."

"So there you go—consider this your revenge."

She laughed, leaning back against the higher stair like Ben, avoiding eye contact. I'm sure Ben was thankful for the shift. She took in the sky before beginning.

"So yes, Veronica stole my boyfriend—my first boyfriend mind you, Logan Chase, and while he may not seem like anything special now, he was the hottest guy on the beach back then. It was a big deal, because you may be shocked to know that I was not the hottest girl on the beach—that was my sister."

Ben interjected with the requisite, "I doubt that," to which Bea patted him on the arm appreciatively and continued.

"I was so angry that I went up to school early and refused to come home for Thanksgiving. I was depressed and exhausted all the time, and just wanted to sleep for the break. My parents were upset. It was a big deal not to come home, but they figured I would be back for Christmas soon enough and they would deal with the fallout between me and Veronica then. About a week later, my best friend from the city, Dana Blum, showed up at my door. She was one of the few home friends I had confided in about the shit that went down with Veronica, and she was worried about me when I hadn't come home.

"I'll never forget it. I was wearing vintage railroad-striped Guess overalls and Dana wanted to try them on. I felt like I hadn't taken them off in a week. When I did, she freaked out. I was about five months pregnant with a belly the size of a small basketball. I hadn't even noticed it or realized that I hadn't gotten my period since the summer."

I was surprised that Beatrix could be like one of those girls who goes to the bathroom with a stomachache and comes out with a baby. From my experience in the short time I was pregnant, I didn't get it—but it happens.

"Dana made me call my mom, whom I made promise not to tell my dad, which I am pretty sure she took to her grave."

"Wow." Ben finally spoke.

He was an awful secret keeper, which was most likely the source of his "Wow." He couldn't keep a single thing from me—let alone hold on to something like that for life.

Bea continued, "I know. I feel guilty about it now. Making her hold something back as big as that from her husband must have been awful. She arrived in Gambier the next day. I'd never even been to the gynecologist until my mother took me then."

"No wonder you're still mad at Veronica."

"That's not even all of it. I carried the baby to term, hiding my pregnancy the whole time from everyone but my mom and Dana. It wasn't so hard; I'm on the heavy side, and the trend at the time was oversize flannels and leggings. I got a research job for one of my professors over winter break, so I had an excuse to stay put.

"The baby was born about two weeks before graduation. My mom flew down in advance—'Bea is depressed again,' she told my dad. I gave birth at a birthing center in Mount Vernon on May 3 to a beautiful baby girl. Six pounds, three ounces with a thick patch of black hair and a dimpled smile just like mine and my dad's. I held her for a few minutes before they swiped her away from me. And that was it. I graduated two weeks later with a big fat Kotex pad stuck between my legs."

She looked over at Ben and laughed. "Sorry. TMI."

He looked stunned, and not on account of the Kotex.

"That's awful, Bea, I'm sorry."

"I know that I made all those choices myself, but I still daydream about what would have happened if Veronica hadn't slept with him. I swear I would have kept that baby and married Logan Chase. I'm not saying we would have lived happily ever after, like I had pictured us doing at the time, but I would have my daughter."

"And you never had kids," he said, sadly pointing out the obvious.

"Nope. And my sister has two, who I don't even know. I just met them at my mother's funeral for, like, two seconds."

I couldn't imagine being estranged from Nora like that. Not that *my* mother would ever allow it.

"Have you ever thought about finding your daughter?" Ben asked.

"More like have I ever not thought about finding her? As luck would have it, the adoption agency burned down years ago, which didn't much matter because it was a closed adoption."

"DNA tracing?"

"I did 23andMe—no close match. And you know, if she wanted to find me, she would have done it too—so there's that."

"Well, maybe. I mean, closed adoptions are pretty rare, even back then. There's a chance she doesn't even know that she's adopted. I'm sorry, Bea."

"It's OK." She reached over and took Ben's hand. "I wish I could find her, but what else can I do? I'm happy in my life, I love my job, and my students feel like my children, plus I'm dating a really great guy right now, a professor too—American history."

"I'm glad you're happy, and don't worry. Your secret's safe with me."

"I think I'm done hiding it. Especially now that my mom's gone and my dad can't get angry with her for keeping my secret."

She stood and stretched her legs.

"Maybe it's time I tell the world, maybe that's the only way I'll find her."

She patted Ben lovingly on the shoulder.

"I should get back, help Dad get settled in."

"I'm gonna miss him," Ben admitted.

"There's still a few more days of summer."

"I may stay here for a couple of months this fall and write."

"That's great!" she said, flashing her dimpled smile. "What's the new book called?"

"I have no idea," Ben responded, but this time his eyes lit up. It gave me hope that something was brewing.

thirty-eight

Chasing Dolphins

The next morning Ben got up early and pulled his paddleboard out of the back shed where he had left it untouched for the entire summer. In the past, when I heard him rise in the morning to board, I would ask about the conditions. He wouldn't know what flag it was till he got up to the beach and looked toward the lifeguard stand, but he always consulted a weather app before leaving the house. If the wind was somewhere around five miles an hour, I would roll over and go back to sleep. If it were closer to twenty, I would throw on shorts and come along in order to keep a watchful eye on him from the shore. Not that I could have saved him, but I could always scream for help, or at least die trying.

Ben didn't necessarily appreciate my vigilance. In fact, I'm pretty sure he resented it. I brought a fear along with me that was palpable, and no doubt jangled his nerves. It wasn't good to have jangled nerves on a board in the middle of the ocean with twenty-mile-an-hour winds and God knows what swimming beneath you, just so your five-foot-nothing weak swimmer of a wife could grieve your death with less guilt.

As he pulled on his wetsuit, I thought of my first and last attempt to paddleboard on the Atlantic. I was so excited when Ben had presented me with our anniversary-of-meeting gift, an occasion we rarely marked with more than a good bottle of wine. With the proudest look-how-good-I-did-with-this-gift face, he dramatically unveiled his and hers paddleboards so that we could continue and improve what we had just begun getting the hang of in Lanai.

"It's a perfect day to try," Ben had preached. "Green flags and winds near five miles an hour."

I was filled with nervous energy as I carried my board up over the beach stairs. I pictured myself standing at the water's edge, facing the horizon, board lassoed to my ankle. Once there, I would find my spot, time it perfectly, and without hesitation jump on and paddle over the shore break, just as I had done in Lanai.

"Our mission today is chasing dolphins," Ben had exclaimed, bouncing from foot to foot like a kid. I had shivered with excitement at the thought of it. I'd heard Fire Island boarders talk about the rare charge of witnessing a pod of dolphins circling them in the middle of the ocean. We had once seen a whale in Lanai. It was far in the distance, but close enough that we could hear it slapping its fins as it breached. It was magnificent—even Ben seemed tiny in comparison.

I took a deep breath in and pushed away the nerves that were forming in my belly as we got close to the intimidating shoreline. My heart raced while my mind fought to keep my anxiety at bay (where I wished I had been instead—the bay would have been much more my speed).

You can't do this, Julia. No way! my realistic side chimed in. *You're not one of those surfer girls.*

By the time I stood my board up in the sand at the shore, my hands were trembling in fear. "I can't do it," I admitted out loud. "I'm sorry."

"Yes, you can. You got this!" Ben assured me. His pep talk did nothing but annoy me. It felt like his encouragement stemmed more from his eagerness to get on with the adventure than concern for me.

"These don't seem like five-mile-an-hour winds," I stated, to bolster my case.

I knew from other boarders and surfers that circumstances switch quickly on the water. You had to always be ready for a north wind to come off the bay out of nowhere, pushing you farther out to sea, and making it hard to come back.

Kind of like cancer, I thought now, looking back.

"It's so different from Lanai," I'd pointed out.

I hadn't thought of the difference between the conditions before. The place we learned to board at in Lanai was in a cove, making it more akin to a lake than an ocean.

Ben wasn't having it.

"It's the same, in theory. Just find the sweet spot. Don't hesitate. Jump on your board—nose to the wave."

Not to sound dramatic, but when you stand facing your own mortality at the ocean's edge, getting into the water at just the right time, with the waves pounding the shore, proves quite terrifying.

"Follow me, babe—you got this!" Ben yelled, entering the surf with ease.

I tried, I really did, but barely stepped forward. When he realized I hadn't followed, he waded back, clearly not happy. It felt like some test of endurance that I had no desire to take, and couldn't believe he was expecting me to pass.

We ended up having our biggest fight ever, with him repeatedly trying to coax me through the dramatic timing of navigating the heavy waves at shore break, and me ending up sitting on my board in the sand, crying. It was a bad day and, after that, I never attempted paddle boarding again, not even on the bay.

But today was different. It was Ben who seemed hesitant about entering the ocean, while my anxiety and fear of death were no longer a factor. He successfully made his move, and I jumped right on and sat at the end of his board. My legs hung off the sides, each pushing through the water like the rudder of a sailboat. It was exhilarating.

The sun was just right; the wind was perfect and, without fear weighing me down, I slipped between Ben's powerful chest and his outstretched arm as he paddled farther and farther from the coast. I had never felt more alive.

As we glided out into the open ocean past the second break, my heart sang.

My God, I'm gonna make it! I'm gonna survive!

And even though I was already dead, my thoughts never strayed from that vibe. Ben stopped paddling after the third break of waves and we stared out as far as our eyes could see, which felt quite far. It was a unique perspective of ourselves, so small compared to such a vast sea.

Sound is different on the ocean. It was quiet except for the repetition of the small waves lapping on the edge of the board and the crashing of the huge ones on the shore in the distance. The light bounced off the water, changing what we could see and what we couldn't by the second.

"Wow!" I said, out loud.

"Wow!" he agreed.

It was the first time that Ben had been completely alone,

without even Sally, since I'd died. He seemed to realize it. A weird expression came over his face, and I couldn't determine what he was thinking. I hoped he was enjoying it. I had rarely seen him enjoy anything that used to make him happy. Last week he bit into a Mallomars cookie (his favorite) and broke down in tears. He had to spit it out, couldn't even swallow it.

He stood in the center of the board and yelled out my name as if screaming to the heavens, in a barreling, heart-wrenching voice, "Julia!"

He slowly lowered himself down onto his knees and then straddled his feet on either side of the board. Tears poured down his cheeks.

I spun around and whispered in his ear, "I'm here, I'm here," then looped my legs over his. Face-to-face, I whispered, "I love you Benjamin Morse and always will. Losing the baby was no one's fault, especially not yours."

It seemed impossible to me that he didn't feel my presence. I felt so entwined with his.

We sat on the paddleboard in the same pretzel-like fashion for a long while, staring at the vast ocean. His feet were cold and waterlogged, mine warm and perfectly smooth—another perk, I thought. It was definitely time to head back and get ready for the big game, but it seemed as though he had no intention of doing so.

"I'm sorry we didn't see a dolphin, Jules," he said out loud.

"It's OK, baby. It wasn't in the cards for me."

Just when we had given up, a dorsal fin appeared in the distance, maybe twenty feet away. As it swam closer, I could see that it was on the back of a creature that looked at least as long as our board. I couldn't tell if it was a dolphin or a shark, and wondered if Ben, who had reported seeing both before, could tell the difference. I held my breath as the fin came closer. When you go up against nature, you never really know what it's going to throw at you, and this seemed like one of those instances.

Ben took the paddle and tapped it on the board. "Come 'ere buddy," he said, leaving me to presume it was a dolphin. Though in his state, I couldn't be sure.

The creature glided through the sea and leaped through the air less than ten feet away, as if to say hello. It *was* a dolphin! As the sun danced on the water, it kept disappearing from sight and reappearing a few minutes later, somewhere completely different. We looked around for the rest of its pod, but it seemed to be on its own.

"It's an Atlantic bottle-nosed dolphin," he told me, "a big one!"

"Huge!" I said, surprised at the size of the friendly creature.

I've heard that dolphins have saved humans from drowning, that they can feel and understand human distress and struggle. The dolphin reappeared, swam underneath our board, and brushed its back against the bottoms of our feet, as if expressing empathy.

Ben's mouth dropped open in awe. And then, that twinkle—the beautiful, youthful, magical twinkle that I had missed so dearly—returned to his eyes. Mine welled with tears—which surprised me in my current state, until I realized they were tears of joy.

The playful dolphin swam around and up to our board for quite some time before jumping high in the air again and swimming away, its fin finally disappearing in the distance.

I saw a familiar look cross over Ben's face. His aha look, I used to call it.

"Oh my God—I got it, Jules, I got it!"

He stood with a new strength and paddled us back to the shore.

Sally was waiting for us on the sand. As soon as she saw us approach, she began zooming in and out of the water until we were safely on land. Ben pulled down the top of his wetsuit and let it hang from his waist, tucked the board under his arm, and headed toward the house. A couple was sitting on the top step of our block, deep in conversation.

It was Renee and Tuck.

thirty-nine

For Your Consideration

I've spent so much time making sport of dissing Tuck that I've neglected to mention his good points. He does have his good points. Like, for example, he loves to read and is very neat—not like neato neat, but actually tidy. Truth is, if none of this had happened and Renee and Tuck had been sitting on the beach, let's say forty-odd years from now, and Tuck had finally decided to swim and been taken away by the undertow or had choked to death on the olive in his martini, people would have said he was a good man, a loyal man. They would have noted his long and faithful marriage to his wife, Renee, his strengths as a father, and by then, I'd imagine, a grandfather, and how, when his mother was alive, he visited her every Tuesday night at the home with her favorite pea soup and rugelach.

Renee would have thought back to their many family vacations, her favorites being Maui and Norway, and the time they took a bike trip through Tuscany. She would have reflected on their early days with Matty, the two of them armed with the notes they had meticulously taken at a new-parenting class at the 92nd Street Y—one of them nervously barked out the diapering and bathing and feeding instructions while the other attempted them. She would have remembered the time they stayed up all night when Matty had croup or rushed him to the emergency room when he had fallen from the top of the pyramid at the playground near the Met—seven stitches. And she surely would have waxed nostalgic about Tuck's sweet marriage proposal, when he had taken her to Paris and got down on one knee on the Pont des Arts, after attaching a lock of their own to the famous bridge. The proposal might not have been the most original, but the thought of Tuck meticulously painting their initials and a heart on the aforementioned lock with her jar of Essie Geranium Red nail lacquer made her heart melt.

And she wouldn't have had regrets, because spending her life with Tuck, dull reliable Tuck, had been just what she had thought she needed. A fulfilled life.

Unfortunately for Tuck, who wanted his old, fulfilled life back, Renee now knew better.

It was a lesson on the dangers of infidelity—not a scare-the-shit-out-of-you lesson, like that famous scene in *Fatal Attraction* with the boiling bunny, but a lesson just the same.

"I want my family back more than I've ever wanted anything. If you forgive me, Renee, I will spend the rest of my life making it up to you—and to Matthew."

Renee was silent for a beat, then snapped into lawyer mode.

"When did you realize this, Tuck—and why?"

"I made a mistake. The biggest mistake of my life. I know how people look at me. I know I'm a short, balding know-it-all. I see people glancing at their watches when talking to me at cocktail parties or in the market. I wasn't looking to be unfaithful to you, really, but Lola looked at me in a way no one ever had, and so I looked back. In the end, that was really all it was. I woke up one day a few weeks ago desperately missing my family."

"And Lola?"

He laughed. "You suddenly care about Lola?"

"I'm just asking. The last I heard from Matty, you two were going to become engaged."

Her line of questioning was curious. Was she leading the witness, thinking Tuck would say that Lola dumped him, and that's why he wanted to come back home? I hoped that wasn't the case. Whether she let him back or not, I hoped she would feel vindicated by him wanting her in the end for reasons of his own, not because he was dumped. I've seen people take back husbands or wives after infidelity and go on to have many wonderful years together, but she certainly didn't deserve to be a consolation prize.

"I realized the engagement idea was a big mistake. I told her I missed my family and let her have the rental house in the Hamptons to herself for the rest of the season." He surprisingly rolled his eyes, adding, "I'm sure she's having the time of her life."

Just when I thought things may go the way of reconciliation, Renee pivoted.

"Do you know what I loved most about you, Tuck?"

"I don't." He smiled, also hoping this was going in the right direction.

"That I could always count on you."

His face dropped.

"That is gone, you know, that trust that meant more to me than anything else? It's gone. My biggest fear, being lied to and left, like I watched happen to my mother, it came to fruition, and I survived it. There isn't much that you bring to the table now, aside from the fact that you're the father of my son."

She was completely disenchanted with him, or more so unenchanted, as if she was just now realizing how low she had set the bar to begin with.

It was harsh. Tuck was speechless. Until he finally asked, "Wait. Is this about that drummer? After everything you said to me about Lola, you're choosing that child drummer over me?" He laughed scornfully, his colossal ego reemerging again, overriding his brief foray into self-awareness.

"Well, I'm hoping the drummer—Gabe is his name—will stay around for a while longer, because I *really* enjoy his company, but I am not 'choosing' him." Renee made little air quotes when she said "choosing," and ended with a Benjamin Morse novel-worthy pronouncement.

"I'm choosing me."

Ah! Just the ending I would have written for her. My inner editor beamed with satisfaction, and my inner BFF with pride.

Renee stood and walked toward the house, turning back to him once more, to leave things on a more civil note. "See you at the game, Tuck!" she yelled with a smile.

He stared at her blankly before sinking back onto the stairs to lose himself in the ebb and flow of the one thing that could weather any storm.

forty

The Big Game

Whereas on any other summer weekend, the stands on the ball field were filled with patches of onlookers who came and went, doing more chatting than watching, the big game carried a much grander, more competitive vibe. It was an event, a culmination of the summer, and an annual tradition that marked the passage of time.

Seated on the left-field set of bleachers, we had the people rooting for Bay Harbor, on the right for Oceanview. The men, and this year one gutsy woman, were divided as well: Bay Harbor in blue, Oceanview in red. Usually the teams are a mixed bag—this is the only game of the summer that pits one town against the other. The air was tense with competition. I'm not joking or imitating my sportswriter husband's vernacular, it really was. Aside from the glory and the bragging rights, the winning team gets their name inscribed on a giant trophy (think Stanley Cup) that sits in the winning town's market until the following Labor Day.

Both teams warmed up together on the field as each player took a turn at BP (batting practice). Joel passed out T-shirts that read, *BAY HARBOR VS. OCEANVIEW HOMEOWNERS' GAME.*

With *SPONSORED BY VIAGRA* written on the back.

Everyone looked at them and laughed—except for the one woman.

I will do my best with the play-by-play. It's not really my thing, but I have been sufficiently schooled in it over the years. So, here it goes:

Eddie stepped up to the plate for BP. Matty was on deck. Ben was catching.

"How you feeling, pal?" Eddie asked Ben while kicking up the dirt a little—as one does.

"Pretty good today, thanks."

It may have been the first time he wasn't lying. The dolphin-induced sparkle in his eyes was still in play, and while his shoulders remained hunched from the weight of the world, I recognized the very specific look he got when his brain was working on a new idea. You could almost see his mind trying to keep track of all its thoughts while still concentrating on the game.

The ball crossed over the plate, and Eddie hit a pop fly into the outfield. Shep caught it and did a little celebratory dance, holding his mitt in the air. These type of shenanigans were short-lived—everyone would get serious once batting practice ended and the actual game began. Very serious. Traditionally, it's painful to watch.

"Good timing with him getting that bike back," Eddie noted, regarding Shep's great catch and happy dance.

"More like getting his dignity back," Ben agreed.

Eddie took a few more swings before handing the bat to Matty, who immediately hit what would count as a home run in the actual game—up and over the rooftop of the second house in right field. I say up and over because this is often a field-clearing argument. Some of these men like to argue even more than they like to play ball. Not Ben, he's more the peacemaker, but boy, a lot of them really get into it. Unlike the calamitous repercussions for hitting it over the left-field net onto the tennis courts, right-field shots are fair game. The general rule is, if it's over the rooftop of one of the right-field houses, it's a homer; if it hits or goes under one of them, it's a double, and if they can't decide if it cleared the roof or hit the house, they will argue for five minutes before compromising on a triple.

Matty did a casual victory lap around the bases just for fun as Ben pulled down the catcher's mask and yelled, "Beautiful hit, Matty!"

Rico looked up from making the roster, shouting, "Save it for the game, kid!" with Shep countering proudly, "My boy's got plenty more where that came from. Don't you worry!"

The guys all stood around Rico as he put the finishing touches on the batting order and fielding positions. It's a real ego thing with these guys. Aside from one just being seen as better than another, there is also the age factor. Two older men who had a ten-year rivalry over first base were both disappointed when he gave that position to Matty.

Matty hid both a smile and his nerves.

"Look at that. A ten-year conflict resolved for the greater good."

"Maybe we should send Rico to the Middle East."

Matty slipped on his shirt proudly as Joel patted him on the back.

"First time in the big game, kid. You nervous?"

"A little. Mostly psyched."

"Good luck, Matty" was heard from all except the rival first basemen, who were suddenly commiserating with each other like best buds.

Dylan arrived, and Matty lit up.

"It's time to get serious, boys. It's been three years, and I want that trophy back!" Shep proclaimed passionately.

Bay Harbor was up first, because in this game home-field advantage goes to whomever won the year before. It's called an advantage because the team that bats second gets last licks.

Rico grabbed his clipboard and announced, "Top of the order. Tony's up, Joel's in the hole."

The game began with a triple and a double, putting Bay Harbor in the lead. Oceanview got one run and then out, and things went that way, back and forth and back and forth, until the fifth inning. At this point I lost track, until the ump changed the score on the board and announced, "Bottom of the fourth, five to three—Oceanview."

Rico read out the order for the inning, "Matty, Ben, Shep."

Matty stepped up to the plate. He let the first pitch fly by. He swung at the second and missed. The third hit his bat with a piercing crack and the ball ascended straight over the house in right field. The now huge crowd cheered; yelling an array of classic ball game jargon that I never quite understood.

"It's a dinger!"

"It's a yard job!"

"It's a Texas leaguer!" as Matty casually took his victory lap.

Ben was warming up on the sidewalk when Josie showed up on my yellow bike, squeezing the ducky horn to get his attention. Her friend was riding a tandem behind her and had stopped to talk to someone she knew.

"Hey, Ben, I found your street!" Josie called out, following it up with her beautiful smile.

Ben's face softened when he looked at her. It was one of the few times since my death that I had seen the pain leave his gaze. He answered her, uncomfortably, as opposed to apathetically. I considered it a win.

"Oh, hey, um, OK. You could just put it in my shed, if you don't mind. I'm up next."

"I'll watch first," she said sweetly, before catching eyes with Pam and Andie in the crowd. By the time Matty reached home plate, Josie was sitting in the stands with them, bouncing baby Oliver on her knee.

Matty partook in a round of celebratory cheers and high fives, and Renee and Tuck both proudly embraced him in a family hug. For a second, they looked as if they had reconciled, and I could feel all eyes on them. Renee could too, I'm sure. She took a step back and waved excitedly to the drummer in the stands.

He waved back at her, yelling, "Way to go, Matty!" He was again wearing shoes.

Ben breathed through the pressure and took his stance at home plate. Roger pitched. Ben swung low and missed.

"Strike one," said the ump.

"What are you, golfing?" Eddie quipped.

Ben swung again.

"Strike two!"

"C'mon, son, get some wood," Shep encouraged.

"You got this!" his new friend Josie piped in feverishly from the stands.

It made Ben smile. A hush came over the crowd. The next ball was pitched and then—*Ding! Boom!* Right over the tree in right field! The crowd went crazy, shouting more joyous ballplayer lingo as Ben ran the bases.

"It's a moonshot over the bush."

"Two in a row!"

"A back-to-back!"

As Ben rounded home, he and Matty jumped in the air and bumped back-to-back in victory. Josie stood and clapped vigorously for Ben, who clearly got a kick out of her unbridled enthusiasm.

Shep got up to bat. A young kid, his designated pinch runner, stood to his right. As always, Shep ignored the first pitch completely. Then came the second:

Pitch—swing—*zing!* And miraculously the ball flew just over the house in right field.

It was a big deal, a man of Shep's age hitting a ball like that. When he was younger the guys would yell "Big stick" and "Move back" when Shep approached the plate. But it had been years since he'd even gotten a double. He told the pinch runner, "I got this one, kid."

And he jogged the bases, milking it for all it was worth. It was worth a lot. The crowd on both sides went nuts, and Beatrix clearly had tears in her eyes. Our side was wild, yelling, "Three-peat" and "Back-to-back-to-back!" and "Trifecta!" The other team was comically countering with calls of "Steroids?" and "Get me the first aid kit—I want to do a urine test!"

Shep strode past home plate, and the three men bumped their backs together in victory. As they separated, Josie came down from the stands and approached Ben.

"Wow, that was great!" she said, clearly meaning it.

"Yeah—that happens all the time."

"Really?"

Ben laughed. "No, absolutely not."

They both laughed some more. Josie glanced at her watch.

"I wish I could stay for the rest of the game, but we're catching the next boat out."

"That's OK," he said.

"Wait, I almost forgot." She reached into her pocket and discreetly slipped Ben a tutti fruity condom.

"Amazing! Thank you so much."

"See you next summer?" she asked, looking straight into his eyes.

His pupils widened, and his eyes lit up in the way they did when tasting the perfect bite of steak or when he figured out the ideal word or plot twist.

He answered, "I hope so," before adding more confidently, "Yes, that would be great."

A warm, wide smile erupted on her face in response.

I don't know if I can pin it all on Josie's beautiful smile; I suspect the other events of the day: the dolphin sighting, the home runs, and the hope that comes with those first sparks of a new idea all came into play. His expression softened, and his shoulders released as he placed down the sack of boulders, my visual for his pain and suffering. It was only a brief moment before he picked up the miserable load again and threw it back over his shoulder, but in that moment, I made my escape.

"Julia!" Nana Hannah called out, madly waving at me from behind the bleachers.

This time I ran to her.

The game fell back into play as we embraced. I felt a tingling warmth throughout every inch of my body. The smell of her, the way her small frame always lined up on par with mine, allowing for the best hugs I'd ever known. I couldn't believe I was feeling them again.

"I kept thinking people were waving at me, but you actually were!" I laughed.

She laughed too, and we embraced again. I knew it was time to go but asked for a little more.

"Can we watch the end of the game?" I asked, not wanting to spend eternity without knowing its outcome.

"Of course, bubbala," she said.

Oceanview scored one run in that inning and one in the next. The ump approached the scoreboard and announced the score. "Top of the fifth, seven to six, Oceanview."

Three Bay Harbor guys managed to get on base, and two got out—so bases were loaded and there was a full count. The pressure was epic, and Matty was up again.

"Bases loaded, two outs, Matty. This is big," Eddie instructed him, as if he didn't know.

"No kidding."

Matty took a few practice swings on the side as Joel added, "A home run would put us in the lead, kid."

"Leave him be," Shep stepped in, adding quietly, "Remember everything."

"Batter up!"

Matty took the plate as his mom, Tuck, the drummer, Dylan, Bea, Ben, Shep, and the entire rest of the town and me and Nana Hannah looked on anxiously. So, no pressure. On the mound, Roger looked at his ball and slowly threw it out of play, yelling, "New ball!"

"He's like a human rain delay," Ben moaned, his first contribution to baseball-speak all summer. As a sportswriter, he was normally the lexicon king. It was another sign of his brain actually working again.

A new ball was retrieved from the wagon and opened up,

while Matty waited patiently, trying not to succumb to Roger's attempt to psych him out.

"Don't take the first pitch, kid," Shep reminded him for the hundred thousandth time.

Matty nodded respectfully. Roger pitched. Matty swung, surprising everyone on the field, none more than Shep, and the powerful first shot took off in the air—going, going, gone, right over the forty-five-foot net and on to the tennis courts.

The silence was deafening until the ump broke it with, "And he's outta the game!"

The crowd erupted in protest or accolades, depending on which town they hailed from. Matty was shocked. He looked at Shep and mouthed "Sorry." Shep just shook his head. Matty looked down the line at everyone's solemn, angry, or pleading faces. It was a sad day on the Bay Harbor field—until someone got the big idea of enlisting Little Les as Matty's replacement.

Joel and Rico coaxed Little Les off the bleachers and begged him to step in for the last two innings. Both teams were thrilled that he agreed to play. There wasn't a guy there who hadn't followed the ecstasy and agony of his career. Even with the hiatus, they still insisted he bat lefty.

Everyone stood and gave him a standing ovation as he jogged out onto the field. He looked down at his sneakers when he got out there, kicking the ground a bit as he did, clearly trying to keep his emotions in check. When he looked up at the stands at his wife and little boy, his signature killer smile spread across his face.

Ben reached into his pocket and planted Josie's gift in the palm of Matty's hand and whispered, "Think of baseball."

Matty's eyes nearly popped out of his head. He found Dylan at the end of the bench and unclenched his fist, giving her a quick view of what he was clutching.

"Tutti fruity?" she asked curiously.

He just shrugged.

"How many more innings?"

"Two."

"OK, that should be plenty of time. I'll slip away first. You follow in a few," Dylan instructed him, as always, in charge of their adventures.

forty-one

Tutti Fruity

Within minutes of Dylan and Matty's departure—not enough minutes, I should say—Jake arrived to catch the end of the game. He was carrying a big box from the freight boat. He looked to the stands for his daughter and in the field for Matty. I witnessed their absence calibrate on his face and told Nana Hannah, "I'll be right back."

I raced ahead of him to warn them, praying I'd have more success than I did on that now infamous night on the dunes. I rushed in to find them making out right on the living room couch. Matty broke away and looked into Dylan's eyes. He had an urgent look on his face. The sounds and cheers of another home run grabbed his attention, and the look faded as he shifted his focus to the noise of the game, suddenly appreciating Ben's instruction to think of baseball.

He asked, "You ready, Dyl?"

She nodded.

"You sure?"

She nodded again. More cheers erupted in the background, and they laughed at the timing, while I did my best to knock down Jake's vast collection of vintage glass bottles to disrupt them, with zero luck.

Dylan grabbed the condom from the table. A hand-painted clamshell with the words *Happy as a Clam* caught her eye. She stared at it reflectively before handing Matty the condom.

Matty smiled at her; she smiled at him, but, just as he ripped open the flamboyant packaging, she uttered meekly, "Wait."

He froze. "Wait?"

She breathed in and out and in and out trying to wrangle her feelings into words when the telltale sound of cowbells ringing on the front gate sent them flying to opposite ends of the couch.

Jake appeared in the doorway carrying the large box. He placed it down on the floor.

"What are you two up to? I heard Matty got tossed from the game."

Dylan was cool, Matty not at all.

"Yeah, he was upset about it, so we were gonna watch a movie."

She reached over to the side table and grabbed the remote.

Matty suddenly realized he was holding a condom in his hand and quite obviously shoved the contraband behind his back. Jake noticed that he was hiding something. It was hard not to.

"What's in your hand?" he asked suspiciously.

Matty was speechless. I'm sure he wished it was a joint. Hell, even an ounce of crack cocaine would be better than a condom. He looked like he was going to cry.

Dylan, always the one to save the day, remembered the packaging, TUTTI FRUITY.

"Bubble gum, Daddy, tutti fruity."

Matty took her cue and popped the hot pink condom in his mouth as Dyl inquired, in all of her innocence, "You want a piece?"

And with that Matty somehow stretched the pink latex over his tongue and blew a bubble. An actual bubble. It was cinematic.

"No, I don't want a piece." Jake laughed, pushing the carton out of the way with his foot.

"What's in the box?" Dylan asked.

"Stuff for you—I searched on Pinterest under 'Things I Wished I Brought to College.'"

Their mouths dropped open. The words *Pinterest* and *Jake* didn't really fly.

"It's a case of fairy lights, one of those mattress toppers, and a box of condoms."

They both nearly fainted, and I laughed so hard I could swear they heard me.

Jake realized the reason for their expressions. I doubted he had even said the word *sex* to Dylan let alone discussed protection.

"They were on the list," he added, real casually as if he had ordered Band-Aids or bug spray. "You know what I say, Dylan—you should always be prepared."

He quickly changed the subject.

"Want to catch the end of the game? It's too nice out to be inside."

The three of them couldn't get out of the house fast enough.

Shep filled them in when they arrived at the field.

"Looking good. Bottom of the seventh—no outs, man on first and second. Eddie is up, Little Les is in the hole!" With Nana Hannah adding for me, "It's a real nail-biter."

"I hope it's a win—for my last game and all," I told her.

"You'll be back if you want to." She touched my cheek and added, "It's just like baseball. You have to leave home in order to return to it again. Look up there!"

Nana pointed to the rooftop on right field. It was filled with years' worth of Bay Harbor and Oceanview softball fans. I was very surprised to see them all.

"The Rabbi told me there are three generations of past relatives at weddings and bar mitzvahs. I never thought the Homeowners' Game would rate."

"I guess for some, like you, it does."

Eddie hit a powerful line drive and headed to first, loading the bases as everyone cheered. Little Les was on deck. It was as close to a sure thing as possible. It was tense, but bases loaded and no outs was a damn good place to be. Still, no one breathed.

Little Les stood at the plate looking like a major leaguer. He waited out the first pitch.

"Strike!"

And then the second.

"Strike!"

No one dared to make a peep as the third pitch flew from the mound. He connected with it, and the sharp welcome sound of a solid hit reverberated through the air as the ball barreled down the third-base line. The third basemen reached down his mitt and picked it off before it flew by, nearly burning a hole in his glove. He tagged out the runner heading home, stepped on third base for a forced out and then threw the ball to first. The first baseman caught it with ease and stepped on the bag, just seconds before Little Les arrived—smiling at the amazing play. If there was anyone on the field that day who cared more about being in the game than winning it, it was Little Les.

The crowd went wild.

"Triple play!"

"Oceanview!"

"We won!"

"They Lawrence Welk'ed us!"

Nana had to explain the triple-play reference to the old bandleader to me.

"An' a one, an' a two, an' a three!"

Oceanview was ecstatic, Bay Harbor in shock, and Jake, not one known for his humor, surprised them with an excellent joke, "Wow. That came out of left field."

He was full of surprises today.

Matty and Dylan laughed, because it was funny and because it came from Jake. Jake smiled knowingly as Joel yelled out, "Come on, guys, there's always next year!"

Ben and Shep looked at each other and reluctantly agreed to the concept of making it till next year. Shep patted Ben on the back.

"I was thinking of hanging up my cleats, but I guess I can do one more."

The teams lined up on the field to shake hands. I watched as Ben took it all in: Andie holding baby Oliver, who was sucking on a clean softball, Dylan and Jake petting Charlie, the drummer putting his arm around Renee, and Tuck chatting up Lisa Marlin-Cohen-Fitzpatrick at the end of the bleachers—though something told me he didn't like pie.

Big Les and Winnie made a surprise appearance when word got out that Little Les was playing. They pulled up in a golf cart turned mobile hot dog stand in honor of their son being back on the field. Everyone helped themselves to dogs and cold beer.

As the group broke up, Shep noticed a young boy, around eight, standing on the left field foul line, next to the game ball. He called out to him.

"Hey, kid, throw me that ball!"

The young boy whipped it at Shep, who caught it hard in his glove.

"Come here, kid," Shep beckoned.

He inspected the kid's mitt, matching the boy's hand against it.

"This is too small for you. Get your dad to buy you a bigger glove over the winter."

"My dad's not into baseball. He wants me to play tennis."

"Tennis is for pussies, kid."

The kid's eyes widened. Shep smirked and pointed to his own house.

"See that house over there? That's my house. Bring your new mitt to me first weekend you're out next summer—I'll oil it up for you and teach you a few things." He tapped the smiling kid's baseball cap and walked off toward Ben and Matty, who were chatting on the corner.

"So?" Ben asked Matty.

"Let's just say all was not lost today," Matty joked.

It was clear that there was more to the story, but Ben thought it best not to pry.

Instead, he preached, "We always said you shouldn't swing at the first pitch anyway."

Matty smiled, and Ben rustled his hair.

Shep reached them and tossed Ben the game ball. "This is for you, son."

"Really, why me?"

"'Cause you deserve it!"

Ben smiled like a kid.

"Was the woman you were talking to the one from the other night?" Shep asked.

"Yeah."

"Pretty lady. Maybe you'll see her again."

"She comes back every year. I told her she can find me in the same place next summer."

"I sure as hell hope not!" He put his arm around Ben's shoulder and gave it a squeeze. Ben smiled at the love and his spot-on humor.

"You guys heading for the beach?" Ben asked.

"Nah, I'm gonna go home, the drummer—Gabe—offered to show me a few things on my bass," Matty said.

"You play bass?" Shep asked, skeptically.

"I haven't in a while, but I've been wanting to pick it up again. Girls really seem to like musicians, and I've been thinking . . ."

The old man laughed and patted Matty on the back in approval.

"I'm heading home too; Bea has something important to talk to me about. I have no clue what."

Ben had a clue. Shep was in for some surprise. Somewhere out there was a dark-haired young woman who may even be a home run hitter like her grandfather.

"Well, I'm gonna go in and work on my new book!"

They both patted him on the back for encouragement before all going their separate ways.

As Ben headed up our walk I called out to him, "Ben, wait!"

The game ball fell from his mitt and rolled back down the walk.

I am the wind, I thought again, this time truly believing it.

He came to retrieve the ball. As he stood on the sidewalk, I wrapped my arms around his waist and whispered in his ear.

"It's time for me to go."

I could feel an energy, almost a bolt of electricity, leave my body and enter his. It sent a chill up his spine. He quivered as it did.

He felt it. He felt me. I hoped he knew.

Tears filled his eyes, big tears, before pouring down his face.

He knew. He most definitely knew.

"I'll carry you with me always," he said.

"I'll carry you with me always," I said.

We stood as one for a minute more, breathing in the moment. It would never feel like it was time to go, but I knew I had to. I took a step back, and a small sigh escaped Ben's lips. After a moment he turned and headed back home without me.

The Love Shack sign swayed from left to right and left to right as the gate swung closed. I stood there for a beat, staring at the words. Though their meaning had changed during this, my last full summer on Fire Island, they may never have rung more true.

Part Three

What the caterpillar calls the end of the world,
the master calls a butterfly.

—RICHARD BACH,
Illusions: The Adventures of a Reluctant Messiah

forty-two

On Fire Island

Ben kicked off his cleats and splashed some cold water on his face. The house was quiet, and after a full summer of the opposite, it felt like just what he needed. He poured a second cup of coffee, sat down on the lanai, and opened up his iPad. His eyes widened at the sight of the blank page in front of him. He couldn't type fast enough.

He wished it would be as easy to write the following chapter in his life as it would to write this story, but maybe he had to go backward before he could go forward. He stretched out his fingers on the keyboard and typed the title of his next and final book.

On Fire Island

by

Benjamin Morse

And began.

Prologue

In ancient Hebrew, the word for *tomb* and the word for *womb* are one and the same. This is what the Rabbi (and bestselling author) I met at the Random House Christmas party pointed out to me when I told her I was dying.

"We are born twice," she assured me. "Once from the womb and once from the tomb."

forty-three

Two Summers Later

Ben pulled into the narrow gravel road of Wellwood Cemetery and parked in his usual spot. He came there often, but not to the point of concern. It was, after all, right on the way to the ferry. He eventually joined the bereavement group that Julia's Rabbi had first recommended and then insisted on. There, he learned that Julia's Nefesh (the lowest part of her soul) remained in her grave, and that visiting her there helped to elevate her spirit. Aside from that, he found spending time at the sacred space cathartic. Ben had realized quite quickly after Julia passed that she was right: death was not the end. Their love would live on, eternally.

Ben usually sat on the grass in front of Julia's headstone and talked to her about nonsense while Sally lay by his side, her head intuitively in his lap the entire time. He relayed the ups and downs of writing his now very successful sports column, In the Locker Room with Ben Morse, and caught her up about everything that had been going on with their friends and family, spewing it all out in one long soliloquy, not unlike the girls behind the register at the market.

Things like, *Matty had a great freshman year at Pomona College—remember when I had that kooky publicist who went there—and*

Dylan is returning from a whole year at the Galápagos Marine Reserve. Word is she's dating a herpetologist, but don't worry, it's not what it sounds like, it's a turtle expert—and Renee finally outgrew the drummer, she left him somewhere in Ohio on tour. I saw her on Hinge. I haven't swiped left or right on that thing yet, but I'm thinking about it. Oh, and there's good news and bad news—what do you want first? The good news, of course! Andie is pregnant with a baby girl, and guess what they are planning to name her? Julia! Yes, I know your sister will name her baby that, but there can never be too many Julias in the world! The bad news is that Shep's daughters are no closer to reconciliation, and Bea no closer to finding the child she put up for adoption. She's coming out this summer for sure though, so back to good news!

But today was different.

Today, he pulled out a copy of "their" final novel, *On Fire Island*, and leaned it on her headstone.

"You're gonna love this one, Jules—an instant bestseller—and the reviews have been out of the park."

He pulled the *New York Times* from his bag, along with the *Wall Street Journal* and that week's *People* magazine, and read the best parts out loud. When he was through, he placed a perfectly round stone on the *J* in Julia before running his finger over the rest, as if smudging a name on a birthday cake, for luck.

And he left, possibly for the first time without shedding a tear.

An hour later, Ben climbed the stairs of the Fire Island Ferry, a large clam chowder in hand. He looked around to see who he knew—oddly, no one—and grabbed a seat up front. It was quite windy, and the benches were already damp from the spray of the whitecaps on the bay. Ben grabbed the squeegee from its usual spot, like the seasoned Fire Islander that he was, and dried off his seat.

As the island came into view on his inaugural trip of the season, his heart swelled past the parameters of his grief for the first time in a long while. He took in a deep breath of the salty sea air and smiled. He was looking forward to summer, but it felt significantly bigger than that. He felt like he was looking forward.

ACKNOWLEDGMENTS

To my friends and neighbors on Fire Island, my muses, thank you for creating the most inspiring community to both live in and write about. And to my favorite Fire Islander, my husband, Warren, thank you for turning right instead of left in town all those years ago. You make it so easy to write about true love. To our daughters, Raechel, Melodie, and Talia, for completing the dream and filling our home with joy, laughter, and an abundance of ABBA.

To my whip-smart agent and friend, Eve MacSweeney. Lucky me! Lucky me! Lucky me!

To my editor, Amanda Bergeron, who possesses the highly unusual combination of genius and charm. I am so grateful for your time, wisdom, and belief in me. And to Sareer Khader for all you do, and all I don't even know you do!

A special thank-you to Claire Zion, for your invaluable input and insight.

Thank you to the one and only Jin Yu, my ride or die, and to the wonderful new addition to my team, Elisha Katz. Many thanks to the dynamic duo of publicity, Danielle Keir and Tina Joell: your smiling faces over Zoom never cease to make me smile in return. I love working with you both. Many thanks to the talented Vi-An Nguyen for the cover designs, and to Katharine Asher for the beautiful illustration. And to the rest of the team at

Berkley, including but not limited to Ivan Held, Christine Ball, Jeanne-Marie Hudson, Craig Burke, Lindsey Tulloch, and Christine Legon. Thank you!

Endless gratitude to Rabbi Dovid Katz of London's Chabad of West Hampstead for his insightful course on the kabbalistic view of the afterlife, Journey of the Soul. For this being a course about death, I actually took away many beautiful things about life. Thank you to my dearest friend, Lauren Breslauer, for the wonderful introduction.

To my trusted (and loved) first readers, Linda Coppola, Andrea Levenbaum, and Melodie Rosen. Endless thanks for your time, your grammatical prowess, and your insightful commentary. And last but certainly not least, the wonderful literary community of authors, book reviewers, podcasters, and Bookstagrammers, thank you for the endless support. I can't imagine doing it without you.

On Fire Island

JANE L. ROSEN

READERS GUIDE

BEHIND THE BOOK

On Fire Island is the story that has lived in my heart for years, and I am so happy to finally be sharing it with my readers. In many ways, it is my most intimate story yet, encompassing my strong love of place, specifically Fire Island, and my personal relationship with death.

I have been grappling with how to intertwine life and death since I was eleven and lost my dad in a horrific accident. How would I keep him with me throughout my life? How would I not be fatherless? I had similar thoughts when my sister passed away from breast cancer when I was in my early twenties. I needed to keep the connection to them both alive in order to go on to live a healthy, happy life. I needed to believe that they were still with me. It was from that perspective that I set out to write an uplifting take on a heart-wrenching experience—the death of my narrator, Julia Morse, and its effect on her grieving husband.

And what better place to live through immeasurable grief than in a small beach town surrounded by people who love you . . . on Fire Island.

I have spent the happiest days of my life on Fire Island. It is the place where I fell in love with my husband of thirty-one years, and the reason I had my third daughter induced a week before her due date, because summer was slipping by and I couldn't bear to stay away from it any longer. It is where I have made some of my closest friendships and my happiest memories. As I walk barefoot up and down its walks, I am so familiar with each step that I could do it blindfolded. Every ball game, beach walk, bike ride, and barbecue in the pages of this book is steeped in personal memories. Each and every character on its pages is a compilation of each and every character on the beach. The urge to keep this magical place a secret versus wanting, as an author, to write about the things that matter most to me left me conflicted. Obviously, telling the story won. I hope my neighbors still speak to me.

DISCUSSION QUESTIONS

1. The afterlife! Are you a believer?

2. Were you all in with the narration from the afterlife, or were you skeptical?

3. Do you believe in signs and intimations from a world beyond? Have you experienced any?

4. If you were given a two-month post-death stay, where would you go?

5. How important are rituals in the practice of mourning and coming to terms with loss? How have rituals and traditions helped you recover from a loss?

6. If you had to choose between sad or uplifting, how would you describe this novel?

7. If you could hear the same story from another character's point of view, who would you choose?

8. Intergenerational friendship is a big part of this book. Is that something that figures into your life?

9. How did you feel about Renee's choices?

10. Beatrix and Veronica fell out over a lifeguard in their teens and never made up. If you were Beatrix, what would it take to forgive your sister?

11. How did you feel about the way Dylan and Matty's story ended?

12. How did you interpret the ending of the novel? Did you believe that Ben was writing a work of fiction, nonfiction, or some combination of the two?

WHAT'S ON JANE'S BOOKSHELF

Take My Hand by Dolen Perkins-Valdez

Signal Fires by Dani Shapiro

Same Time Next Summer by Annabel Monaghan

We All Want Impossible Things by Catherine Newman

Community Board by Tara Conklin

The Five-Star Weekend by Elin Hilderbrand

You Were Always Mine by Christine Pride and Jo Piazza

Everything I Never Told You by Celeste Ng

On Beauty by Zadie Smith

The Year of Magical Thinking by Joan Didion

A Tree Grows in Brooklyn by Betty Smith

To Begin Again by Naomi Levy

Photograph of the author © Captain W.

Jane L. Rosen is the author of four novels: *Nine Women, One Dress*; *Eliza Starts a Rumor*; *A Shoe Story*; and *On Fire Island*. She lives in New York City and on Fire Island with her husband and, on occasion, her three grown daughters.

CONNECT ONLINE

JaneLRosen
JaneLRosenAuthor
JaneLRosen1